KING SIZE

LEXI WHITLOW

D1311351

Cover Design:
Mayhem Cover Creations

Photo Credit:
Wander Book Club

Find me on Facebook at facebook.com/lexiwhitlow and in my group Bad Boys Wanted.
Subscribe to my mailing list for free exclusive content and the hottest new releases!
Click here to sign up!

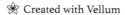 Created with Vellum

For all the NICU moms and their little princes and princesses.

1

"**A** fucking art opening, Duncan?"

"Why, yes sir. It's the kind of thing you said you liked to do in Paris."

"When exactly did I say that?" I grab a martini—or whatever they've named the martini style drink of the evening in this overwrought, annoyingly trendy Paris gallery —and down several gulps. The vodka is mixed with something else—melon, grapefruit—and it's surprisingly refreshing.

"Well—sir—this morning." Duncan puffs up, and I give him a wide grin. Normally I don't act too terribly princely with my ever-patient bodyguard, but I can't quite help it. Duncan glances at my face and gives me a long-suffering sigh.

"I like art. And art galleries." *And the artists themselves, sometimes.*

I survey every face and figure in the room as I walk through and take in the art. There are tall black-and-white photographs of the city, initiation impressionist paintings with modernist flair, and some interesting sculptures in a style I don't entirely know how to describe. The women are usually the more interesting aspect of gallery openings and big events like this one.

Even last year, I'd find a girl to take home in a heartbeat, but this gallery is full of women of a certain sort... I should have known before I even had Duncan drive me here. In the corner, I spot three towering goddesses, each on stiletto heels. Beside them stands a creature built for the Paris runway—a doll. Her figure has been starved for the benefit of designers and photographers who prefer the look of a young child to the figure of a grown woman. Her lips are full and puffed with restalin or collagen or whatever people are using these days.

"Go home, Duncan," I say, waving him off. "I don't need any company."

Duncan gives me an appraising look. He's been told to accompany on this trip to Paris as a protective measure. He doesn't want the type of paparazzi reports from my last trip to Amsterdam to visit my cousin Matthias. And he doesn't want to bear the weight of responsibility if I take off on my own.

"Seriously," I urge him. "I just need to find some art for the new apartment here. Just... go."

I feel the need to be overly formal with Duncan—my princely self. I'm not really that person. And this whole art event isn't what I had in mind. Come to think of it, I don't quite know what I wanted. Not one of the long-haired goddesses, or one of the Paris fashionistas. Maybe—as my mother told me many long years ago, I simply need someone to have a decent conversation with.

Funny idea, Mother. That's not exactly who I am.

I laugh at the idea as Duncan hesitantly leaves me. I

watch as he walks out into the cool Parisian night. I know he'll sit in the car, waiting for me a block or two away.

I wait for him to round the corner, and then I take a step outside myself, taking one of the contraband cigarettes out of my jacket pocket and putting one between my lips. I breathe in the smoke, cognizant of the fact that I'm probably actively taking thirty minutes or so off of my life with just one puff, but that's the beauty of it. I'm doing something just because I want to.

I glance over my shoulder at the women inside, each one more beautiful than the last—and all of them "acceptable" dates for a man like me.

"Boring," I mutter. And even more boring if they know who I am.

I fish around in my jacket for my iPhone, and I open up the screen. There's one app I've been meaning to try—Sparc.

It's for *dating*—well, fucking, primarily. I'd certainly be banned from doing something like *this,* which is why I want to. I have a dead profile with the fake name "Collin" on the thing I set up months ago, but I open it up anyway.

"The whole of parliament would have a fit," I say, laughing. "And the tabloids..."

I type a few words about myself as I smoke the last of the cigarette and stub it out against a tree. I don't expect to find anyone intriguing as I scroll through the profiles with the little green circles attached to them. Since it's based on location, a few of the women inside the art gallery opening pop up. Apparently the girl with the collagen lips is "ready to party."

That might have been appealing at one time in my life. But, as I stand out and face the glittering Paris night, I can't help but feel that I'm done with all of that. Done with models and stiletto-heeled goddesses of all kinds. I'm about to close the app when a new green light pops up, a couple of blocks away.

I click on her profile, and there's a picture of a girl with sandy-blond locks of hair, cascading around her shoulders. She's standing next to a painting, and her whole shirt is smeared with the paint.

Artist-adventurer-thrill-seeker. That's all it says.

I click the *yes* button on her profile and wait. After several minutes of staring off into the night, the phone buzzes again. She's seen me, and she's clicked yes as well.

I tuck the phone inside my jacket—along with the pack of cigarettes. And I step off into the night towards the slightly seedier part of Paris downtown, just a few blocks away. The galleries there are nothing like this one. And Duncan wouldn't mind—after all, I *am* just going to look at art. I keep my pace brisk and my head down. I don't want to be seen by the people from the opening I was just at.

When I reach the gallery—it's more of a bar turned into a gallery—I look behind me to see nothing and no one. The bouncer lets me inside with a fee of twenty euros. I give him a tip and tell him not to let anyone know I came in. He shrugs.

The floor is cement, painted red, and the tables are the kind of dark, old wood that always looks sticky. But each and every surface is covered with some kind of art—small sculptures on each table, paintings and graffiti covering the walls and countertops. And there's some kind of experimental dance troupe performing on stage as people mill about, laughing and talking and *actually* having fun.

I order a beer without the bartender recognizing me, and I take off my jacket, rolling up the sleeves. Even if *she's* not here, this place seems like it's a good time, and not a total snooze.

Then, I turn, and I see *her*. My cock stiffens at the very idea of meeting a woman like this. So long, I've suffered through arranged dates, boring ballets, overly fancy dinners, and all sorts of palace theatrics.

It's not just that.

She's *different*.

There's nothing painted or artificial about her—her beauty is genuine. She doesn't have puffed lips, and she's not tottering on heels. Her blond locks are wild with curls, gathered in a messy bun. She's dressed in clingy black leggings, Doc Marten boots splattered with paint, a fitted undershirt, and a wispy, thin tunic concealing just enough curve and silken skin to render her fascinating—and far more beautiful than any woman I met at that gallery.

Duncan would be *horrified*.

Her eyes meet mine, and I give her a genuine smile—no artifice there either. There's something mischievous about how she looks at me, like she's undressing *me* with her eyes. She leans over to the man she's been talking to and quickly departs, walking my way with a wide, un-self-conscious stride.

"I'm Collin," I say.

"Norah." She absentmindedly pulls her hair out of the bun, and it spills over her shoulders in a sunny cascade.

"Artist, adventurer, thrill-seeker?"

"All of the above."

"And you're... American, I take it? What brings you to Paris?"

"Getting away from old habits... and looking for new stories."

"Found any yet?"

"No, but I'm still searching."

"Maybe I can be part of a good one," I say.

"Maybe." She grins at me. "But I already have an exciting night planned. Just wanted to... meet someone afterwards."

"You've already met him. And he already likes you." I can't help it—the words come out of my mouth unbidden. Maybe it's the couple of drinks I've had, but the words definitely feel right.

"Don't make such a quick judgment. You've been talking to me for about thirty seconds."

"Hopefully more. I'd like to stick around longer than..." I take out my phone and tap the screen. "Just one date."

"You say that now." She steps closer to me, and I smell the tropical scent of her hair—floral and coconut. I *do* want to know this girl just a little bit better, I realize. But my position as prince doesn't often afford me such opportunities.

"Let me get you a drink." I signal the bartender and walk over to the bar with Norah. She gets whiskey—straight. I like watching her drink it, and I feel something tighten deep inside me as her lips pull upward into an enchanting smile.

"I, um, haven't used that thing before. Sparc. Not to meet someone for—" She shrugs and raises an eyebrow.

"The app?" I take a swig of beer. "I haven't either. But I'm glad I did tonight."

"Me too. My ex—er my sometimes stalker—Eric—has been following me around. He's going home next week, and he just ditched me here at my art show." She pauses. "Not that I've been sleeping with him or anything—he's just been following me around." She looks around nervously, like I'm going to judge her for finding me on the app.

"Glad he's gone. I'd like to get to know the artist-adventurer-thrill-seeker for myself."

She laughs. "Okay, well, you want to stay for my painting? Then we can..."

I nod. "Your painting?"

"Consider it foreplay," she says cryptically.

God, yes. Uncomplicated. No strings attached. I look her over. Her breasts are round and full beneath her tunic, and her ass is a work of art in and of itself. I let her lead me over to the stage, near where she was standing.

There are stage hands clearing away the hippie-style dancers and rolling out canvas all over the stage and behind us. Stage hands are bringing out buckets of paint.

"What is all this?" I start laughing. "Are you going to..."

She nods. "I'm a broke artist." She leans into me for a second, eyes sparkling. "And I don't intend to be wearing any of these clothes later."

I watch her as she helps the stage hands prep. She hasn't recognized me yet, and if she hasn't, she won't. Perfect for one night together.

Her eyes glint and crackle as she gets up on stage, and their fixed on me. There's a sexual, sensual energy pouring off of her as she arranges the paint cans. A bucket of red sloshes up and spills onto the edge of one black boot, and she laughs, letting it ring out long and loud. Everyone in the entire place turns to her, eyes locked on her pristine clothes and her body.

"*Merde.*" She looks around the bar and grins. "That's French for 'Oh fuck, I spilled this paint.'"

There are laughs all around. She kicks another can over. Green this time. And then orange. The colors swirl together in a rainbow sea. My heart beats faster as I watch her. It's madness, and her boots are utterly covered in paint. She slides as she walks, tracing ridged lines over the canvas in all manner of colors.

"Is this artistic enough for you?" She yells through the din of the bar.

"Not quite!" Someone yells from the back. She takes her white tunic off, revealing the tops of her perfect, round breasts, poured into the tight black tank-top she's wearing. She throws the tunic at me, and I catch it. I drape the gauzy fabric over my arm, but I don't move. I'm mesmerized, watching her.

The lights in the bar dim, and a purple spotlight falls on her.

I can't quite remember her name from the app. Was it ... Cora? Something old and Gothic. Dickensian.

Paint pours from the ceiling, one can after another— purple, blue, green, iridescent black. It splashes like waves hitting the shore, natural and unstoppable.

She raises her arms in celebration, kicking the paint and letting it splash on the canvas, on the floor, into her hair and all over the untouched black of her outfit. It's an explosion of color and sound. She stomps, dances, turns—and then she lies down in the middle of it, rolling and moving her body over the canvas.

My eyes are locked on her. It seems like hours have passed when her performance ends, and the weirdos in the bar clap wildly for her. I do the same, like I'm in some sort of erotic trance.

When she stands again, her nipples are hard, pushing through the lace of her bra and camisole. Green and blue paint trickles over her breasts in tendrils. Her hair is a mass of red and ochre and silver.

As the canvasses are cleared and hung to dry, she comes and stands beside me.

"What did you think, pretty boy?"

"I'm a pretty boy?" I grin wickedly. "I came to this bar and watched you do... whatever that was."

"You did. I guess that gives you some credit." She pauses. "I don't really know how this works. But I live right on this street. It's... Not much." She shrugs like it doesn't matter where she lives, like nowhere is really home. And she's talking so fast, I'm not sure if she's asking me back to her place, or if she's just making conversation.

"You asked me what I thought," I say slowly. I pause, and she looks up at me with those glinting eyes. "I think you're not like anyone I've ever met."

She takes my hand in hers, getting green paint on my skin, and she pulls me down towards her, kissing me. Her body collides with mine in the middle of the bar, and I'm covered in color. Consumed in it.

I have the passing thought that I won't know how to explain this to Duncan, but I'm not sure I care.

"We're going back to my place," she whispers. She pulls me through the bar and out onto the street in a mad dash. I nearly forget to grab my coat, but the bartender throws it at me at the last second, and I catch it, smearing it with paint.

It's so unlike the art opening I'd attended earlier this evening that I have to laugh. Norah laughs too.

"I'll be moving on in a week," she says, the wind whipping through her sandy blond, paint covered locks. "It's not much but...it's enough for right now..."

I take her then and kiss her, my tongue glancing off of hers. "Don't care," I murmur. She walks with me along the dark Parisian street, arm in arm. Like we're lovers, old friends. But we barely know each other—and even better, she has no idea who I am.

She practically drags me up the stairs to her place. It's a

bohemian hole-in-the-wall, and she probably has at least five other roommates. Thankfully, they seem to be absent—though there could be one lurking behind one of the Turkish wall hangings or behind the clearly broken cappuccino maker.

But we don't pause for a tour of her living arrangements. Inside the apartment, she barely manages to turn on a lamp before I lift her and carry her over to what I assume is her bed. She squeals in delight and kisses me again as I hold her, suspended in midair like some paint-covered sprite.

I throw her down on the bed, and she kicks off her boots. They land in a wet thump on the floor and she laughs. "I don't think I'll be getting back the security deposit."

I pause for a second. "What will you do?"

She lifts up onto her paint-covered elbows. "I'll think of something. I always do. I've got a few accounts here and there."

There must be a concerned look on my face, because she takes her shirt off and throws it away. And then, she pulls me down towards her waiting body. "Shut up," she says. "We're not here to chat."

I peel off her paint-covered leggings, and her milky white thighs spread willingly for me. I can feel the heat of her body rising to meet mine, and my brain tweaks into that place—the one where I become hunter instead of man. My cock rises to the occasion.

Her body is perfection—skin pliant and soft, reactive to each touch. I kiss her again, slowly this time, trailing my lips over the line of her chin and down to the tender flesh of her neck. My tongue traces the goosebumps rising on her flesh, and I take one nipple in my mouth and then the other.

She moans softly, then whimpers in need.

My fingers descend, tugging her panties to the side and slipping inside her delicate folds. I feel her clit, swollen and ready for my touch. Her back arches as I slip one finger inside of her, and then another.

"Let's get this done," she says, putting one hand to the bulge pressing against my jeans.

"I think I can manage that," I say, unbuckling myself and letting my cock free.

She slips my jeans off and kneels before me, looking up at me with those curious, glinting eyes. Her hand wraps around my cock, and she presses her fingers gently against my flesh, stroking me, tracing the ridges and contours with careful attention.

"Lie down," she instructs.

She stands and presses *me* back into the bed this time. "You have a way with words," I say.

"I'd rather not exchange any more of them," she says, almost haughtily.

She's not timid. She straddles me, her naked skin against mine, her hands working my cock. Gently, slowly, she lowers her lips to the head of my shaft and goes to work, swirling her tongue around the tip, and bringing my rigid length into her mouth. And she *looks* at me as she does it, bringing me to heights I didn't think possible.

This isn't something that happens. The girls I see use this kind of thing to get in my head, if they do it at all.

But Norah is just *having fun.*

She brings me to the very limit and backs off, slowing the movements of her mouth and tongue and bringing her cherry-red lips back to the head. There are still flecks of paint on her face and hair. They make her look more beautiful, more like the wild thing she is.

She builds me up again, licking and sucking, taking me to the back of her throat and swallowing gently, time and time again, like she wants to milk me dry. I'm unable to hold on any longer. My balls seize, and an orgasm made of light and liquid gold fills every nerve ending in my body. I come hard, lifting my eyes to watch her as she swallows every last drop.

Normally, I might leave in this situation. I'd be done.

But I'm not satisfied. I want that body—I *need* to know it. I pull her next to me.

"That was..." I murmur. *Earth-shattering. Unexpected. Insane.*

Before I can think of a word, she brings a finger to my lips. "Shhh. You'll ruin it."

I grin. "You might be right. I'm told I *don't* have a way with words."

"Still talking," she murmurs, curling her fingers in my hair and yawning. Lazily, she moves her naked, paint-flecked body to straddle me again, positioning herself above my chest.

"I need *something* to shut me up, don't I?" I pull her closer towards me until she's sitting just above my face.

She laughs. "I like how you think."

She lowers the pink lace of her panties closer to my lips. I smell her, kissing her thighs as she sits above me. My tongue begins to explore her skin. She's salty with sweat, her scent rich and dark and wholly inviting. I take it in, breathing deep, and I feel my cock stirring again.

Nearly driven mad, I grab her thighs and begin licking and sucking at the thin lace barrier that separates me from her sex. I use my tongue to find the tight, hard bud of her clit, and I suck it between my lips. Each moan and each involuntary movement of her hips makes my cock—impossibly—harder. I use one hand to yank her panties to the side, and I feast on her, covering her clit with my mouth and moving my tongue around that sensitive button in rhythmic circles as she bucks hard against me, her voice building as her own orgasm grows, deep inside of her core.

I'm vaguely aware that she's raised her hands to her nipples and that she's riding me faster and faster now. She's crying out, arching her hips again and again. Her legs shake, and I know she's coming with my tongue inside of her. I'm buried in her taste—and I haven't been this satiated or this *hard* in years.

Just as she's coming down from the high of her orgasm, I throw her back on the bed and move her to her hands and knees.

She's laughing, her wild hair hanging over her face. She combs it behind one ear and looks back at me. She takes one look at my cock. "*Again?* You're hard *again?*"

"All your fault," I whisper, stroking myself. Her pussy is dripping, and utterly inviting.

"I don't have a condom," she murmurs. "But I'm ... taken care of."

"Good."

I nod with a wicked grin on my face. I take her light body in mine and position her on the bed, her perfect ass in the air. I let my fingers explore her, dipping inside of her soaking wet pussy, and up over her tender, swollen clit.

"Ohhh...." She moans. "Don't stop..."

I press my cock to her entrance and slide inside her, bit by bit. She's impossibly tight, impossibly hot.

"God, you're big," she groans, wrapping her legs around me and pulling me in tighter. "More... please, more."

I almost lose it then. Her sharp taste is on my lips, and the feeling of her mouth on my cock is still with me. I've wanted to come deep inside of her since I first laid eyes on her in that bar, and I'd stroke my own cock a thousand times thinking of her rolling around in that paint, nipples hard as diamonds. But I hold myself back.

I fuck her with long, measured thrusts, each movement designed to draw out her pleasure.

Usually I'm thinking of my own, but this time, it's different. I ride her as she comes again, her body shaking from exhaustion. Once she's come just one more time, I let my balls seize up again, and I fill her up with my liquid hot essence. She moans, bucking hard against me.

We collapse together, and I fall asleep draped in her arms and legs, tangled in her body heat, my skin slick and perfumed with her scent.

I went out tonight to get art and a beautiful woman.

I definitely got both—and far *more* than I expected.

MY PHONE IS RINGING. I hear it from a long way off, the tones familiar, melodic. "Purple Rain." A song from another time, another prince.

"Jesus, what the hell is that?"

It's Norah's voice that wakes me, not the sound of my phone. I sit up, confused and blinking back sleep. The room is bright with sunshine and barely furnished, scattered with dirty clothes and books.

My phone keeps ringing; it's the ringtone I've set for palace security. It's the only tone I know I can't let go to voicemail. They don't call without a good reason.

I scramble in the back pocket of the jeans I dropped in a rumpled heap last night. I swipe to answer, hoping I've caught the call before it disconnects. If that happens, a whole different set of events get put into motion, none of them good, especially considering I'm naked and in a strange girl's bed. I don't need a mass of armed men bursting in under the assumption I've been kidnapped, ready to shoot first and ask questions later.

"Yes?!" I say, relieved to hear live air on the other end of the connection.

"Your Highness, this is Rowling. I'm sorry to disturb you, sir, but we have a situation developing at the palace. Your mother has requested your immediate return."

"What's wrong?" I ask. "Is she alright? Is she ill?"

"No, sir. Her Royal Majesty is in fine health. I'm sorry sir —I can't discuss this on an insecure line. When you get to the plane, we'll have a secure connection and I'll brief you. The jet is standing by at the airport. Is Duncan with you now?"

I struggle out of bed and to the window, peering down at the street. Duncan leans on the closed driver's side door, looking up at me from behind mirrored aviator sunglasses.

"Yeah, he's here," I say. "Not in the room, but here."

"He has instructions to take you directly to the airport. There's no time to be lost."

"Very well." I end the call, then look at the phone in my hand. The last time I got a call like that was when my father died six months ago. That ringtone makes my guts clench and my heart race. I don't ever want to get a call like that again—it means everything is falling apart.

Something big is going down at home. Something—*I know*—to do with my brother and his bizarre behavior. That's the only reason they'd call me. He's the heir. I'm the spare. They're never supposed to need me, and I'd like to keep it that way.

"Everything okay?"

I turn. Norah is sitting up, her knees pulled to her chest and the sheets drawn tight, covering her from shoulder to toes. Last night she was wide open, shameless. Now, in the mid-morning light, she's the picture of demure—if slightly rumpled and paint-speckled—reserve.

In the new light of the day, I realize she's the most beautiful creature I've ever laid eyes on.

Game over.

"I've gotta go," I say, reaching for my jeans and pulling them on, then searching for my shirt.

"Why?" she asks, confused. "I thought we'd go out for coffee... or..."

But I cut her off. "I've *got* to go."

What I want is what she wants: I want to stay, have breakfast, hang out with her, get to know her. That's never happened before—and it can't happen now. It's better to nip any expectations she might have in the bud.

Forty seconds later, I'm on the stairs headed down to the street and back into the over-bearing care of my patient, ever-loyal bodyguard, Duncan.

2

NORAH

"**W**hat an utter ass," Chantal snips in her sexy French accent, then downs half a glass of red wine to punctuate her statement.

She doesn't need to say it—I'm in perfect agreement. "I didn't even get his last name," I admit, lowering my voice. "And I went down on him—*voluntarily!* I've never been so comprehensively dissed in my life."

"No, *mon Dieu!*" she cries, wagging her finger at me. "Never do that the first time. You must build them up to it. Otherwise it takes the mystery away."

"But I *liked* it. A lot." I give her a grin.

We laugh about it, which eases some of the sting. But I'm still chafed, mostly because Collin was blisteringly hot and a rocking great lay. He made my toes curl. There was something else about him, too, something I can't put my finger on. He's the first guy I've met in a very long time who I *wanted* to take the trouble to get to know better.

Oh well. Collin-With-No-Last-Name is an ass, and I'm done wasting tears and heartbeats on asses. If I ever see him again, he can kiss mine.

I even *tried* to find his profile again, but it was gone.

"So Norah, now that Stephen's art-fest is over, what are you going to do? Are you staying in Paris, or going home?"

"I can't stay. I'm moving out in—" I check a fake watch. "Like today."

"So what is the plan?" She says "the" like a French villain in a movie. *Zee.*

I shrug. "I'm not going home yet. I'm thinking of doing a tour of the UK and the rest of the islands. I've always wanted to see Ireland, Anglesey, Scotland. I could Airbnb my way across the North Atlantic. I don't have to stop until I get to St. Petersburg."

Her eyebrows raise. "If you're going to St. Petersburg, get there before summer ends, otherwise you'll be iced in until next June."

I grin, sipping my wine while a crew of men a few tables away ogle Chantal's long, shapely legs. One of the men winks at me, flicking his tongue suggestively. I lift my middle finger, smiling. "Fuck off," I mouth clearly, so he doesn't mistake my intentions.

I swear to God, unabashed shit like that doesn't happen with such frequency back home. We've got our problems in the states, but at least I can sit in a café with a friend without being subjected to obscene gestures from strange men.

Chantal turns to see who I'm insulting. She turns back, rolling her eyes. "*Les cochons,*" she smacks. "Pigs. They snuff for truffles in the dirt. They'll never taste *my* truffle!"

We almost burst our sides giggling at the *cochons* sitting paunchy, balding, and humbled just tables away.

"French men are pigs," Chantal observes, and she should know. "I prefer the English. They have manners."

That settles it. I'm going to tour the British Isles, with a lengthy visit to the northern island of Anglesey. I have a good friend who lives there, and I've always wanted to visit anyway. It's where my ancestors on my mother's side come from. The place is a fairytale, loaded with history and castles, ancient baronial manor houses, and the last surviving absolute monarchy in the developed world.

I lift my hand to the garçon, offering my credit card in the air.

"Will your ex follow you?" Chantal asks, leaning forward. "He's made quite the point of being by your side these last few weeks."

I shake my head. "Thankfully I think Eric has to be back at work next week," I say. "Unlike you Frenchies, in America we get two weeks' vacation—max. He's on day eleven, so I think I'm clear of him for a while."

"He's the reason you met that guy on Sparc, isn't he? You were trying to get him off of your mind?"

As much as I hate to admit it, Chantal is probably right.

"You know, that sort of thing only makes a man dig in. Making him jealous will only lead him to desire even more what he can't have."

She's probably right about that, too. Eric called me the afternoon after Collin, offering to take me to supper. He said he saw me leave with someone—the fucker had been watching me.

I was still licking my wounds from Collin leaving and needed to get out of the flat, and I stupidly went with him. He spent the entire evening reminding me in endless, tedious detail how successful he is. How long our families have known one another. How one day soon, when I get bored with being a "flighty artist, searching the world for poetry that doesn't really exist," I'm going to see the logic in settling down with someone familiar, someone who understands me.

Eric will never understand me.

I don't give a shit about his money or his seat on the New York Stock Exchange. I don't care that his father and my father are golf buddies, or that we've attended the same private school since kindergarten. I'm never going to be the girl who's satisfied with an acre lot, a white picket fence, and a brunch table at the country club. I grew up in that world, and I've had enough of it. It's soul-crushing. It's for people who lack the capacity to imagine more for themselves.

I'd rather be dead broke—seeing the world, meeting fascinating people—than spend my life in a cocoon surrounded by well-dressed Stepford wives and their spawn.

"*Mademoiselle, je suis désolée... em...* I am sorry. Your card was declined. Perhaps you have cash?"

Fuck. I thought I had at least a hundred euros still there.

"It is not a mistake," the waiter assures me sternly. "Cash or another card, *s'il vous plaît?*"

"I can get it," Chantal offers.

I wave her off. "I've got cash," I say, producing a handful of euros. "The card must have expired or something."

I keep it cool, but inside, I'm shaking.

BACK IN THE apartment I'm about to lose, I call my parents. That account was linked directly to *them*. And I need to get shit straight.

But my father's voice is shaky when I call him. It appears that my account isn't the only one that's utterly fucked.

"Barney's disappeared, honey," my father tells me, trying to keep his voice even.

"What do you mean, he's disappeared? You invested everything with him!" I say to my father.

"He's gone," Dad says. "He's gone, along with every asset in the company's holdings. Every investment. Every checking and savings account. *Everything.* The FDIC and the SEC, along with the FBI, are tearing his offices apart. They say he's left the country. Gone to the Emirates. He took billions with him. Honey, *we're broke.*"

I try to process what my father has said. Barney Mackoff, long-time family friend, investment counsellor, owner of Mackoff Bank and Investment Trust, the man who has managed my family's finances since before I was born, has stolen everything, disappearing into the murky underworld of international money launderers, oligarchs, and mobsters.

"We're broke?" I repeat. "Not just me? I'm the one who deserves to be broke—not you guys. Shit. Oh *shit.*" I think of the profundity of it. My parents, who worked *hard* for their money—they're just like me now. They were able to give me every opportunity and let me follow my dreams, and now their own dreams are *dead.*

And they're the last people who deserve it.

"I'm going to try to sell the house on Pawley's and the apartment in New York to raise some capital," Daddy says. "Thank God this house is paid for."

"This house" is my mother's, inherited from her grandmother. It was paid for before the first shots were fired at Fort Sumter. *It damn well better not be mixed up in this bullshit.* I never did trust "Uncle" Barney. He tried to put the moves on me when I was just thirteen. He's a creep.

"You need to come home, Norah," he says emphatically. "Your allowance has to be stopped. Your credit cards are all cancelled. I can probably scrounge up just enough cash for your plane fare."

"I'll deal with it," I say. "I have some cash put away. I'll be

fine. I'm not going to take money from you right now, Dad.
I'm just not."

When the call concludes, I sit down at my kitchen table,
regarding the small, untidy apartment that I was about to be
kicked out of anyway.

I'm not a complete idiot. Unlike my father, I didn't put all
my eggs in one basket: I have almost six thousand euros in
cash here, along with another bank account at home with
forty thousand dollars in deposits. My parents thought I
spent my summer job and internship money on clubs and
clothes. *I banked it.* And since their allowance was always
more than enough for my needs, I banked some of that, too.

My only problem is, I can't get to that account from here.
The other problem is that I no longer have a functioning
credit card, and it's impossible to make travel reservations
without one. It's impossible to do almost anything without
one. And I can't get a new one because I don't have a permanent address in Paris. I'm a tourist, and Paris banks don't
extend credit to tourists.

"YOU NEED TO COME HOME," Eric states. "I'm leaving the day
after tomorrow. I'll book you a seat on my flight."

I shake my head. "No, I still have things I want to do,
things I need to see. I have some money—I just need to get
at it. And I need a credit card."

"You're being unreasonable," he says. "Your parents are
in a crisis. They need you back home."

My parents are *fine.* My grandfather was careful. She has
assets separate from my father's investments. Papa never did
quite trust his son-in-law to take care of his only daughter in
the style in which she was reared, so her trust fund is safe,

well-managed, and accessible only by her. My father can't touch it, though Lord knows he's tried (and failed) before.

I would have talked to Mama when I called, but she was at the club. I'll catch up with her soon enough. I know she wouldn't have me freaking out or changing my plans just because Barney Mackoff turned out to be a conman.

"I can get you a credit card issued from my firm," Eric says. "But it'll have a low limit, and I'll need your account details at the credit union in Charleston where you have your savings account."

I could kiss him. *But maybe not.* "You can do that?" I ask.

He nods. "If I co-sign on the account," he says, then leans in. "The thing is, if I do this, when you get home I'm going to need you to thank me appropriately."

What does that mean?

"Norah, I'd do anything in the world for you. All I want is to make you happy. You can make me happy, too. Go ahead: sow your wild oats. But when you're tired of sowing, come home. We'll have beautiful children, a nice home. We'll make our parents proud."

My parents are already proud of me.

"How does the co-signing thing work?" I ask him, skirting his plans for my entire life.

"Don't worry about it." He waves a hand. "You'll have the card in two days."

Outstanding.

ANGLESEY IS the most beautiful country I've ever seen. I realize this within six minutes of landing on her shores. I flew into London a month ago, then worked my way west, dropping in at every tourist destination along the way. I've visited grand old houses, sumptuous estates, cathedrals, and tiny, antique villages. At Liverpool I boarded a boat—a steam-powered ferry that looked and felt like a vessel from another era—to cross the Angle Sea to Cymrea, the capital city of Anglesey. I disembarked on a magnificent stone dock built in the 12th century by a king whose name has so many vowels I can't possibly pronounce it. A half-mile from this broad dock sits the Castle of Beaumaris, a 13th-century fortress with ten-foot-thick walls enclosing the principle palace of the Anglesey monarchy.

I have precisely one friend in Anglesey: Sinead. We were in school together at the London College of Art & Fashion. After college, I went on to Paris to work with fashion photographer Stephan Aubauchan prior to his retirement, culminating in the show last month. Sinead married an earl who's heir to an estate in the west country of Anglesey. He has connections to the nobility and a civil service job in Cymrea that's not too many stations removed from the highest echelons of power.

"You haven't changed a bit," Sinead cries, wrapping me in her arms. "Oh, I've missed you, and school, and all the times we had in London. I'm so glad you're here!"

Three hours later, just as I'm settling into my spacious bedroom (which is three times larger than my Paris apartment) in the west wing of this sprawling old manor house, I am notified by the housekeeper that dinner is to be served at eight o'clock sharp.

The table is laden with all the good things this rather exceptional country can conjure. Steamed crabs, shellfish, and roasted salmon fill serving dishes and our plates. Potatoes, leeks, and carrots make delicious sides. A sputtering, steaming serving of bread reminds me very much of my grandmother's corn-pone. At least now I know where cornbread comes from; it's basic food, no matter where in the world your people call home.

"Prince Owen is hosting a large party at Saxony this weekend," Sinead's husband observes between formal courses. "There's a rumor about that he's on the hunt for a wife." The Earl smiles mischievously as he butters his cornbread. "There's another rumor about that he may very well be the next king, as the Prince of Merioneth has gone off his rocker and is as likely to abdicate as he is to be deposed."

"Innuendo!" Sinead exclaims, thumping her knife gleefully on the tabletop. "Treasonous language!"

Her husband grins. "I only repeat in private what I hear in private. Time will tell. Anyway, we're off to Saxony for the weekend. It should be a splendid party, rumors notwithstanding."

It *is* a splendid party. Saxony is a picturesque port town on the far west coast of Anglesey, a small city that appears frozen in time. Its row houses are all Tudor design, with crossbeams and mud-fill walls, peaked roofs shingled in heavy slate, and cantilevered upper floors hanging precariously over narrow, cobbled streets.

The prince's party is held on the grounds of Brynterion Castle, a palatial country estate built in stages between the 13th century and the early 20th. It's the official residence of Prince Owen, Duke of Brynterion, the younger brother of Crown Prince Lloyd.

The castle is astonishing to look at, even from a distance. It's a massive pile of white stone sprawling over acres, with more columns and windows than a reasonable person could count in one sitting. Luckily, I don't have to count them. Sinead, the Earl, and I are situated in a VIP tent on the castle grounds, alongside a few hundred other lower nobility who've been invited to this fête, but not granted access to the main house.

We're comfortable under a sprawling tent with plenty of food and drink, a band playing, and games provided for our amusement.

As the evening wears on, after I've met a thousand earls, dukes, marques, duchesses, and ladies—enough to fill a Grimm Brothers' fairytale—all I want to do is find a comfortable bed to lay my head on and go to sleep. I'm just about to excuse myself to the modest quarters of our weekend guest house when a young man wearing a very fine suit and a microphone wired into his ear walks up to me directly. He looks just like a secret service agent, or maybe James Bond.

"Miss Ballantyne," he says, bowing discreetly, "His Royal Highness Prince Owen requests your presence tomorrow at five o'clock on board the royal yacht. You may bring one guest. Dress is casual."

He places a card in my hand; it's stamped with the royal seal. *What the fuck?*

"Oh my Lord!" Sinead exclaims, her eyes wide with disbelief.

The young man draws back, bows again, then turns and walks off toward the palace.

The Earl steps up, peering over my shoulder at the card. It's a simple card, made of expensive linen paper, with nothing except the imprinted royal seal and the time, "5:00 p.m.," written in blue ink in an elegant hand.

"That is quite a compliment paid to you, Norah," The Earl says, watching the suited young man disappear into the darkness of the grounds between our tent and the palace.

"It certainly is," Sinead concurs. "Good Lord, what does

one wear to a command appearance aboard the royal yacht?"

I look at Sinead as if she's joking. "You don't think I'm going to this, do you?"

The expression both she and the Earl return is one of horrified disbelief. "Norah, you must attend," the Earl informs me, his tone firm. "You can't say no to a member of the royal family."

"I'm not his subject," I protest.

The Earl smiles coolly. "You are a guest in his country, and as such, you act at his pleasure. When the prince requests you come to his party, you damn well come to his party. *And you like it.*"

"But..."

SINEAD IS much happier about this odd turn of events than I am. In truth, I'm sorely pissed on two accounts. First, I don't relish the idea of spending an undetermined quantity of my precious time with a gaggle of posh, self-important *peers*, who—*no doubt*—will be looking down their pointy noses at me, wondering who let the rabble in the back door.

The second reason is far more practical: I despise spending my hard-earned, painfully limited resources purchasing clothing I'd never buy for myself in a million years, and will never in my life wear again. "Dress casual" apparently means something very different in Anglesey than it does in Charleston or New York.

Before Sinead is done outfitting me for this shindig, my bank account's a thousand dollars lighter. When Eric sees my credit card statement he's going to birth a cow. He's already laid a few hen's eggs over my meandering tour across England, stopping in every old bookshop I could find, paying top dollar for rare books I'm going to have to ship home on the slow boat.

"There it is," Sinead nearly squeals as we come over a ridge, angling down toward the port. "Isn't it splendid?"

The object of her extreme approval is less of a yacht and more of a Carnival cruise ship. It's huge: it must have four or five decks, two giant smokestacks, satellite dishes, and all manner of weather and navigation gizmos hanging off the bridge. I expected a luxurious party boat, but this thing is the length of a football field. There's even a helicopter pad —with an actual helicopter parked on it.

"Impressive," I mutter.

The Earl glances at me in his rearview mirror, clearly amused. He's almost as excited as Sinead; I think he's pleased that his wife may get an opportunity to meet the prince, although he cautioned both of us to manage our expectations.

"His Royal Highness will most likely remain on the uppermost decks for the entire cruise. It would be unusual for him to put himself forward to linger among the bulk of the guests."

This morning, after our shopping adventure had concluded, Sinead and the Earl put me through my paces, giving me a crash course on how to behave if I find myself confronted with royalty. I now know how to curtsy properly, and to whom. I know to keep my hands to myself, my eyes down, and to speak only when spoken to. If I'm asked a question, I must always begin or end my response with "ma'am" or "sir," even if the royal in question is a toddler asking to "go potty."

It's all very pretentious and confusing. I'm counting on the idea that I won't need to deploy any of these new skills, and maybe I'll be able to return most of the clothes I purchased for the outing.

Just as we're about to head up the gangway to board the ship, the Earl seizes Sinead's hand, pulling her back for a big, warm hug. "Have a wonderful time, my darling. And please don't do anything to get your photo in the papers."

They have a good laugh as they part. He calls out to me, already far ahead, "You either, Norah. Behave yourself!"

I don't think the Earl has much to worry about: I'm the least likely of all the people who've been invited to this party to put myself forward. I've brought a book with me, and I intend to get some reading done.

3

OWEN

My mother, "Her Royal Highness, Co-Regent to the Crown Prince, Princess Dalia, Duchess of Merioneth, Duchess of Dowlais"—*and a royal pain in my ass*—is nothing if not efficient. She's determined to see me married, and she's doing everything in her power to accomplish it in short order. There's nothing I can do about it. For the sake of the country and the monarchy, I have to do this.

The House of Cymrea is the last absolute monarchy in the Western Hemisphere, and the only one in the world that doesn't sustain itself through violence or intimidation. The dynasty has lasted seven hundred years, while others fell or were reduced to ceremonial status. We've survived by maintaining a strict family code and hiring disinterested, outside advisors as counsel. We've also managed to keep our heads —literally and figuratively—about us.

And my brother, the Crown Prince who will be made king within six months unless the unthinkable happens, is doing his dead-level best to break everything to pieces. He's either lost his mind, or he's doing a convincing job of acting like it.

Mother wants him to abdicate. If he refuses, she intends to depose him. To accomplish that, the nobles must vote in support of her decision by a two-thirds majority. Only once in seven hundred years have Anglesey's nobles had to vote to select a new king. They didn't back the heir apparent because he was unmarried and had no immediate prospects for an heir. Instead, they chose a nephew of the former king who was married with a son. That nephew is my 21st great-grandfather and the founder of the House of Cymrea.

My mother is determined to prevent history repeating itself. I'd also prefer not to be the jerk responsible for killing the monarchy. It's entirely possible the nobles would just abolish us and get busy dividing the spoils among themselves. Then we'd have a civil war. And as history has shown, that's where these things always go.

Given all that, my life could be far worse. At the moment I'm sitting in the sunshine with a drink in my hand, gazing down at a crowd of mostly beautiful women hand-selected by my mother and her staff. We're taking an overnight cruise around the islands. It's mid-May, which means the sun won't set until almost midnight, and it'll be up again by five in the morning. Judging by the looks of the enthusiastic partiers below me, it's going to be a busy, drunken night.

At some point I may have to get off my ass and inspect some of these "likely wives," but right now I'm lacking motivation. I promised myself I'd pick two or three to try out as potential candidates for a few weeks before making a final decision. That approach seems about right. The challenging thing will be to convince the "lucky girl" that this isn't a fairytale, that I'm not bloody Prince Charming, and that it's highly unlikely either of us are going to live happily ever after.

Just look at my parents as an example. My mother was the lucky girl chosen by the prince. Six months later she realized he didn't choose her—a committee did—and he was in love with a married duchess he'd known since childhood. Princess Dalia was brought in for one specific purpose: to produce an heir. She did it through artificial insemination.

My heir could end up being conceived the same way.

While she was married, my mother was the loneliest person I've ever known. When my father died and their farce of a marriage ended, she came out of her shell and started living again. Just a few months later, Lloyd began behaving oddly. Mother had maybe six weeks of peace before the drama spiked up again.

Which brings us to this—me lounging on the top deck of the yacht, surrounded by security and a handful of cousins, all of us peering down at the rabble to see if anyone stands out in the crowd.

What I wish more than anything is that I was someone else entirely: ideally someone wandering through Europe, brave enough to go and find Norah, wherever she is. I'd beg her forgiveness and tell her I haven't stopped thinking about her since that night. I'd tell her she's extraordinary. That I know she is, even though I can't explain how I know—I just feel it in my bones.

It might not be love, I'd tell her, but I'd like to see where the adventure goes.

"Sir?"

I look up. Duncan's wearing the same deadpan expression, the same gray silk suit, and the same aviator sunglasses he's worn for the last seven years.

"What's up, Dunc?" I ask, returning my gaze to my guests below. There must be five hundred women down there, most of them damn attractive.

"Your mother has a list of prospects she'd like you to look at. She suggests bringing them up for closer inspection."

I level a steely glare at Duncan. "I suppose you have a list? Or files on them, or something?"

"Yes, sir." He retrieves a small stack of files from under his jacket and hands them to me.

My mother has assembled a veritable Who's Who of nosebleed Anglesey nobility. There's Lady Devon Pembroke, Duchess of Swansea. She's eighteen years old, speaks six languages, plays the piano and the cello, raises thorough-breds, and likes taking long walks in the countryside. She's also got a double chin and a hook nose.

The Duchess of Cardiff is lovely. She's also functionally illiterate.

The Marchioness of Hollyhead is also quite striking, but at six-foot-four, I worry she might be tempted to lead when we dance.

I pull her folder and Lady Devon Pembroke's from Duncan's collection, returning the rest to him. "Not on this deck," I instruct. "If anyone's using deck two, clear them out and set it up down there."

"Yes sir." He turns to go.

"And Duncan," I call.

He turns back to me. "Sir?"

"If you see anyone better than those down there, let me know. *I'm dying here.* Bring me someone with some person-ality? Someone interesting?"

He almost cracks a smile. He nods. "I'll keep that in mind, sir."

My cousin David approaches wielding a bottle of expensive Anglesey whiskey. He refills my glass. "Hell of a way to pick a wife," he observes, settling into the empty seat across from me, crossing his legs.

I swallow a generous portion, enjoying the burn of it in my throat. "Hell of a way to run a country."

"Indeed," he agrees. "And speaking of, where is Lloyd? I thought for certain he'd be here."

I shrug. "Different obligations. Besides, I think he'd rather do anything than float around the islands helping me choose a wife."

"So what's the rush?" David asks, prodding where he shouldn't. "Why all the anxiety over your marriage and not Lloyd's? Shouldn't he be the first to marry?"

"I think my mother has just as many schemes for Lloyd as she has for me," I answer, choosing my words strategically. "She always shores up the spot where the weakness is most pronounced."

David huffs out a laugh. "Ah, I see. So she's trying to clean up your reputation. And she thinks she can do that by marrying you off to some pretty duchess. Because that worked so well in your father's case."

I withhold the punch a commoner might throw in response to a dig like that. "Careful, David," I say coolly. "My father was your king, and my mother is co-regent. A modicum of respect, please."

"Of course. My apologies, my prince," he replies with equal coolness.

David is six years older than me and married with two sons. He's next in line to the throne behind me, and should anything happen to keep Lloyd from ascending, it's entirely possible David would become a legitimate contender for the crown.

My mother may be a royal pain in my ass, but she has a keen understanding of just how precarious things are. David's inquiry reminds me I need to buck up and stop working at cross-purposes against her. Things are happening too fast. I can't be the spare flying under the radar any longer. If David decides to compete with me on this, it's possible I could lose more than a crown: I may very well lose my head, and not in the figurative sense.

THE DUCHESSES ARE ALL VERY PRETTY, VERY accomplished, and *very boring*. They're preened and polished to a high gloss, ready to blind me into submission. One of them whose name I forgot won't shut up about some book she's writing about the Austro-Prussian war. I have to walk away from her in mid-sentence in order to regain my ability to think. They all want to talk about themselves, all trying to outdo one another with superlatives, attempting to impress me. The one thing that none of them do—the one thing that would distinguish them in my eyes—is ask me a single question about myself.

They think because I'm the prince, and because I'm famous, because my face is splashed across the tabloids every week, they already know me.

They don't know the first thing about me.

By the time the dog and pony show is over, it's nearly midnight and the sun trails low over the North Atlantic. The water is flat and black against a cloudless sky, glowing in hues of deep royal blue, purple, crimson, and gold. The wind has dropped to nothing as twilight creeps in.

Thirty feet below me, my guests are still going strong: music is blaring, people are dancing, and the alcohol is flowing. The party probably won't slow down until the sun comes up again.

"Sir?"

I've been alone up here on the top deck for quite a while, and I didn't hear Duncan come in. I don't bother to turn around. My mind is lost in the sunset, lost in contemplation of the last days of my freedom, the end of any hope for happiness.

"What's up?" I ask.

He clears his throat. "Earlier today you said if I saw anyone *better*..."

I turn to face him, full of inquiry. Duncan knows me well, better than anyone alive. He knows my tastes and what catches my fancy. "What are you onto?" I ask him.

"This, sir." He hands me his phone.

I look down at the screen. My heart stops. My knees tense. My mouth goes dry. *It's her.* It's Norah. She's here, aboard the yacht. "How? How do you even know who she *is*, Duncan?" I barely mumble.

"It's my job to know such things, sir."

"And why is she *here*?"

Duncan shakes his head. "I don't know, exactly," he says. "I... I saw her on a security camera at the party at Brynterion last night and was pretty sure it was the girl from Paris. When I cross-checked her name against the guest list, the first names matched. I did a quick background check on her, and nothing turned up."

"Does she know who I am?" I ask, fearing the worst: that my fantasy of Norah has materialized into a very real stalker.

"I don't believe she does, sir," Duncan says. "I think it's a coincidence. She was visiting a friend who had an invite to the party, and they just added her name to the list. I took a risk last night and presented her with an invitation to the cruise so I could get a closer look at her behavior."

"And?" I ask, impatient, annoyed I didn't know about this earlier.

"And she's spent almost the entire cruise in the shade of the aft deck, reading a book. She brought a guest, who's been quite a bit more social. Sir, the girl is... She's not here to win friends."

How strange.

"I need to see her," I say. "I need to see her without letting her know who I am."

"Sir?" Duncan asks. "I don't understand."

"Just figure it out. I need to see her, alone, without her getting wind of my identity."

Duncan is baffled, and then I see his gears grinding. He's got an idea. "Come with me, sir."

I LOOK good in a Royal Yacht Crew uniform. Blue suits me.

Duncan hands me his shades. "Keep them on, sir," he says, "until we're through the main deck."

Duncan's plan requires the participation of five members of the yacht crew (all in uniforms identical to the one I'm borrowing), as well as a half-dozen members of the security team. We hustle at pace straight through the dense crowd of drunken partiers on the main deck, through the loud music and flashing lights, and take the staff-only stairs to the second level berth deck. That's where Norah's been assigned her quarters, and at some point she's got to return to her room.

Duncan's plan goes off without a hitch. None of those boozy blue bloods even look up to see what we were about. One girl glances at me, and seeing my uniform, just as quickly looks away. It's just like when I stalk the streets anonymously collecting pretty girls: everyone just looks right through me and I blend into the background scenery.

It occurs to me that this is how conmen and serial killers function. But I'll save that bit of reflection for another time —right now I have a very special girl to reconnect with.

I wait with Duncan and the crew inside a tight, spiral stairwell used by staff to move swiftly and invisibly between decks. It's just like the secret passages in our various palaces, except considerably smaller and less drafty. We wait nearly an hour before I see Duncan touch his earpiece. He's got members of the detail strategically placed, watching Norah, monitoring her every move.

"She's up and walking," Duncan says. A moment later he elaborates: "Headed this way."

Luckily she gave us plenty of time to stage this, and time enough for me to swap shirts back into my polo so I'm not facing her as a ship's boy.

Just as she turns the corner, headed to her berth, I turn the opposite corner, headed straight toward her. Men from my detail are poised at each end of the corridor, preventing anyone from wandering in to interrupt us.

She looks up, meeting my eyes with surprise, then question, then recognition.

She's still the most beautiful woman I've ever set eyes on.

She stops in her tracks. I slow my approach, allowing myself to take her in, drinking up the sight of her. I let myself return to her kisses and the moments we shared in the dark, unconcerned about what the next day would bring —or our titles, or our jobs, or any of the things that complicate life and make us all miserable.

"You," she spits, suddenly coming to life. "You fucking asshole!"

The next thing I know is pain. Not horrible pain, but sharp, humiliating pain. She slaps my face so hard I see stars and my ears briefly ring. If the experience wasn't so damn unexpected and bracing, it might almost be enjoyable. As it is, I'm reasonably certain this is not a great start.

"What the fuck are you doing here?!" she demands. "Don't answer that—I don't even care. " She turns her back, digging in her pocket for a key as she approaches a nearby door. "I should have known when I met you on that stupid app. You disappeared—and oh my God, I should have known. Your *profile* was even gone. I just wanted coffee the next day. I was stupid." She's talking unreasonably fast again.

"Norah, please. Let me explain."

"I don't want to hear it," she says, and that's when I see her hands trembling. "It was just a hook up. I should have known better. I was dumb."

"I had my reasons," I say. "It's not what I ever intended, to leave you that way. It was a family emergency. A crisis. I couldn't stop to explain. And you and me, we were…"

"We were *nothing*," she states, finishing my sentence differently that I'd intended.

"I had just met you," I say, stepping closer. "I wanted to stay. But my world here blew up. I had to go."

She slips her key into the door, opening it. She lingers outside, just paces away. I want to reach out to her, but I don't dare. She may just punch me in the face, and something tells me she has a vicious right hook.

"I saw you on deck. I've been waiting for you," I say. "I've been waiting a long time so we could talk."

She turns toward me, eyes dark, liquid with repressed

tears. "Who the hell are you?" she asks. "And why are you here?"

I nod to the door in front of her. "I'll tell you. Let's go inside so we're not broadcasting this whole thing to every berth guest on this deck."

It's an amusing fact that I've been on board the royal yacht more times than I can recollect, but I've never ventured to the low decks where nobility is housed when they come aboard. I've been to the galley and the engine rooms. I've toured where the work gets done, but never once have I stepped into these narrow corridors where my subjects lay down their heads. The rooms are small, with low ceilings and narrow views of the ocean beyond the patio doors.

I wonder why the rooms are so small. This is another bit of reflection more appropriate for another day.

"I thought it would be a one-night stand," I say. "Maybe hang out and get breakfast or something. That's all I was about. But you..."

"I made you want to bolt within fifteen seconds of waking up beside me?" Norah slams her keys on the bureau, then yanks her overnight bag from the closet, tossing it on the bed. "I don't even know why I'm mad. But your dumb, stupid face makes me *mad*. I hate that I wanted you to stay. And I hate that I'm upset. Now, tell me *why* you need to talk to me at *all*."

She crosses her arms.

"No," I insist. "I *couldn't* stay."

"Why?!" she demands. "Why not stay five minutes and explain it to me?"

"I'm trying to explain it now," I say. "People I care about very much were in trouble. They needed me here in Anglesey. Norah, I was trying to pass as just a random guy that night, but I'm from an important family here. I had to come home. I couldn't wait—it was too important."

"Who are you?" she asks.

I need to think of something. I can't let her know. Not yet. "I'm a duke. A noble," I say. "With responsibilities and estates and more obligations than you can imagine."

"Are you married?"

I shake my head. "No, I'm not married."

She raises her head as if she understands. She doesn't.

"But you're here. Maybe I could make up for it?"

For just a second, I think she's considering my proposal, but then she shakes her head. "That would be an awful idea," she says. "Besides, I've depleted my savings doing my fancy tour of the UK. I need to go home soon. My own family is having a bit of a crisis themselves, and they need me back soon."

This is useful information. "What kind of crisis?"

Norah fills me in on the highlights. I heard something about this Mackoff character on the news.

"I think you need to go," Norah says. "I don't know what you expect, but you're not going to get a repeat of our night in Paris."

Her words cut me to the quick. "I don't expect that," I say. "I'd like to start over. Take you to dinner. Roll around in paint."

She smirks for a second and then goes back to her stern face. "You missed that chance by walking away from me. You didn't even tell me your last name."

Norah walks to the door, opening it, showing me out. "I still don't know your last name," she grinds out between clenched teeth. "It's time to go."

"You don't know my last name because I don't *have* a last name. The House of Cymrea was established in the Middle

Ages, before last names were required. We've always been monarchs, princes, and kings. A king doesn't need a last name."

She rolls her eyes dramatically.

"That a shitty excuse. Go."

"How did it go, sir?" Duncan asks once I'm safely returned to my sprawling apartments above deck. Bright rays of sunshine stream in, bathing the rooms in glowing golden hues.

"Not well," I admit. "She called me a 'fucking asshole.' Then she slapped me. Then she told me to get the fuck out."

Duncan is unmoved, but there's a flicker of amusement in his eyes. "Should I have her arrested, sir?"

I offer him nothing except a tired smile. "No, Duncan," I reply. "Just get me everything you can on her, and her family. This isn't done yet. Not by a long shot."

The truth is, I admire Norah for standing up for herself. She did exactly right. I treated her with shameful disrespect, I broke her trust, I hurt her. She has every right to regard me with disgust.

The ball is in my court to regain her faith, earn her forgiveness, and try the best way I know to show her I'm not the sociopath I behaved as. I'm not a bad person; I'm just a normal person trapped in an abnormal world who—out of frustration, or boredom, or a blind sense of entitlement—occasionally does stupid, hurtful things. Something tells me that Norah might bring some balance and sanity to this gilded cage we call the House of Cymrea.

4

NORAH

W hat an epic, entitled asshole. Every time I think of him my heart races, my brain seizes, and my fists clench. I should have slugged him or kneed him in the balls. My upbringing kicked in, checking me from venting my full rage. Honestly, I should have broken his nose. That said, his nose is too pretty to break. And as much as I despise him, he's still easy on the eyes.

When we finally got home and laid our heads down to sleep after that endless, tedious midsummer night's cruise, all I did was dream about Collin. I dreamed of his exquisite build, those broad, muscled shoulders, and his phenomenally skilled cock making my toes curl in a tangle of sweat-drenched sheets.

I'm incorrigible. There's no hope for me.

After a fitful night's sleep, I'm awakened by my phone. The Caller ID says it's Eric. I'm too exhausted to process the idea of just letting it roll over to voicemail. Foolishly, I answer.

"Three hundred sixteen dollars and thirty-seven cents

on clothes from three different shops in Saxony? I hope you got to meet the king?" His tone is incredulous, spiked with outrage.

"The king is dead," I blandly inform him, my brain still cloudy from lack of sleep. I refuse to justify buying several pairs of jeans and renting an AirBnB. "But I did get to attend a very nice party on the royal yacht."

"Fuck, Norah. *What are you doing?* Your credit union account has less than twenty-five thousand in it, and you're over there behaving like a jet-setter."

"I am not," I say. I let the pause go on, silence blooming between us.

"You'll come home *now*," Eric demands. "You'll come home now, or I'm shutting this whole shitshow down. I'll cancel your card."

"Do it." I realize I'd rather be dead broke than deal any more with this asshole.

"Watch me." I hear the ice in his tone. "Call me to book a flight home when you're ready to end this nonsense."

How can my account have less than twenty-five thousand in it? I've been living off the largesse of the Earl and Sinead. Except for clothes, I've spent almost nothing. I had thirty-five thousand when I got here.

Something's not right.

～

I RELAY my username and passcode to my mother over the phone. She types the digits on her laptop while I wait. "I've got it," she says. She's logged in successfully. "Honey, there's nothing there."

What?

"Your account balance is zero. It looks like everything

was transferred to an account in New York a week ago. Do you need me to send you some money? I don't have a lot, but I can get you home."

"I may need that, Mama," I say, feeling the full impact of her revelation. "I probably should come home."

The one person I trusted—Eric—has deceived me and stolen from me. I'm stranded in a foreign country without any resources.

"Book me a ticket out of London," I say, hearing the defeat in my tone.

"I'll try," Mom says. "All our credit cards were cancelled, and I've hesitated to have one issued from my trust account because I'm afraid of the damage your father would do if he got hold of it. If your friend Sinead has better access, you might try her first. We can reimburse her with cash."

Damn. That could be an awkward conversation I'd rather not have.

SINEAD HAD a fantastic time at the party, and she hasn't stopped filling her husband in on every single detail. At dinner she's still going strong, dropping the titles and names of every royal and blue blooded noble she managed to rub shoulders with. The Earl is entertained but unimpressed.

"You didn't meet Prince Owen," he observes dryly. "Did he even show up? Was he even there?"

"Oh, he was there," Sinead assures him. "Perched on the top deck, looking down his nose at us. His cousins came down to mix with the guests, but he never did. There was a rumor he had some girls brought up to him."

"Which girls?" the Earl asks, intrigued.

Sinead shrugs. "No one I know. I only heard about it third-hand."

The Earl turns to me. "And how about you, Norah? Did you see the prince? You've been awfully quiet since we got home. Did you have a good time?"

Sinead smiles awkwardly for my benefit. She knew she was on her own as soon as the loud music started. I hate crowds and loud noise; that party was not my scene at all. That, and running into Collin put me in a bad mood.

I didn't tell Sinead about that, because honestly, I'm ashamed of myself. I'm ashamed I hooked up with a total stranger who ditched me, who lied to me, and who I can't stop thinking about. The whole sordid thing paints me as pathetic.

I shouldn't have even been *mad*. I used a dating app. But I can't explain it.

"I had an okay time," I lie. "I've never been to anything like that before. It was... interesting."

The Earl smiles sympathetically. "I'll be honest with you, Norah: I'm not much for those sorts of soirees, either. And I'm probably less impressed with princes and dukes and the whole lot of nonsensical pretense than most of my countrymen." He glances at Sinead, then back to me. "It's why I married a good Irish Republican girl. She comes from a country that's done well at keeping kings and queens in their proper place."

Sinead laughs. "You know my father's an Orangeman, a devout loyalist."

He nods. "Yes, but I also know you've got your mother's common sense, and she's as green as Irish clover."

Before Sinead can reply, the dining room door opens and the butler appears, his face strained with anxiety. He moves toward the Earl, then leans down, whispering something in his master's ear. The Earl's face goes white as a sheet. His entire body tenses.

"What's wrong?" Sinead asks.

The Earl takes a breath, nodding to his butler. "In the parlor. Give us a moment."

As soon as the butler departs, the Earl turns to me. "You have a visitor," he says. "And I am all astonishment."

"I have a visitor?" How can that be? I don't know anyone else in this country... *except Collin.*

I feel my head cocking to the side. I feel my blood beginning to boil. That *asshole.* He tracked me down here. What is he, some kind of stalker? I really should have punched him in the nose.

Well now I have a second chance.

I'm on my feet before the Earl can elaborate. I'm in the wide, marble-paved foyer before he or Sinead can follow me. I'm in the parlor before the butler can clear his throat to announce me. And I am in Collin's very shocked face, giving him a piece of my mind, before he can open his mouth.

"Are you out of your mind?!" I demand accusingly, the anger palpable in my tone. "What in the hell are you doing here? Who in God's name do you think you are? You've got some nerve. You're worse than an asshole. Yesterday you were just an asshole—now you're a certified creep, stalking after me like..."

"Norah!" the Earl calls behind me.

"...like a damned criminal!"

"Norah," he calls sharply, "shut up!"

No one tells me to shut up.

Collin smiles. His eyebrows cock with amusement, his blue eyes flashing brightly. He's not even looking at me. He's looking past me.

I turn. Sinead and the Earl are behind me, both kneeling, heads down, eyes to the floor.

"Rise, please," Collin says. "Go on, get up. Nothing fancy. I'm just an asshole."

What in the ever-loving fuck is going on?

The Earl stands first, helping his lady to her feet. Still, neither of them lift their gazes.

"At your ease," Collin says.

The Earl looks up, swallowing hard, his face now bright red. He glares at me as if I've stabbed him in the head. Sinead just looks horrified.

Collin steps around me, approaching the Earl. He offers his hand. "You are John Hereford, Earl of Herefordshire?"

"Yes, Your Royal Highness," the Earl says, his voice trembling slightly.

What?

Collin turns his gaze to Sinead. "And your lady, sir?"

The Earl nods, "I'm pleased to introduce my wife, Lady Sinead Hereford, formerly Hewson of County Down, Republic of Ireland."

Collin offers Sinead his hand, and by the looks of her, I'm pretty sure she's going to faint. She's shaking like a leaf, as pale as death.

"I'm very pleased to meet both of you," Collin says. "And I beg your pardon for interrupting your dinner with my unannounced visit."

"Not at all, Your Highness. Your visit is the highest compliment of our lives. I... I... I apologize most emphatically for the way you were first treated. My guest... Sir, I have no explanation. I beg your forgiveness."

"There's no problem," he says. "I'm apparently in the wrong, according to Norah."

This is crazy. I don't understand.

Collin returns to me. There's something new in his demeanor, a haughtiness that wasn't there before, a self-importance that isn't attractive at all. "Forgiven," he says. "Miss Ballantyne and I, as you may suspect, have met previously—under very different circumstances."

He comes to me, facing me, staring into my eyes. "She's not to be reproached on the matter. She's a foreigner. She doesn't know any better. And I may have..."—he grins arrogantly—"I may have misled her as to my true identity."

What a fucking catastrophic asshole. 'Collin' is Prince Owen.

Sinead wavers on unsteady feet. Then, quick as a hummingbird's heartbeat, she drops to the floor like a sack of potatoes, out cold.

The Earl looks down at his wife, then at me, then at the Prince. He sits down next to his wife, trying to revive her, looking like he might faint as well.

Collin's brow furrows. He blinks. "I guess I should have called ahead," he says, deadpan. "Or maybe sent a card. It's rude to just drop in unannounced."

Norah rolls her eyes at me, shaking her head in disbelief. She glares at the her friends, then huffs out a string of expletives.

"You motherfucking imposter. Fucking dirtbag," she seethes and crosses her arms. "Biggest cunty asshole in the land of fucking cunty assholes."

"You have a dirty mouth," I observe. "And that's one of your better qualities."

"Oh, shut up and help me with these two," she insists, going to her friend's side, checking for a pulse—as if she has the first clue what to do to revive her.

"Where's the butler?" she asks Earl Hereford and then look to Prince Owen. "Do we need an ambulance?"

The Earl is too out of it to respond, and Owen just shrugs.

"I don't know. How should I know?" She's clearly irritated with me. At least she didn't slap me again.

I step into the foyer and call out for the butler's assistance. He responds dutifully, hurrying in with a footman and maid at his heels. By the time he lands on his knees beside Earl Hereford, the man is chatting nicely with him and helping his wife to sitting. A moment later his wife pops back to life with animation, waving her arms in the air as if trying to swim to the surface of some deep pool she's found herself in.

"Your Highness, I'm mortified," the Earl says once he's collected himself sufficiently. He tries to stand but finds himself still unsteady.

"Take a moment," I say, trying to reassure him. "I'm not in the least put out." Satisfied that no one is the worse for wear, I return to the point of my visit. "If it's not too much bother, I'd like to take a short drive with Miss Ballantyne. I have a few things I'd like to discuss with her."

"I'm not going anywhere with you," Norah protests.

The Earl shoots her a stern look. "Norah! Remember our conversation. You're a guest in my home, and in *his* country. You will do as you're told."

"Norah, please behave," Sinead pleads. "This is serious."

She's fuming and angry as hell. And just as sexy as she was when I first laid eyes on her.

I offer my hand. "Shall we?" I say, motioning toward the door.

"Where are we going?" Norah demands, slipping into the back seat beside me. Duncan is driving.

"I want to show you where I live, and talk business," I reply, turning my gaze toward my window so I won't be tempted to study the curve of her knees or the shapely arc of her calves. Her legs are diverting, especially when I recall how nice they felt against my chest, with her heels hooked over my shoulders.

"What business could we possibly have?"

"I'll tell you when we get there," I reply. "I'd prefer to discuss it in private, as I'm sure you would."

Duncan shoots me a hurt look from the rearview mirror. He knows exactly what I'm up to. Hell, I think he cooked this idea up himself and just convinced me it's my idea. He's clever like that. I'm going to need to make him the Minister of Defense before this is all said and done. I'd hate to have him working against me.

Norah turns on her seat toward me, laying her open palm down on the soft leather between us. She leans in, eyes narrowed, *judgy*. "And what is the deal with the high-brow, posh manners and tone back there with Sinead and Earl Whatsit? You're faking it! You're faking it with me, or you're faking it with everybody else. But one way or another, you're a complete fake!"

She's got me there.

"At least I don't have a dirty mouth like you," I reply, ignoring her rebuke. "Do you kiss your mother with that mouth?"

"Ew," she says, drawing back. "I don't kiss my mother at all. That's... *gross*."

Americans. They're so... *conflicted*.

It's well after nine in the evening when we arrive at Brynterion, so it's quiet. Half the staff have gone home, and the night staff are mostly busy with their duties. While I would love to try to impress Norah by walking her in the front door, giving her a grand tour of the castle, that runs the risk of drawing a great deal more attention to her visit that either of us are ready for.

Duncan deposits us in the back, inside the courtyard by the stables.

"Where are we going?" she asks again, this time less annoyed, more intrigued.

I lead her into the stables past fifty stalls occupied by curious, noisy thoroughbreds.

"They're beautiful," Norah whispers, knowing not to speak loudly lest she startle them.

From the stables we enter the mudroom, and from there I lead her through a false door into the "hidden" halls and passages connecting every room, corridor, and chamber inside this massive, ancient fortress.

"Are you taking me to the dungeon?" she quips, referencing the shadowy darkness and the scent of wet and mildew on the stone walls, ceilings, and floors. These halls have a dungeon's feel to them, but the actual dungeon is much creepier than Norah might imagine.

"Not yet," I reply. "But don't give me cause."

"Asshole."

The stairs leading to the third level are narrow and winding, the walls dripping with condensation. Sound carries up the space, our footsteps echoing, amplifying in the chill air. When we make the third floor, Norah is breathless. I lead her on at a quick pace, noting the cameras overhead that are certainly recording our presence here.

Finally, we arrive at the entrance to my apartment. I pause at the door, letting Norah catch up.

She comes alongside me, looking up at me oddly. "What is this?" she asks. "And why am I here?"

I open the door, showing her in.

My rooms don't exactly fit the traditional idea of a royal residence. Aside from the heavily decorated ceilings and overabundance of molding, carved paneling, and complicated geometric designs made into the glowing hardwood floors beneath our feet, everything else is all my own. I favor a minimalist approach to interior decoration, or perhaps a "functional" approach is a better definition. If it doesn't serve a purpose, I don't want it cluttering my world.

"Damn," Norah says, spinning around in the room—my parlor, for lack of a better word. "This is cool." She stops spinning when she sees the next room over, visible through a set of ornately carved wooden doors, set open.

"My library," I say. "Being a royal is boring. I have a lot of time to read."

Norah wanders into the library. I follow.

She studies the shelves, scanning spines for titles. There's everything in here from 16th-century cradle works to modern fiction. Lately I've been reading a lot of medieval history.

"Fascinating," Norah says, her voice low, contemplative. "I wouldn't have pegged you for a reader."

"Why's that?"

She shrugs, still inspecting. "I dunno. Preconceived notions, I guess. And I always heard royals were inbred dullards."

"Inbred... maybe," I reply. "Dullards sometimes, but not always."

This is fun, but it's not why she's here.

"We should get down to business," I say. "I have a proposition for you that I think you might be interested in. I hope you'll consider it."

I show Norah to a table at the far end of the library, pulling out a chair for her.

"I'd like a drink," I say, realizing I need one to prop up my courage. She may slap me again before I get through what I'm about to propose. "Would you like a drink?"

She waves her hands, rolling her eyes. "Whatever. Apparently I've got nowhere else to be."

I pour two glasses of the best thirty-year-old Anglesey whiskey money can buy. This is the King's Reserve, distilled and aged according to a recipe that's three hundred years old by the only distillery in the country licensed to use the royal seal or claim the prestige of the name.

Norah lifts her glass, taking a cautious sip. She takes a sip and then a deep breath, then halfway smiles. "That's very good."

I give her another moment to accustom herself to the beverage before I get to the point. "I'd like for you to hear me out on this before you react, or freak out, or slap me in the face, or whatever you ultimately decide to do. And I mean hear me out all the way. Can you do that?"

Norah frowns. "It depends on how wordy you are and how pretentious you sound while you're telling me."

"Fair enough," I respond. I take a deep breath, trying to gather my thoughts. "So my father died last year—six months ago, to be precise. It's law that a new king, his heir, must be crowned within a year of his death. My elder brother, Lloyd, is in line for that, and he's currently serving as co-regent with our mother."

She already looks bored.

"The thing is, while my brother is the new king for all intents and purposes, he's out of the country in an unofficial capacity, and I'm being forced to step into his role —*temporarily*. It's an unusual situation, and I can't go into a lot of detail, but it's a long-held custom in this country that the king must be a married man. If I'm going to take on the role even temporarily, as second son I have to demonstrate that I'm at least on the *path* toward marriage."

Norah's eyes grow wide. She clenches her jaw tight.

"Of course, it's all very temporary and just for show," I say, trying to reassure her. "As soon as my brother comes back, which will only be a few months from now, I can go back to being the invisible spare and no one will care about my relationship status."

"What does this—any of this—have to do with me?" Norah asks.

"I'd like to put you forward as my girlfriend. Nothing more complicated than that. Except instead of being my girlfriend, you just have to play the part. And you'll be... well-compensated."

She's looking at me like I have three heads.

I lift my drink to my lips, hoping it gives me the resolve to finish this. "I'll tell you everything you'll need to do to fulfill your part, and then you name your price."

"Why me?" she asks. "You had a boat load of girls at your feet yesterday who would have paid *you* for the chance to be your girlfriend. *Why me?*"

I'm glad she's asked. It's one of the first absolutely honest responses I can give her. "You're different," I say. "You're not an obsequious sycophant trying to climb the royal ladder. You're not interested in getting your name engraved in the Peerage Registry. And honestly, even though you think I'm an asshole—and rightly so—your manner and lack of shits about what I think is the most refreshing thing I've encountered in my whole life. I grew up with dukes and lords kissing my ass, treating me like... *royalty*. It's good to just be treated like the asshole I am."

Norah regards me and my answer a long while before she responds. Her eyes glint like steel. Like hard diamonds —intelligent and knowing. When she does, it's as if she's gotten inside my head and read my thoughts. "That's the first truthful thing you've said to me so far, isn't it?"

I don't reply. Instead, I finish my drink and pour another. Then I continue, detailing exactly what this very big job entails, from the clothes she wears to the way she walks and speaks, to accompanying me to social and ceremonial events, to living inside the palace walls where we can provide security, to having every aspect of her personal life, her background, and her family and friends' lives dissected, examined, and scrutinized by the press.

"We've already done comprehensive backgrounds on you, your employers, your family. So far nothing has turned up. Can you think of anything you or someone close to you may have done that would be catastrophic if it came out in the press?"

Norah shakes her head without pausing long on the question. "No, other than my father being stupid about money, or the fact that I had a one-night stand with a total fraud and conman, I can't think of anything else."

"That's fair."

"I have a question," she states, "and I need an honest answer."

"I'll do my best," I reply.

"What happens if your brother skips town, decides he doesn't want to be king?"

I try my best not to reveal just what I think of the question. "My brother will do his duty; it's what he was born for. He's just sowing the last of his wild oats right now. He'll be back soon, and we can all go back to the way things were."

She asks a few more questions, the last being, "Am I allowed to say no? Or is this a command performance like the party on the yacht, and making me come here to hear you out?"

"You're allowed to say no," I assure her. "But I very much hope you'll say yes, and I'm willing to go to some lengths to get you to yes."

"I'm listening," she says.

"First, I think I can part with one of the smaller royal estates under my care. I'll let you choose which one. After that, we could probably work out a grant or two to get you started in business for yourself. I believe you're a fashion photographer as well as an artist?" She nods. "Cymrea doesn't have a big fashion industry, but London does, and it's possible we could pinch some of that work and send it your way. Plus, being on the arm of a prince helps get clients for that sort of thing."

She's listening alright. A smile—the first real, full one all night—turns her lips ever so slightly.

"And as a final inducement, I believe an upfront cash payment is appropriate, followed by a final payment at the conclusion of our business. That, in addition to a generous allowance to cover expenses like your everyday clothes and such. The household will cover the cost of gowns and formal wear for the events you'll attend with me."

"How much are we talking?" Norah asks, trying to put a price on her freedom.

"You open the bidding," I say, allowing a small, self-satisfied smile. She's taken the bait. I've hooked her. Now I just need to reel her in.

"A hundred thousand dollars," she says.

I can't stifle the laugh that slips out. "How about... *a million euros*? Half now, half when we're done."

She grabs the arm of a chair and slowly lowers herself down. "A *million* euros?"

I may have given her a stroke.

She swallows hard. She looks down at her hands, and seeing them tremble, presses her palms flat on the table. "Good Lord," she whispers. "Good Lord."

"Is that a yes?" I ask.

She nods. "Yeah. Yeah. That's a yes."

I would have gone to three million.

"Outstanding," I say, lifting my glass. "It's a deal. But there's just one last thing you have to agree to."

She cocks her head at me. "What?"

"You can't ever call me an asshole in public again. You're welcome to do it in private when no one else is within earshot, but from here on out, you have to at least act like you like me, even if you hate my guts."

Norah grins, lifting her glass to touch mine. "Fine, if you say so. Just know that wherever we are, no matter how much I'm smiling or fawning for the cameras, I'm thinking the whole time, '*what a fucking asshole.*'"

"WE HAVE TO MAKE A SMALL DETOUR," I say, showing Norah into the car. "We need to get this show started, and the fastest way to do that is to let the press open the speculation. That'll get my mother's attention, and she'll insist on meeting you."

"What do you have in mind?" she asks as Duncan pulls off, headed toward town rather than back to her friend's house.

"Just a little PDA on the boardwalk, under the lights," I say. "The paparazzi know I'm in town, and they're all hanging around. It'll take about ten minutes before we're flashbulb central."

"Good God," Norah says. "This is crazy."

"You have no idea how crazy," I laugh. "It's gonna get crazier. Take me at my word."

Duncan parks the car in a public lot above the board-walk, overlooking the beach. The sun is just starting to make its way down, but it's still plenty bright, with a warm, gentle breeze coming from the southwest. I take Norah's hand in mine, leading her down the steps to the walkway. The air is clean and salty, the water blue out to the horizon, and high tide is rising on the sandy beach twenty feet below us.

As a child, I loved coming here with my nanny. We could do that then because no one knew who we were, as my mother did an excellent job of keeping our faces out of the spotlight. We were just two little boys on the beach with a woman everyone assumed was our mother. Today, it's rare that I get to come out in public. I miss it.

"Penny for your thoughts?" Norah says.

I smile, pausing at a wide stone post installed hundreds of years ago when the first seawall went in. It's four feet high and three feet square, made of solid granite. It occurs to me that this stone would look good with Norah's lovely ass planted on it. I lift her up, setting her onto it before she knows quite what I've done.

She laughs. I don't know if she's laughing with me, or at me. I don't care.

I step close, spreading her knees between my hips. "You really are beautiful," I say, which is the second truthful thing I've said to her today. Three glasses of whiskey, and I'm letting my guard down.

"Shut up, Your Royal Dickness," she says.

"No, it's true," I say. "If it wasn't true we wouldn't be here."

I lean in, finding her mouth, slipping my hand around the back of her lovely head. I part her lips gently, more gently than I did last time we were this close. Instead of citrus and spicy peppers, I taste peat bogs and orange wood. I taste strawberries and cream. I taste Norah, her precious heat. She kisses me back, slipping her arms over my shoulders. She sucks me into her, breathing me, even though she thinks I'm a "fucking asshole."

"Prince Owen!"

Right on cue.

"Prince Owen. Who's your girlfriend?!"

The flashbulbs are blinding. There are at least three of them, all shouting at us, all snapping shot after shot.

In a nanosecond, Duncan is between them and us, and I'm hustling Norah back to the car, back to safety.

"Jesus," she huffs as I pull the door closed against more paps and their cameras. "They're like piranhas."

That couldn't have gone better if I'd staged it.

My mother is going to wake up tomorrow with headlines giving her something else to think on besides my crazy brother and the fact that I'm twenty-seven years old and still not married. When she confronts me with it, I'll confess that Norah and I have been seeing one another secretly for more than a month—which is sort of true—and that I'm installing her as my Official Companion, which is my prerogative.

Mother may not like it. Norah's not one of her chosen duchesses, but she's better than any of them, and she'll do just fine for *both* our purposes.

Sinead lays the paper down on the table. She gapes at it, then up at me. "Seriously?" she insists. "Are you for real? You're seeing the Prince, and you've been keeping this a secret?"

The lurid photograph splayed across the top fold of *Today's Mail*—the worst tabloid in all the Northern Isles—would lead one to the conclusion that Prince Owen and I are more than just casual acquaintances.

Earl Whatsit stares at me with unrestrained horror. "This is insupportable," he states indignantly.

I have no idea what that means. I signed a non-disclosure agreement. I signed a detailed contract. I can only give them the "official" story.

"We met in Paris," I say. "We hit it off, but things got complicated. Then we reconnected again, and... yeah... we're dating."

We're "dating," and this afternoon a car with a security detail is going to show up to escort me, my suitcase, and three boxes of books to my new residence inside the palace grounds at Beaumaris Castle in Cymrea. Collin—Owen—

informed me of this as he sent me off after our brief but exciting stroll down the boardwalk at Saxony.

"I'm headed home to Cymrea tomorrow, and you're coming with me," he said, squeezing my hand between his.

He's paying me a million euros to relocate, and I really can't complain. I've worn out my welcome with Earl of his Holy Whatsitface, anyway.

I'VE ENDURED a week of fittings, elocution classes, and a crash course in Anglesey history. If I thought Sinead and the Earl put me through my paces ahead of the royal cruise, I was sadly mistaken. This world I've entered is beyond comprehension: everything is artifice, pretext, and staging.

If I'm dressed in blue, it means I aspire to marrying into the royal family. If I wear yellow, it means I'm just a friend. Red signifies I'm simply a passing fling. Green is the color of revolution and opposition to the monarchy. Orange implies I'm a fascist, bent on enslaving the whole nation.

What's left? Apparently I'm to be outfitted in fifty shades of gray with a few highlights of teal, as no one seems to have assigned any symbolic intrigue to that hue.

Owen—I've finally gotten used to calling him that— staged three more clandestine outings where the photographers caught us engaged in absurdly public displays of affection. He's adept at building a solid case for this fake relationship. Everyone thinks we're the real thing.

Today, for the first time in eight days, I have the afternoon to myself. My apartment at Beaumaris is wonderful, but it lacks a few things—like a toilet brush and dish rack— to make it perfectly functional.

"Where are we going, ma'am?" Duncan asks as he drops his shades low on his nose.

"Is there a Target?" I ask. "Or something like it. I need to get some household things. Wal-Mart would work."

Duncan looks confused.

"Ikea. Ikea is what I'm looking for. Tell me there's a fucking *Ikea*."

"There is no Ikea in Cymrea," Duncan says haughtily. "There's one in Bristol, but I'm certainly not crossing the border to England to deliver you to a sodding Ikea." He pauses. "*Ma'am.*"

I sigh. "Then take me to whatever most closely resembles a *sodding* Ikea."

Duncan delivers me to the only thing resembling a department store on the entire island. It's a place reminiscent of a five and dime, a time capsule from another era.

I locate my dish rack and my toilet brush, then make my way to the check-out counter. That's when things move south—quickly.

"Miss? Excuse me, miss!"

I turn toward the strange voice calling me. The next thing I know I'm framed in a reporter's viewfinder, flash-bulbs popping off in my face like strobe lights. I'm holding a toilet brush in one hand with a look of absolute shock on my face. I'm sure Owen will be thrilled.

"*If Crown Prince Lloyd abdicates, do you and Prince Own plan to marry?*"

"*Prince Lloyd is rumored to be suffering from a mental break-down. Is Prince Owen going to be the next king?*"

"*Have you and Prince Owen set a wedding date yet?*"

One photographer becomes three, and then ten. They shout questions at me rapid-fire, pressing in too close. Duncan steps between me and them, but they surround us.

The next thing I know, Duncan has a gun in his hand, backing them off with the barrel pointed straight ahead. "Let's get you out of here," he says, pulling me under his arm, hustling me back to the car while the photographers stalk twenty paces behind.

Speeding off, he glances at me in his rearview. "Are you okay? That was much too close."

I'm fine. A little shaken. I nod at him.

"We're going to have to rethink your security protocol," Duncan says. "I'll speak with the Prince about it today."

Why would they think Crown Prince Lloyd is having a mental problem? Why would they think he plans to abdicate?

Right after I arrived in Anglesey, Earl Whatsit said there was a rumor afoot about Owen succeeding to the throne, but he made light of it, like it was a joke. Maybe there's something to this. Maybe Owen's been leading me down a merry path.

I need to get to the bottom of this.

"Duncan, tell His Royal Pain in My Ass that I need to speak to him posthaste, or our deal is off, and I'm going to the press with some deep palace intrigue."

Duncan nods without expression, keeping his eyes fixed on the road ahead. "Yes, ma'am."

∾

"DUNCAN PASSED YOUR MESSAGE ALONG," Owen says. "I'm sorry about the paparazzi, but it's no reason to get testy or start making threats."

He's standing over me with his arms crossed, peering down his nose at me like I'm an errant child. He's infuriating, and infuriatingly handsome. It would be so much easier to *really* hate him if he weren't *him*. Six feet, perfect, slightly messy hair. Deep set blue eyes that look almost thoughtful if you catch him off guard. And the lean, muscular body of a swimmer. His easy manner can change from formal and appropriate to downright dirty at a moment's notice—and I catch myself almost liking him.

"Where is your brother? And why do the tabloids think he's having a mental breakdown?"

If he clenches his jaw any tighter, he's going to chip some of those perfect pearly whites. "I told you, he's out of the country on a personal issue," Owen says. "It's none of your business."

"Oh, it's very much my business when I'm accosted by a rabid gang of bloodthirsty reporters who only back down when guns are drawn," I snap back at Prince Pompous. "It's my business when the whole world thinks I'm your intended and you're going to be king, which makes me a prisoner for life inside this fake romance you've dreamed up. Tell me what is going on."

Owen slumps, then slides into an overstuffed chair in the middle of the parlor. He looks deflated. He may even be pouting. It's hard to tell. He's delicious, even when brooding like a brat.

"Okay," he relents, shaking his head, letting it fall back on the cushioned chairback in utter defeat. "My brother is in Bora Bora, hanging out with a bunch of lunatics with shaved heads who fancy themselves The Exalted Order of the One True Toth. They worship a statue of a baboon, chant at the thing all day long, and believe the world is going to end on the thirty-first day of February, 2037, when Toth will magically appear from the heavens to take them to some planet hiding behind the moon."

Wait. What?

"But there is no thirty-first day of February," I say, then

realize the absurdity of my own statement. Laughter comes to me; I can't suppress it. Giggles peal out as I try to process what the hell he's just said.

"Go ahead," Owen sighs, staring up at the ceiling, not reacting. "Laugh. Lord knows I've laughed about it enough. But no one's laughing anymore."

"You're serious? Your brother, the Crown Prince of Anglesey, has joined a cult? The next king is going to be a baboon-worshipping Hare Krishna?"

That's rich. That's awesome! That'll be fun to watch. Get me some popcorn!

"Probably not," Owen says, resignation dragging his tone to the dungeon.

"What do you mean?" I ask, still snorting back giggles.

He sits up, his face now stern, serious. He folds his hands together between open knees, his eyes fixing mine in a steady gaze. "I mean he's either going to voluntarily abdicate, or he's going to be declared unfit to rule and be deposed. There's a committee of twenty-seven judges, nobles, psychiatrists, my mother, along with several other members of the royal family, secretly flying to Bora Bora right now. So far he's refused to come home. One way or another, he's coming home now, even if it's in a straightjacket. We were going to give him some time to come to his senses, but the idiot gave an interview to some reporter. We were able to suppress its publication, but that stunt was enough to put everything in motion. My mother is apoplectic."

"Oh my God," I say, realizing exactly what this means. "You're going to be king."

Owen heaves a heavy sigh. "Maybe," he says. "I've got a few cousins who might arm wrestle me for it."

"How could they?" I ask. "You're the king's son, too."

"I'm the king's unmarried second son," he replies, still holding my gaze. "If I'm to have a prayer of becoming king, I need to be married, or at least engaged."

"That isn't part of our deal," I say, feeling the Earth tilt beneath me. I need to sit down; I feel queasy. "This was supposed to be temporary. This isn't even real."

"It's become very real, very quickly," Owen says. "I'd like to re-open our deal, throw some things in, convince you to marry me. When Mother returns from this trip and the news comes out about Lloyd, I want to have a fiancée and a wedding date ready to announce, to put as much of a positive spin on this fiasco as I can."

He's lost his mind.

"I'm serious," Owen insists. "Your father lost everything to that conman Mackoff. I can restore what he lost and then some, along with paying off your family's debts."

"You're serious."

"I'll give you Brynterion as your own private residence, so when you decide you've had enough of me, you'll have somewhere to retire that's befitting of your status."

What?

"Of course, you'll become Duchess of Brynterion, which comes with an annual income of sixteen million euros. I can probably throw in a few more titles and smaller estates to round the numbers up."

Oh. My. God.

"And I think your friends, the Earl of Hereford and his lovely wife, Sinead, would appreciate being elevated to the Marquess and Marchioness of Westmoreland, with that estate and its income at their disposal. The Earl inherited a title and a nice, very ancient house that's badly in need of repair. He didn't inherit the money to keep the place up.

Unless he wins the lottery, he's going to be the last earl to ever walk those halls."

That's awful.

"What more can I offer you?" Owen asks, something akin to pleading in his expression.

I always hoped someday I'd meet the *one* guy who was meant for me, that we'd fall instantly in love, have a whirlwind, romantic courtship, and then live happily ever after. But I've known for a long time that only happens in fairytales.

I don't love Owen. I don't even like him sometimes. But he's not a bad person. I could do so much worse for myself and my family. This would make everything right again for them. And think of the good I could do in the world with a platform like this one, and the money I could spend on worthwhile things. I'd have to be a fool to say no, and my mother didn't raise a fool.

"You don't need to offer me anything more," I say. "We'll figure it all out. But yeah, I'll be your real fake fiancée."

"Really?" he asks, optimism lifting his tone. "You'll do this?"

I nod. "Yes," I say, half-smiling. "I'd be pretty stupid to say no to becoming an instant duchess, now wouldn't I?"

7

OWEN

"He's completely lost his marbles," my uncle Rupert says, peering through the one-way mirror at my brother, who sits cross-legged on the floor, dressed in a saffron robe, chanting some gibberish at the top of his lungs like a cat in heat. He never could carry a tune.

It's hard to look at him. According to the doctor, he's been living on a diet of white rice and tree bark. He's bloated *and* emaciated, pasty-looking. His head is completely shaved, and he has a hieroglyph tattooed on his forehead right between his eyebrows, which are plucked into razor-sharp points like some Japanese anime character.

"He's batshit crazy," my cousin David observes with no small amount of glee. "He tried to bite me when we were putting him on the plane."

"He tried to lick me," my aunt says. "He's lost his wits."

Lloyd has refused to sign the abdication papers; he wants to be king so he can change the official religion of Anglesey to The Exalted Order of the One True Toth and convert Beaumaris Castle into a baboon sanctuary. He even suggested he might appoint me Minister of Cage Sweepers. I thanked him for thinking of me.

There is no doubt that my brother is bonkers, but it remains to be seen what's going to be done about it. Six different psychiatrists have examined him, and all six agree he's completely detached from reality. Being crazy has never been used as a reason to depose a prospective king in Anglesey before. To do it, the nobles are going to have to be on board.

My mother has been working the phones all day. She's calling an emergency meeting of the House of Lords to put the question to them. I haven't seen her or spoken to her since she returned with Lloyd late last night, but she's summoned me to her apartments for a meeting at three o'clock. According to everyone I've spoken with, she's in high dungeon, ready to start stripping titles and lands from any noble who opposes her.

I need to calm her down. The last thing we need to do is piss off the peers—not when we need them to back me as the next king.

When I'm shown into her library, I'm surprised to find her in a good mood. She's sitting cross-legged on a gilt Louis XIV chair, tapping her toe to a Mozart concerto playing in the background. "Ah, Owen!" she greets me. "Finally."

"I'm glad you've returned safely," I say, kissing her cheek, then taking the seat across from her.

"Have you seen him?" she asks.

I nod.

"He's deplorable."

"In a word," I agree.

"That's not why I asked for you, however," she says, setting her teacup down, neatly folding her hands in her lap. "I hear there's a girl here, living in the Official Companion's apartments, and I hear she's wearing a certain sapphire ring that belonged to your grandmother."

Word travels fast. I nod again. "I was waiting for things to settle down a bit before telling you," I say. "We haven't told a soul yet."

"Yes, well, staff pay attention to these things, and I pay them handsomely to report everything to me. And you've been all over the papers."

She's taking this better than I expected her to.

"She's no one I know," Mother observes. "She's an American. Where did you find her?"

"We met when I was in Paris a couple months back. We've been seeing one another ever since."

"Really?" she asks, offering a discreet, doubting smile.

"I care a great deal for her, Mother. I know you would have preferred some duchess or a Swedish princess, but new blood might be just what we need to reassure the public we're not all inbred, raving lunatics."

She cocks an eyebrow at me. "You might be right," she admits. "And since I know she passed the background checks you so wisely performed before letting this relationship leak, I'm not going to make a fuss. I need you wed by Christmas, and we need her knocked up by sometime next year. She'll do just the trick."

Oh boy. What else do I have to horse-trade with Norah to get *that* thrown into our deal? I think I've already thrown all my chips down.

"One thing at a time," I suggest. "Let's make sure the House of Lords vote goes our way first."

Mother smiles. "It's going to go our way," she says confidently. "I've had the assurance of every duke and marquess in the chamber. Your cousin David did some early lobbying of his own, threatening to bring back the guillotine if he didn't get named heir. It didn't go over well. Your other cousin, Martin, has no interest in being king, much to his mother's dismay. He's in a rock band touring South America. He said he couldn't possibly come back for a coronation."

If I do become king, my first official act will be to banish my cousin David from the realm, seize all his assets and titles, and give them to our cousin Martin.

"You're certain?" I ask. "Absolutely certain?"

"I'm certain," she says. "You'll be King Owen by your twenty-ninth birthday. And then we'll get you happily married."

I'm not sure why, but I can't wait to share this good news with Norah. I know she'll have some smart-ass comment, and she'll find a way to make it bad news while insulting me in the same breath. For some odd reason she's growing on me; her quips and jabs entertain me. She's challenging, and I find that more attractive than I ever expected.

She looks good on my arm, too. I like studying the paparazzi photos of us: we're a striking couple, and we look like we belong together. Sometimes I worry I might be falling for her, especially when I think about how perfect we were in bed back in Paris. I keep reminding myself that this is an *arrangement.* Norah is in it for the money—not for me. She can barely stand me.

I wish, sometimes, that it weren't that way. But it is.

"Dinner is at eight," Mother says. "Bring the young lady to meet me. I want to get a good look at her before we make the announcement."

～

"WHAT IF SHE HATES ME?" Norah asks, checking her hair and dress in the tall mirror in her bedroom.

She's nervous, and she's beautiful, too, flitting around to make certain she looks perfect.

"She's not going to hate you," I say. "Unless we're late."

Norah glares at me in the mirror. She's changed dresses three times, making me turn my back while she decides which one among a dozen is right. They all look wonderful; she'd look like a princess even if she dressed in a brown paper bag.

"How do you know?" she asks. "She's Princess Dalia, the 'World's Princess,' the most popular, most beautiful royal on the planet—and I'm just frumpy Norah from Charleston."

Norah is so far from frumpy the idea makes me laugh.

"You laugh!" she gripes. "But if I screw this up, you're going to sue me for breach of contract."

"She's going to like you just fine," I assure her.

"How do you know?" she asks again, fiddling with an errant strand of wild, curling hair.

I step up behind her, gazing into the mirror, taking in her lovely figure, admiring the arc of her hip, the bow of cleavage peeking from beneath her neckline. "Because *I* like you," I say. "And even if she is the 'World's Princess,' she's also my mother, and she wants me to be happy."

Norah stills, gazing back at me in the glass. Her expression is perplexed.

I've rendered her speechless. That's a first. "We should go," I say. "It would be better not to keep the 'World's Princess' waiting."

The poise and elocution classes have paid off. When I present Norah to my mother, she perfectly executes a knee-deep curtsy in her high heels and fitted dress.

My mother graciously—and unexpectedly—offers her hand.

Norah shakes correctly, then returns her posture to hands clasped, eyes down, waiting to be addressed before making eye contact.

"Norah, I'm very pleased to meet you," Mother says.

"Thank you, Your Royal Highness. I'm honored." She's forgotten to breathe and is turning pale.

"At your ease, darling," Mother says. "I promise, I'm genuinely pleased to learn that someone has finally, at long last, caught my son's heart. I was starting to think I was going to have to pay someone to marry him."

Norah tries not to smile, and I see her relax a little. I almost expect her to pop off with some smart-ass remark, but I begged her to behave. She seems to be minding me.

"She's lovely, Owen," Mother says to me. "You didn't tell me she was so lovely."

At dinner, Norah uses the correct fork and the correct spoon at all the correct times. She's dropped her American table habit of spearing her food, adopting our more refined manners. Mother asks her leading questions about her family and her work, which Norah answers with the grace of a seasoned diplomat.

I stay out of the conversation, letting them banter, until Mother turns to me with a stunning suggestion. "Darling, you know, there's absolutely no reason whatsoever that Norah should be banished to the Official Companion's residence in the back wing of the palace. She should move into your wing, attached to your residence. I certainly have no issue with it, and if I approve, that settles it."

I stare slack-jawed, trying to figure out how to respond, when Norah begins giggling like a school girl. I love her harpsichord ring of laughter; it melts my heart. I can't help but smile whenever I hear her laugh. I can't help but laugh with her.

Mother looks to Norah, who's trying not to laugh and failing miserably. Then she looks to me. She folds her hands over her plate with a self-satisfied smile, shaking her head. "You two really are rather adorable. It's been a great while since this palace has seen a real love match. It's long overdue."

Norah gives me a look that I can't quite place, and then we move on to dinner.

8

NORAH

I reach forward, pressing my fingertips into the smooth, taut flesh of Owen's chest. The heat of his skin warms me deep in my bones as I trace the firm muscle of his shoulder. He watches me while I touch him, regarding me with perfect contentment. I could sit just like this, the two of us naked together, exploring one another forever. He's my beau ideal. Our bodies were made for other another. When he lies atop me with his cock inside me, whispering against my ear, he feels like the half of me that's been missing my entire life, returned to my core where he always belonged.

He makes me nearly come with the way he looks at me, the way he possesses me completely. The scratch of his stubble against my skin is electric. I get wet just catching his scent...

I'm yanked awake, pulled out of my bliss by an unwanted ray of bright sunshine poured over my face with the same bracing effect as a bucket of ice-cold water.

"Mmmmm..." I complain. "I want to sleep." *I want to dream of him.*

"I'm sorry, ma'am," says Sally, my maid. She fluffs the

curtains she's just opened. "I thought you might like to see this."

I pull up the covers, spreading them flat to make way for the tray table she's brought with my coffee and toast.

She's also brought the morning papers. Usually I could care less what the papers have to say, but it's been a tense week with Lloyd going under public scrutiny, being interviewed by the House of Lords on live television, demonstrating to the entire world that he's a complete basket case, incapable of rational thought. He chanted and howled while the lords tried to question him. When he did speak, it was nonsense. The hearings ended yesterday, and the lords went into convocation to decide what to do. They can't leave the debate chamber until they've legally deposed Lloyd and selected the next king, or decided to leave Lloyd in place, surrendering Anglesey to the baboons.

Owen and his mother are confident the outcome will go the way they want it to, but anything could happen.

Sally opens the paper, laying it by my side. The headline reads "HRH Crown Prince Lloyd is Crowned No More. DEPOSED! Lords Like the Sound of 'Long Live King Owen!' Coronation Set for 7th of August."

"Thank heavens!" I exclaim, lifting the paper, admiring the official palace photograph of Owen in his striking military uniform.

"Yes, ma'am, we're all very pleased," Sally says, smiling broadly. "Everyone's been on tenterhooks the last few months. We're so happy to have it resolved."

"Is Owen around?" I ask, taking my first sip of coffee.

"No, ma'am. He left early this morning, as soon as the news arrived. He had to go to the House of Lords to sign documents, making it all official. He should be back soon."

This is really happening. It's still so hard to believe. *King*

Owen. And I'm marrying him. We're announcing our engagement to the public tomorrow night at the Mid-Summer Gala. Princess Dalia told the lords about us, just to bolster their confidence in Owen, but no one knows outside the court. I haven't even told my parents, which I'm going to do today.

But first I want to see Owen.

"Let me know as soon as he returns, okay?" I ask Sally.

"Of course, ma'am."

While still incredibly pompous, entitled, and irritating, Owen has endearing qualities. He never ceases to give me new material to laugh at. He never ceases to amaze me with the bottomless depths of his expectations. I learned over lunch a couple days ago that if everything goes according to plan, we're going to need to get pregnant next year.

"And precisely how is that supposed to happen?" I ask him, mustering all the indignation I can manage, yet truly curious about the answer.

His Royal Cockiness grins at me. "Well, there's this thing called fertilization that occurs when the man's sperm reaches..."

I kick him under the table, making him howl.

"You bruised me!" he whines like a brat. "You really are mean."

"And you're an asshole," I remind him. "You're an entitled asshole with a mightily overblown ego."

"I'm entitled," he quips right back. "If everything goes as planned, I'm going to be king. And our son is going to be crown prince. And that's that."

"I think not," I say.

Owen, resigned to my taunts, replies, "Don't worry, Duchess. In this family we make heirs and spares the old-fashioned way: with artificial insemination."

That's somewhat disappointing news. "Are you serious?"

He nods, regarding me with amusement. "Deadly serious. Haven't you ever wondered why all the royals have boys before they have girls, and how the babies are conceived so swiftly, with no trouble at all, so soon after the wedding?"

"Now that you mention it, that is odd."

Great. I'm going to be a fake fiancée, a fake wife, *and* a fake mother. I wish someone could guarantee me a fake, pain-free childbirth. Maybe we can hire a fake surrogate.

"You know, Prince Conniving," I say, "you're not *all* bad. There was that one time in Paris..."

Owen sighs, offering a heartened smile. "Why Duchess, I think that's the nicest thing you've ever said to me."

"Don't get used to it," I huff back. "Just offering to do my duty for crown and country, no matter how awful the duty might be."

It's late morning by the time Owen appears, looking panty-melting hot in a fancy tailored suit of shiny gray silk. He doesn't dress up often, but I guess when you're going to the House of Lords to sign papers making yourself king, it's best to look the part.

"You're dashing," I say, meaning it. "Silk suits you."

He offers me a wide, princely grin followed by an unexpected, brotherly hug. "It's done," he sighs over my shoulder. "It's finally done."

When he pulls back he keeps his hands on my shoulders, fixing my gaze. "As of this morning, I'm the acting king of Anglesey. Mother even resigned as co-regent, which wasn't required and was certainly unexpected."

"Do I need to curtsy?" I ask, only half teasing.

He drops his hands, laughing with me. "No," he says. "But you do need to make a strong showing tomorrow night when we announce our engagement. We're going to be scrutinized. Every glance will be analyzed for subtext. We'll need to put on a convincing performance and engage in a little bit of PDA for the guests and the cameras."

I can think of worse ways to spend my time. "Fine," I say. "I don't care. I just need some assistance picking out a gown. Your mother had seven sent in for me to consider. Will you help?"

Owen smiles. "Of course I'll help," he says. "But can it wait until this evening? I've got a meeting with the privy counselor at noon, and another with the royal comptroller at one. That one's important, as I'm giving him instructions on getting your parents' debts cleared and payments made to them, as well as the payments I owe you. After that, I have a third meeting at two o'clock to interview the three most promising candidates for the job of my private secretary. And I'm sending Lloyd off to Switzerland for a thorough psychological examination to see if anything can be done for him. I won't be free until at least four-thirty."

"You're so very important now, Your Royal Hoity-Toity," I observe drolly. "Yes, I can wait until this evening. Bring a bottle of something expensive so we can celebrate your grand achievement: being born rich, male, and royal."

"Of course," Owen says. "Expensive red, white, or whiskey?"

"You choose," I tell him. "That's the only thing you know more about than I do."

~

THE CALL with my parents goes surprisingly well. My

mother is shocked, and she keeps asking me if I'm happy and if I love him, which I assure her I do because I don't want to break her heart. I am happy, so there's no fudging there. I'm having a good time being Owen's fake everything.

And I'll be able to save the two people who saved *me* time and time again. All of this is the only thing I *can* do.

My father is just as shocked, but his reaction stems from a different root. "He's paying you?" he asks with disbelief. "Like a dowry? He's paying *us?*"

"Yes, Dad," I say. "In fact, just this afternoon Owen is meeting with the comptroller to get the money transferred to you. Try to hang onto it this time. Maybe manage your own investments?"

"You're marrying a prince?" my mom says. "A real prince."

"I'm marrying a real prince who is about to become a real king," I remind them. "We haven't set a date yet. But we will soon. I'll let you know and book your travel."

"I LIKE THAT ONE," Owen says, peering at me from his seat halfway across the room. He's got a glass of fancy scotch in his hand and a scandalously lurid smirk on his face.

"Stop ogling me and zip me up," I instruct. "Make yourself useful."

He sets his glass down and rises, coming behind me to help with the zipper. When he's done, he pauses, looking me over in the mirror, hands lingering at my hips. "That's the one," he says. "It's beautiful. You're beautiful in it."

I wonder what he'd do if I turned around and faced him right now? I wonder if he'd kiss me the way he kissed me in Paris?

I need to stop thinking these thoughts. I need to focus on the task at hand.

The dress is a fifty-thousand-dollar gown designed by someone whose name I can't pronounce. The fabric is so fine and soft to the touch, it's like stroking a newborn lamb's ear. The cut is perfectly tailored to my figure. It fits like a glove, made just for me. The color is so close to the color of my eyes it's almost haunting to see myself wearing it. It makes my eyes shine bright, as if they're illuminated from within.

"I should have hired a less attractive woman for this gig," Owen says, still taking me in. "Every man in Anglesey is going to fall in love with you. I think I might just get a little bit jealous."

I roll my eyes at him. "There's not a man in this entire country who would look at me twice," I say coldly. "I'm stamped with the royal seal. I couldn't get laid if I walked through Cymrea Central Prison stark naked. Every man in Anglesey knows you'd hang, draw, and quarter anyone who even gives me a sideways glance. Duncan won't even make eye contact since you got made acting king."

"Duncan's a smart man," Owen observes, reaching to lower my zipper. "That's the dress you're wearing tomorrow. Send the rest back."

With that royal proclamation, he turns and walks away without another word.

I find myself wishing that, for once, he would stay.

THE MID-SUMMER GALA IS, I'm told, second only to the Christmas Gala in the long list of holiday parties hosted by the monarchy. The palace is decorated with flowers at every table and hung from every stone archway. The ballroom is festooned with bouquets and vases spilling with blooms. The sun still shines brightly, hanging high overhead at eight in the evening when the first parade of guests arrive in a train of limousines stretching from the front steps, around the main drive, out toward the palace gates, pouring onto the city streets.

From my balcony, I watch people step out of their cars: nobles dressed to the nines in tuxedos and gowns, wrapped with furs, crowned with jeweled tiaras, diamonds glittering on their fingers, throats, and wrists.

"It's almost time."

I turn, surprised. Owen stands in the open doorway behind me. He's dressed to the nines as well, wearing a royal blue tux coat with sharkskin lapels over a stiffly starched, tab-collar shirt. With his broad-shouldered, narrow-hipped build, he could almost be a male runway model for clothes like those. He was born to wear them.

"I'm ready," I say. I've been dressed for an hour; I'm anxious to get through this evening and get past it. It's a big "coming out," and once it's done I hope everything will get a little bit easier.

"Not quite," Owen says, half-smiling. "You're not finished dressing."

"What?" I ask him, not understanding.

He reaches into his jacket pocket, producing an oblong box. The box is hand-sized, wrapped in royal blue velvet. "You're going to be the most beautiful woman in the palace tonight, so you should have the most beautiful gems to adorn you."

He opens the box, revealing a necklace composed of the most stunning array of sparkling blue sapphires and diamonds I've *never* seen before, not even in the movies. "Let me put this on you," Owen says. "Turn around."

The necklace is heavy. It's perfect, and gorgeous, and absurdly opulent. I'm astonished by how lovely it is and how well it complements the dress.

Owen smiles at me in the mirror. "It belonged to my grandmother, and before her, her grandmother. Now it's yours."

For tonight, at least.

"You're still not completely dressed yet," he says, giving me a boyish grin. From another pocket he produces a smaller square box, also wrapped in blue velvet. "This one," he says, opening the lid on a matching sapphire and diamond bracelet, "didn't belong to anyone else, as I had it made just for you."

He releases the clasp, slipping the bracelet onto my gloved wrist, then secures it. "Now you're dressed."

I think I ought to change my panties.

"It's time to go," Owen says, threading his fingers into mine. "Showtime."

Because the place is overrun with guests, crowded with people in every room and corridor, security takes us, along with other members of the royal family, into the tunnels to make our way to the ballroom. It's quite the silly adventure: a dozen over-dressed blue bloods in tuxes and ball gowns walking on delicate high heels over uneven, raw stone floors and through dank, seeping passageways toward our destination.

There's one member of the royal family missing: Owen's cousin, David. As we're hustled up a narrow, spiraling stone stairway, I ask Owen where he is.

"He's in Paraguay," he says with a smirk. "Running a logging camp."

"That sounds horrible," I exclaim, trying to navigate on my heels, holding tight to Owen's strong hand, which is the only thing keeping me upright.

"Better that than the castle tower," he quips, referring to the jail used in an earlier era to confine traitors prior to their executions. "Or the gallows."

"Remind me to never *really* piss you off," I reply in a low voice.

Owen smiles, squeezing my hand. "I don't think there's anything you could do to get you banished to Paraguay," he says. "The Shetland Islands, however, are looking for a new duchess—just in case you get out of line."

The first hour of the gala is the most awful, tedious affair I've ever endured. It consists of a reception line with Owen at the head, his mother to his right, and a string of royals in order of precedence shaking hands with and greeting every single guest invited to this shindig, from the highest to the lowest.

I'm banished to a position all by myself behind the family, my hands clasped in front of me, eyes straight ahead, just waiting for the monotony to end. I see a thousand eyes fall on me, all of them curious, inquiring, examining. I feel like a speck of mold on a beautifully decorated cake. I'm the taint of sour in the otherwise pristine cream.

"You're doing just fine," Duncan whispers in my ear when I begin to fidget. "Hang tough. This part is almost over. After tonight, you'll never have to do this again. You'll be where Her Royal Highness Princess Dalia is now— second only to the king."

I look up at Duncan, who's staring straight ahead into the crowd. "Thank you," I say. "Thanks for boosting me."

Duncan lets a hint of a smile. "Ma'am, it's my pleasure. You're the best thing to come into this creaky old house in years. You're the best thing that's happened to Owen since I've known him. Keep it up. Whatever you're doing, it's good for him."

What in the world can he possibly be talking about? I haven't done a thing for Owen except agree to be his fake fiancée, his fake wife, and the fake mother of his royal heir.

Once the reception line is done, Owen returns to my side. He lifts my hand in his, asking me to remove my gloves. "When I take the stage to make the announcement, everyone needs to be able to see the ring," he says. "We can't hide it behind formal wear."

The ring he gave me is stunning. It's a gigantic sapphire wrapped in an oval of diamonds, set in platinum. This, like the necklace, belonged to his grandmother. The press is going to want pictures.

"I'll call you onto the stage," Owen says. "All you have to do is come up, stand beside me and be lovely, which you already do without thinking about it. Okay?"

I nod, my heart pounding in my chest.

A half hour later I find myself on the elevated stage, unsure exactly how I got there, feeling Owen's strong hands circling my waist, hearing his voice tell the huge crowd of people and flashing cameras in front of us that he feels like the luckiest man in the world.

Ahead of us I see Her Royal Highness Princess Dalia beaming, applauding, curtsying to me. A dozen other members of the royal household follow, dipping low on bent knees. The whole room, a sea of people, go quiet, stooping to kneel. It's the strangest, most stupefying spectacle I've ever witnessed.

Owen pulls me close, leaning into my ear. "Welcome to the family business," he nearly growls. "You're one of us now, Duchess."

Later, after the handshakes and congratulations, after toasts and a thousand strangers bowing to me, saluting my health and happiness, I find myself outside the palace in the shadows with Owen, walking along a torchlit path, hand in hand.

"You did well tonight," he says, drawing me close, under his arm. "You won them all over and looked stunning for the cameras. You're going to be the cover story on every tabloid paper from Madagascar to Tokyo tomorrow."

It's late, and my feet hurt. What I want more than anything is to go to bed.

"You look beautiful," Owen says, slowing on the path. "Even more beautiful that I imagined you would, and I have a vivid imagination."

As exhausted as I am, I'm keenly aware that Owen is turning on the charm, and that we're hardly alone. A half-dozen security men from the royal guard surround us. Plus, the grounds are littered with guests who, like us, are eager to escape the confines of the stifling crowds in the ballroom.

"At some point," Owen continues, turning to face me, "you're going to have to admit we're not a bad match. We may just be a *good* match."

"If irritating me is *good*," I quip, "then you're the best."

Duncan and another of the royal guard stand within easy earshot. Owen glares at me, then he addresses them authoritatively. "Guards, walk away."

They both hop-to as ordered. When they're gone, Owen sizes me up like he's considering a lamb chop. "I told you to keep your opinions of me between us," he reminds me. "Not that I mind irritating you, but letting the help know it does neither of us any favors."

I roll my eyes at him, then conjure a cutting glare.

"Oh, this is going to be so much fun," he nearly growls, smirking at me.

What's he up to?

Owen reaches forward, taking my hands in his, and pulls me with him onto a turn-out in the path leading into a dark tunnel of hedges that close above our heads, blocking out even a glimmer of light.

"Where are we going?" I ask, holding on tight to Owen. "I can't see where we're going!"

"Shush!"

He pulls me around another corner and the hedges draw back, revealing a cloudless, starlit sky. There's a beautiful little stone building in the center of an odd courtyard hidden in the hedges. Owen leads me toward it at a pace that's difficult to keep up with in my delicate heels.

"Slow down!" I beg. "I'll break a heel. These shoes cost a thousand euros!"

"Is that all?" he asks, laughing, and then he sweeps me up in his arms as if I'm a pet. When he puts me down, it's on top of what can best be described as a stone altar in the center of the building.

"What is this place?" I ask him, peering around, taking it in through shadows and reflected starlight.

"This is some old king's architectural folly," he informs me. "Made for moments just like this."

He steps close, placing a hand on my knee over my dress, then pushes it aside, spreading my legs so he can get closer still. A second later, his other hand slips up my leg, coming under my skirts. He reaches my thigh, then turns inward, his hand lost to view but very much present in my awareness. It's so dark I can barely see him, but I feel his heat, I smell him, and I hear his breathing.

His fingers graze the inside of my thigh, high up, very

near my most private places—so close that his touch makes me ache. This is what I've dreamed of: Owen touching me, exploring, taking his sweet time, teasing my skin.

We shouldn't do this—not after all the name-calling, the tedious planning.

What would it hurt?

His other hand slides up my bare arm, then over my shoulder, fingers eventually circling the back of my neck. He pulls me to him, opening my lips with his searching tongue, sucking me in with hungry, impatient kisses as his thumb slips higher up my thigh, finding my already-stiff clit. He presses gently over silk fabric, making me moan, making me wet.

His mouth is skilled at drawing me out of myself. I forget I'm supposed to keep a wall up against him in retribution for how he treated me. He melts me under his touches. Every cell in my body fires when I'm skin-to-skin with him. My hand falls to his chest, fingers pressing into stiffly starched fabric stretched tight over firm muscle.

I pour myself into his kisses. My body responds reflexively to his intrusion. I can't hate him when it feels so perfect to be this close to him. And yet, there's so much danger in caring for a man who is such a...

Owen pulls back, breaking our kiss, breaking the spell. He hauls in a lungful of air then huffs out a quiet laugh. "Duchess, if I didn't know better, I'd think you like this. I'd think you like *me*," he whispers, leaning down, trailing kisses and gentle nibbles around my earlobe, down my neck, then over my shoulder.

"I'm a very good actress," I say, hearing the breathiness in my own voice. I'm turned on and tuned up, and there's no way to hide it.

He laughs again, and I feel his smile against my skin

while his thumb probes deeper under the edge of my panties, finding my slit dripping and my exposed clit begging for his attention. "Hummm," Owen purrs. "That's Oscar-worthy acting right there."

He circles my clit with his thumb, pulsing me, drawing me closer and closer to the brink. "Don't come," he whispers, slowing his work, nicking the tops of my breasts with his teeth and lips. "I'll make you come, but not here."

Can I do this with him? Be his fake *and* be his lover? What will it mean? I want him, but I don't want to be just another conquest. Been there, done that, didn't appreciate it. Maybe if we just got it over with I could get it out of my system. Maybe then I wouldn't want him anymore.

He steps back, withdrawing his hand from inside my panties, then casually licks his thumb clean while hanging onto my waist with his other hand.

I groan in agony, frustrated, wanting him even more.

"We should go," he purrs into my neck, pulling my hair back. "Any more and I'm going to haul all those fancy skirts up and fuck you right here."

"That might be okay," I breathe, wishing he would do just that, hoping it'll cure me of him for good.

He doesn't fulfill that wish. Instead he circles both hands around my waist and lifts me, settling me on my precariously high heels in front of him. He smooths my hair and my skirts while trying to collect himself. "Let's go back to the party, say our goodbyes, then go upstairs and have a drink in the library," Owen says, his tone low, edged with tension. "Then we'll see about finishing this."

9

OWEN

Norah appears stunned, and it's a feeling I share. That kiss, staged in the garden for lurking paparazzi, went farther than I planned, and it heated up genuinely.

I thought she was just playing along. I assumed she knew someone was watching. I figured she'd threaten to cut off my hand if I got any closer. Instead she drew me in, surrendering herself rather than shutting me down.

The royal guards fall in line behind us as I lead Norah silently toward the palace. We pass guests who bow as we approach. Making our way inside, among the gilt decoration, surrounded by satin, silk, a bounty of flowers, and the sound of so many voices lifting above the strains of orchestral music, all eyes are on us. I wonder if Norah feels as exposed as I feel in this moment. Every nerve in my body is raw, itching, sore. The only thing that's going to soothe my discomfort is escaping this crowd, getting behind closed doors, and finding out if what happened back there is real and not just wishful thinking.

"Where have you two been?" my mother asks when we

return to the royal table. She's sitting with the Lord Mayor of Cymrea, who nods at me, offering his congratulations on our pending nuptials.

"Thank you, Lord Mayor," I reply politely, then turn to my mother and her question. "We went for a walk," I say. "And now we're going to say goodnight. Norah's exhausted and I'm done in, too."

Mother isn't pleased, as this leaves her with the obligation of closing the ball and seeing the guests off at sunrise, but it's my prerogative and I've got more important priorities just now.

"You looked lovely tonight, darling," Mother says to Norah, taking her hand in genuine affection. "You charmed us all, like you've charmed the Prince. I'm not sure what your secret is, but I'm glad of it."

Norah curtsies demurely, just as she should, then says, "Thank you, ma'am, and thank you for the beautiful dress. I'm not royalty like you, but this dress made me feel like a princess just for tonight."

She's either being entirely sincere, or she's truly giving an Oscar-worthy performance.

My mother—a woman as wily as a fox who can spot a conniving upstart from a mile distant—just melts. "Oh Norah, you're so welcome. What a sweet thing to say."

I think I see a tear form in the corner of Mother's eye. Good Lord, Norah Ballantyne has the "World's Princess" wrapped around her little finger. *Nobody does that!*

Once we're away from the crowd and back in the residential wing of the palace, Norah stops, pausing to take off her heels. "I'm sorry," she says. "I can't take another step. These things have rubbed blisters. It's like walking on razor blades."

I wait, offering a hand for balance as she teeters on one

foot, peeling off the offending footwear. "Did you mean what you said to my mother?"

She looks at me curiously, settling down much more comfortably on bare feet. "Of course I did," she says. "Why would you think otherwise?"

I shake my head, biting my lip. "Norah, you're such a bloody enigma to me. I never know what's real, what's fake, when you're teasing, when you're genuinely angry with me or complimenting me. I have no idea what to think about you."

"Hmph," she snorts, walking past me.

Once we're in the apartment, Norah starts toward her rooms.

"Where are you going?" I ask.

"To go change," she says. "This dress, while beautiful, is damned uncomfortable. I'm sewn up in a corset so tight it would make Scarlett O'Hara feel sorry for me."

I have no idea who Scarlett O'Hara is, nor do I care. "Don't change," I say. "Stay just a few minutes—in that dress. Let's have a drink first."

Norah takes a breath, leveling me in her gaze. I can't tell if she's going to insult me, or tease me, or tell me to go screw myself. "*First?*" she asks. "First before what?"

My turn to take a breath. *My turn to take a chance.* "First, before we finish what we started down in the garden. First, before I take that dress and whatever else you're wearing off you myself."

She regards me with caution. "What are you drinking?"

That's not at all what I expected to hear. "I'm drinking whiskey," I say, allowing myself a small smile. "What would you like?"

"Whatever you're having."

Before I pour our drinks, I soften the lights and turn on

the stereo. A little music might go a long way toward easing us into this. I can't imagine she's going to make it simple; she's going to make me work for it. The thing is, I already know it's worth the effort.

I hand her a cut crystal glass half-filled with golden Anglesey whiskey, then take her other hand, leading her toward the couch. I'm wishing now I had slightly less minimal taste in interior decoration. My couch has metal-framed edges and barely comfortable, stiff leather cushions.

"We could go to my rooms," Norah says as if she's reading my mind. "They've got more functional furniture."

"Fair enough," I admit, happy to accommodate whatever makes her more comfortable.

Her apartment is in keeping with the rest of the palace's décor. The furniture is ancient, ornate, but functional. The walls are covered with elaborately patterned wallpaper and hung with paintings of long-dead royals, landscapes, and still lifes. There's nothing here that speaks to me of Norah or her preferences; I wonder if anyone told her she's perfectly welcome to make changes.

I peel off my tux jacket, open my collar, then settle down on a big, overstuffed couch in the middle of her parlor. I kick off my shoes, as Norah's not the only one with feet sore from wearing stylish footwear. "Come sit with me," I say, motioning for her to join me.

She's taking a play from my book, fumbling with the stereo, trying to get some music on. When she finally settles down, she's anxious, sitting far away from me at the opposite end of the couch, gripping her glass in both hands so tightly I worry she might break it.

I need to address this head-on.

I reach down to the floor, clasping her bare ankles in my hands and lifting them onto my lap, pulling her down into a half-reclining position. She yelps with surprise, almost spilling her drink.

"Oh, relax," I insist as I begin to firmly but gently massage her feet.

It doesn't take long for Norah to melt back into the couch, head rolled on a cushion, shoulders slack. A moment or two later she's purring like a cat. "That feels *so good*," she says dreamily as I work the bones in her feet, pulling toes, massaging her pads and heels with strong hands.

I've bedded a lot of women; I can't remember most of their names. I've never given more than a passing glance to any woman's feet, much less spent serious foreplay time with them. Norah's feet are lovely. Her toes are long and graceful, arches high. The skin is soft, and her nails are buffed to a pretty gloss.

"I'd pay you to do this every day," she moans, closing her eyes, settling her whiskey glass on her belly while she loosely grips it with both hands.

"You wouldn't have to pay me," I say softly. "All you need to do is tell me you want me to do this—*and more*—and I will."

She opens her eyes, watching me. She doesn't say anything for the longest time, then finally asks, "It doesn't have to signify anything, right? It's just fun. Like in Paris?"

I shrug. "Sure," I say confidently, brushing off any other notion. "Just for fun. *Extracurricular fun.* Outside the terms of our contract."

I wish I was as confident as I sound. The girl makes my heart flutter in my chest. She makes me crazy. She confounds me, and amuses me, and makes me overthink everything. More than that, I genuinely like her. She's decent, and kind. The way she spoke to my mother tonight was above and beyond expectations. The way she treats staff like they're friends and family. The way she takes the time to learn every detail she needs to know to do this job, and then executes beautifully. I know she took up this thing to bail her parents out of dire straits and set herself up for a career at some point down the road, but she's taking it all seriously, holding up her end of the bargain better than anyone else Mother and I might have enticed into the job.

I have a healthy, realistic view of royal marriage. I don't expect Cinderella. That said, it would be awfully nice to have a partner in this business who I like and respect— someone I can sit down and talk with at the end of the day, whose opinion I value.

If that happened, this arrangement we have might become the happiest marriage this royal family has seen in centuries.

"I'm game," Norah says, rousing me from my reverie and my gentle, two-handed kneading of her left foot. "But you need to get me out of this dress soon, because I'm about to suffocate."

"I can do that," I respond, feeling my cock stir with heady anticipation long before it should. "Come here."

I pull her forward, settling her on me, thighs straddling my lap with layers of silken fabric, crinoline, and lace piled up between us. She's a vision before me. Reaching hands behind her back to feel for the clasp and zipper, it occurs to me that I've never done *this* in the palace. I've always kept my trysts—*because that's all they ever were*—away from here, away from my family, away from any possibility of my royal life and *that* life intersecting.

I slip the bodice of her gown off her shoulders, letting it relax and gather at her hips. Her pale breasts are bound tight in a corset of satin and fine, handmade lace, reinforced with canvas and bone stays. It's threaded up from behind with silk ribbons stronger than steel wire.

"Stand up and turn around," I instruct her.

Norah slides back on my thighs, putting her bare feet to the carpeted floor. Without getting up, I pull the gown down to her ankles, revealing long, strong legs and her perfectly sexy, heart-shaped ass barely covered by lace panties. Grasping her hips in my hands, I press my warm lips to her right cheek, nicking it teasingly with bared teeth, causing her to stiffen, then giggle in my grasp.

"You're beautiful," I whisper into her warm skin. "And I mean that."

Getting back to the task at hand, I loosen the bow of silk ribbon just above the crack of her ass and begin unwinding the binds that constrain her.

"Oh, that's so much better," Norah breathes, filling her lungs with air. "Oh, that's wonderful. Thank you."

I stand, pulling the slouching corset up over her raised arms and head, discarding it on the floor. She's wearing a strapless, damn-near-transparent lace bra that matches her panties. It will have to go soon, but for now I want to keep it where it is. "Turn back around," I say, returning to my seat on the couch.

She turns in place, standing before me, an angel. Her pale skin is flawless and glowing, her curves and soft places exposed. She's still wearing the sapphires at her throat and on her wrist. The only thing she's lacking to make her perfect is letting her hair down from the tied-up "do" the stylist contrived for her, complaining that her golden locks were far too wild to set loose.

"Come back to my lap," I say.

When she does, I slide my palms up her thighs, then around her ass, scooching her closer, pulling her sex to mine. I'm stiff behind silk suit pants and tight boxer briefs. It's excruciating, and excruciatingly pleasurable knowing her slick heat is so close to my hard desire.

The first time we did this, it was anonymous. Fun. Quick and insane. We barely spoke ten words between us. It was raw sex, just two unfamiliar bodies hurling themselves at one another until we were sated and exhausted.

This is different. This *feels* altogether different. This is personal.

"The night we met," I say to her quietly, drinking her into my mind so I'll never forget this moment and how she looks sitting here on my lap, "do you remember what you said to me, and what I asked you?"

She smiles at me. "I told you I came to Paris to find new stories, and you asked me if I'd found any yet."

I nod, letting my hands trace the contours of her body, from her collarbone to her sternum, pausing at the round of her breast, circling her nipple, then tweaking it between my thumb and middle finger, causing her knees to press against my hips and her eyes to close briefly.

"Have you found any new stories yet?" I ask her, my hand flattening as I palm over her soft, flat belly with fingertips dancing just beneath her navel.

"A lot of them," Norah says, lifting her own hands, reaching forward to undo my shirt buttons. "More than I ever counted on."

When she's got my shirt open, I sit forward, lifting my hands up under her shoulder blades, drawing her to me as I press my face into her soft, fragrant flesh. I kiss her collarbones and her neck, then go lower, nosing the seam of cleavage at her breasts, then lower again to grip a lace-covered nipple in my teeth and lips, making it stiff with my attentions.

Norah moans.

"I hope I give you a lot of stories," I breathe into her flesh, tasting her skin, lapping up her scent. "Good ones."

I reach high into her hair, pulling pins and nets, threading my fingers through a curling mane of golden tresses that falls away, tumbling over her shoulders and down her back. "That's better," I say, running my fingers through the tangle of spun gold. "Wild and unruly, like you."

She huffs an amused smile at me while her hands tug at my shirt-tails, pulling roughly. "You need to be naked, too," she says, mild frustration piquing her tone. "I need your skin on mine."

"By all means," I agree, opening the button on my pants, loosening them enough to set my shirt-tails free. She shoves the thing off my shoulders and down my arms, insisting it comes off. I'm left in an untucked t-shirt. She lifts it, pressing her fingertips into my belly, tracing the contours of my abs, then flattens her palms at my sides as she leans in to kiss me.

Our mouths meet, parting, tongues circling, probing, sucking between hot breaths, noses pressed together. Norah is heat and hunger, her hips pressed tight against me, her mouth locked on mine, arms intertwined, fingers exploring, pressing.

This is personal. This is a first like our first time, only better by orders of magnitude. We fit. Our timing is in perfect synchrony. Even our scents are complementary.

She's bright to my dark. She's smart to my dull, and rough to my sharp. She's hot to my cold, blue blood. She's what I need to feel whole. My life has been a performance, acting the part I believed others wanted me to play while playing at being a normal person. Norah has brought those two incomplete characters together.

Norah's brought me to myself. She's something wholly unexpected—a friend. And a naked one, at that.

She heaves against me, breathing hard, her body tense as her hips grind on top of mine. "We need to go lie down," she purrs between starved kisses. "I want you now."

I lift her with little effort as she wraps her legs around my hips, her arms tightly winding around my neck to hang on. I walk her to her bedroom, then lay her on the bed as I crawl in over her.

"I need to go back to my apartment," I whisper, kissing her neck, her body arching up to meet me. "I forgot the condoms."

"Forget the condoms, Owen," she breathes in my ear. "

Damn. Alright. My cock burns inside my pants, aching for release. *Not just yet.* There's something I need to do first. I hook my fingers in the silk waistband of her panties, pulling them down over her hips, thighs, knees, and ankles, casting them aside.

It wasn't about Norah the last time we were this close—or at least, I didn't think so. This time it *is* all about her: I want to make her come a thousand times, moaning my name; I want her flooding my face with her juices all over again; I want her to suck my fingers insider her and never release them; I want her to know how I can make her feel so she never wants anyone else so close; I want to stamp her with my royal seal and have her wear it as a badge of pride.

I slip a single finger through the seam between her legs, feeling liquid heat pour instantly onto my hand.

"Oh God," she cries at this small intrusion. Her clit is hard, erect in its pocket between pink, hot folds.

I drop down, putting my mouth and tongue to work

against that little button while my fingers probe her depths, stroking her, forcing her tight walls to surrender.

"Oh, fuck, Owen!" she calls, fists gripping my hair, hips riding my chin like a bucking, un-trained thoroughbred. She comes on my face, into my mouth, gushing like the high tide at Saxony, salty and warmed with the Gulf Stream tropics.

"Oh... oh... oh... God." She comes again a few minutes later with more of my fingers put to work while my lips torture her nipples, sucking them hard, making her writhe under me.

I watch her face change as she comes. Her eyelids flutter. Her jaw slackens, then clenches. Her back arches, rising high above the sweat-dampened sheets. Then she just goes soft and limp like a doll in my hand, whining like a kitten. "Come to me," she heaves, her breaths evening against my kisses. "Inside."

It feels as if I've waited my entire life for this invitation. Unsteady hands shove my pants and boxers down, freeing my aching erection from the binds of cloth and elastic. I guide myself to the tightly-enclosed circle of muscles between her thighs, shoving her knees wide apart with my own. Pressing in, the head of my cock jolts alive, electrified by contact with Norah's precious, ringed walls of gripping tension and velvet. Her delicate folds envelop my length in searing, wet heat.

"Oh..." Norah moans in my ear.In a second, everything I know falls away. I'm lost in a world without pretension or order. Everything superficial evaporates inside the heat of two creatures entwined into one thing. There's no need for title, or prestige, or power. There's only this moment and the pleasure of being lost in it forever, with her pressed deep into the sheets, flat beneath me, then on top of me, smiling

down on me, sucking my soul into those artless blue eyes that consume me. This time is fleeting, and forever, consisting only of eyes and breasts, lips and hips, thighs and belly—the parts of her that are now parts of me, all of them having done away with every pretension I ever held dear, rendering me vulnerable and raw to the only person in the world who makes me laugh and laugh at myself, and come aching, crying against her, moaning her name, lost in her golden tresses, lost in her safe embraces.

10

We're sitting up in bed, legs crossed, facing one another, both of us naked, both of us sated and blissfully dazed. I reach forward with outstretched fingers to gently touch the sweat-misted skin above Owen's left nipple. There's a small patch of port-stained skin there, a birthmark vaguely shaped like a cat. I trace its edges, wondering at it.

"My father had one just like it," he says quietly, looking down at my hand. "My brother Lloyd has one, too, except his lion is upside down and backwards."

"An omen," I suggest, only half-kidding.

Own takes my fingers in his, lifting my hand to his lips. He kisses each digit individually, then turns my palm up and kisses that.

We sit a long time together, touching one another, tracing curves and angles, Owen twirling his fingers through my hair, then leaning down to breathe chaste kisses on my knees. Finally, he lies back, pulling me down with him into his embrace. "Should I stay or go?" he asks, his voice low. "I don't want to wear out my welcome."

Of course I want him to stay. I'm also scared of wanting him too much. This arrangement could become painful. "Stay," I whisper, "and tell me what you're thinking."

"Hum," he says, lifting a finger, tracing the round of my shoulder. "You first."

I'm thinking so many things. "I'm thinking this could get complicated," I admit. "I'm afraid of that."

"Don't be," Owen whispers. "It doesn't need to be complicated. It is what it is. When it doesn't work for you, then you get to uncomplicate it."

That sounds so simple. It probably is for him. Just "extracurricular fun" outside the terms of our contract. He's paying me for the pretense of a relationship, not an actual relationship. *Simple.* So simple it makes my heart ache.

"Norah?" Owen asks.

"Yes?"

"Do you know how to cook?"

What an odd question. I lift up, propping on my elbow so I can look at him. He's sleepy, starting to drift.

He opens his eyes, just tired slits, smiling up at me. "That morning in Paris, when I had to go, I was hoping you'd cook me breakfast. I wanted to stay and spend the day with you. That's what I'd planned. I'm sorry it didn't happen that way."

He's delirious from exhaustion. He's babbling. He's also incredibly sweet.

"Yeah," I say, "I know how to cook."

IT TOOK SOME DOING, but I've managed to wrangle my way into the palace kitchen and bully the head cook into letting me make Owen's breakfast. The cook is aghast that I've turned up with Sally, my maid, running interference for me.

"It's quite a romantic thing," Sally says to the cook as I'm scouring various walk-ins and pantries for eggs, bacon, and pancake mix.

"You don't have any grits, do you?" I call out to the cook, who's shouting something incomprehensible in French at Sally. She's blocking his way, keeping him from throwing me out of his private dominion.

I establish that there are no grits in the palace, settling instead for fried, hash-browned potatoes. I merrily begin to whip up a South Carolina style breakfast fit for a king while the cook stalks, swears, and threatens, not understanding a word Sally tells him—until she points out my ring. When he sees that, he takes a step back, takes off his chef's hat, and quietly backs out of the room.

Sally makes coffee while I get everything set up on a nifty rolling cart to deliver upstairs. "I'll take it from here," she says, smiling. "I'll have everything upstairs in just a few minutes."

When I get back to my apartment, Owen is still snoozing to beat the band. He's adorable, all tousled hair and easy-breathing, tangled up in the sheets like a little kid. I slip back in bed with him, sidling up against him, hoping I don't wake him just yet. I want breakfast here first, filling the room with the scents of fresh bacon and sweet pancakes before he opens his eyes.

That hope is instantly dashed when my phone, plugged up on the nightstand beside Owen, starts ringing. He stirs, a frown scouring his handsome brow.

I scramble, reaching across him, stretching to grab the phone and silence it.

"Hummm," Owen mumbles, waking up, catching me

mid-reach. His hands circle my hips. He hefts me onto him, my thighs straddling his hips.

I grab my phone and swipe to send the call to voicemail, noting with no small amount of irritation that the call is from Eric.

"Good morning, Duchess," Owen purrs at me, smiling sleepily, looking me over, hands strong on my thighs. "How come you're dressed? How come you're not naked?"

I feel a stiffness rise, pressing the fabric between my legs.

"Somebody's happy to see me," I say, leaning down to kiss him, nipping his bottom lip. "Sorry that woke you. I was hoping you'd sleep a little longer."

"Why?" he asks, licking his lips.

"Breakfast," I say proudly. "I made you breakfast. Sally's bringing it up now."

Owen wakes up with this. He sits up, propping on an elbow to face me. "*You* made breakfast?" he asks. "How?"

"I bamboozled my way into the kitchen and frightened the head cook off. Sally helped."

He's astonished. "I don't even know where the kitchen is," he confesses. "You really did that?"

I nod, almost giddy that he's impressed. A moment later, Sally shows up with the evidence of my bravery and determination.

Twenty minutes later, Owen is busy slurping down pancakes, dipping forkfuls in runny egg yolk smeared across his plate. "This is excellent," he mumbles, wolfing down a mouthful of greasy bacon. "We should have a kitchen put in our apartment so you don't have to fight the cook. I could get used to this."

I laugh, then pause, realizing he said "our apartment," as if this thing we're doing is real and not just an arrangement of convenience. A kitchen in "our apartment" signifies private time, shared meals, genuine conversation, and time spent together out of preference, not obligation.

Or maybe he just really likes my pancakes.

"Who was on the phone before?" Owen asks, looking up from his cleaned plate. "I meant to ask earlier, but I got so distracted by all this I completely forgot."

I shake my head dismissively. "Only Eric," I say. "Not important."

"Who's Eric?" Owen asks, setting down his coffee cup.

"You remember," I say. "The guy in the art gallery in Paris who dissed you? The blond with a shitty attitude?"

Owen nods slowly, the recollection returning to him. "I do remember," he says. "Why is he calling you?"

I shrug. "Probably because he's heard I'm engaged to the future king of Anglesey, and he's calling to offer congratulations." That's wishful thinking, but I can hope. He's probably calling to cry about his shattered dreams for us and beg my forgiveness for stealing my money and threatening me.

"Were you two together?" Owen asks, that furrow returning to his brow. "I remember he gave me a look that night like I had just stolen his ice cream."

"Never together," I say. "Eric's just a friend."

Owen punches the inside of his cheek with his tongue, the furrow softening just a little. "Well, he wanted to be more," he says, a tinge of jealousy weighing his tone. "If you call him back, keep that in mind. Trust me—I know."

I don't doubt him. "I don't have much reason to call him back," I say. "The last time we spoke, it ended badly. I'd rather leave it at that."

Owen nods, lifting his cup again, smiling at me. "Good. I like that better," he says. "And another thing: your apartment in Paris. You had some photos on the walls. You're a photographer. Where's all your stuff?"

"It's all in storage back in Paris," I say. "I was planning an extended vacation, not a fake royal wedding. I haven't really had time to deal with it. Plus there's nowhere to put most of my things. My apartment here is furnished to the nines."

Owen smiles at me again. "Your apartment is yours to decorate—or not—however you like. It's not a museum. Anything you want to get rid of, call housekeeping and tell them to come get it. I'll arrange for your things to be brought from Paris. I'll also arrange for a decorator to meet with you and help you with any renovations you'd like done."

"Renovations?" I ask. "Like what?"

"Well for starters, like a kitchen for us. You think on it. Anything you want is fine."

Anything? "Can I have... a library?"

Owen cocks his head to the side in question. "A library?" he asks. "We have a library."

"*You* have a library," I correct him. "I have my own books. A lot of them. If I can have a library, I can get my books from home in Charleston. I miss them something awful."

He nods. "Duchess, you can have anything you want."

He could get used to my pancakes, and I could easily get used to everything else that comes with this life.

11

"You're an asshole," Norah spits out, glaring at me over the screen of her laptop. "You're such a fucking asshole."

What did I do? This morning I was Prince Charming, making her laugh with my witty remarks while making her come for the third time.

She swings the laptop around to face me. It's the main page of *Today's Mail*, that rabid tabloid royals love to hate. They've run with the photo from the garden, and it's salacious, a perfect night-vision shot: high detail of me and Norah doing what looks like "the nasty," with her skirts hiked up and me wrapped up in them, my hands nowhere to be seen, my head buried in her tits. Norah's wearing an expression of ecstatic bliss, looking like she's about to melt.

"Yeah, about that," I say. "I should have..."

"You should have told me we were being photographed? You should have told me you set it all up?!"

She's angry. Understandably so.

"I didn't think..."

"You didn't think!" she snaps. "You thought it out well

enough in advance to plot the place, time, and moves. What the hell?"

"I had a good reason. If you'll just manage your moral outrage for a second, I'll tell you."

"This should be rich," she spits. "I can't wait."

"The maids were talking," I say. "They were surprised we weren't sleeping together. There was gossip. Duncan caught wind of it, brought it to my attention. I just set that up to squash any rumors that might have gotten started about us not being... *real*."

"And so finger-fucking me in public in front of cameras —that seemed like the appropriate response?"

"I didn't expect it to go that far," I admit. I sit back in my chair, heaving a sigh. "I kept expecting you to back off or shut me down, but you didn't."

"You're an asshole," she repeats. "An unmitigated, royal asshole." She slams her laptop shut, gets up from the table. She turns her back and storms out of my library, leaving me to consider my options.

"Don't forget our appointment at three!" I call after her. The palace portrait photographer is coming to take our official engagement pictures this afternoon. It's a pain in the ass and an epic waste of time, but it's got to be done.

"Lift your chin up to the left just an inch," the photographer says to Norah. "That's it. So beautiful. Hold, and..."

The flash goes off in our eyes for what seems the billionth time. All I can see are stars and weird-colored orbs floating in the room.

Norah's still upset. She won't talk to me except to bite. I'm back to being "Prince Conniving," and she doesn't mean it in a teasing way. As beautiful and cute as she is when she's seething, I like it better when we're friends. We were doing so well. A return to the cold-shoulder and being kept at arm's-length makes me sad.

And I get it. I wasn't thinking. Or I was. I was thinking of *myself* and all the things people are saying about *me*. I put her reputation at risk, and there's evidence in every single newspaper in this godforsaken country.

"I think that's enough," the photographer says, bowing to us. "Thank you very much for your patience."

"Thank you," I say. "Can you give us a few minutes alone?"

"Certainly, sir," he replies, making himself scarce.

Norah stands up, turns toward me, slips the sapphire off her finger and hands it to me. "You keep that," she says, ice in her tone. "Trot it out as needed for photos and public appearances. We have an arrangement, but it doesn't say I should be responsible for a rock like that. I put the necklace and bracelet in the box in your bedroom where you keep your cufflinks and watches."

"Norah..."

She shakes her head at me. "No—I get it: you need me to be convincing. I'll smile and play along. This is a business deal, nothing more and nothing less. But from here on out, you keep me informed. I don't know what I was thinking. Once all this settles down, you and I can go back to leading our old lives. You can go screw strangers in the park since that seems to be your thing, and I can go back to working on my career after popping out a royal kid or two—as per section three, items one and two of the contract."

"Norah, stop," I insist. "I'm sorry. I should have been explicit about what was happening. I assumed too much."

"Apology accepted," she says. "Don't ever do anything like that again."

"Please take the ring back," I say.

She shakes her head, dismissing the idea. "You know, one day you might actually find someone you really want to wear that ring. And it would be a shame if that girl thought it was a sloppy second. This way you can tell her the truth."

"Norah, you're the girl I really want to wear this ring," I say, telling her what I should have said weeks ago. "I don't want some other girl."

She glares at me, incredulous.

"This started out fake. It's not fake anymore. I think that's why you're so angry, too: because you care about me, and you feel betrayed, and that's an awful feeling. I'd do everything differently if I could."

"You're delusional," she says. "Maybe what your brother has is catching."

"I'm not delusional. I'm smitten with you, and that doesn't happen to me. I've always been a one-and-done sort of asshole. You're different."

She rolls her eyes. "One-and-done assholes shouldn't be kings of places that insist on wives and offspring. It's a bad combination."

I nod, smiling. "That's so true," I say. "Which is why I'm so glad I'm fake-marrying you and not someone else who I'd get sick of. Who would annoy me. Who isn't the most captivating, mercurial, stunningly beautiful woman I've ever met in my life, who makes the most amazing pancakes."

"Oh good Lord, Owen," she sighs. "Give me the damn ring back and stop groveling. It doesn't become you."

I've got one shot at getting it right. I need to not fuck this up. I drop to a knee in front of her, holding the ring in my hand. "Norah Ballantyne, I can't imagine not having you as my best friend, and my foil, and my wife. Will you marry me? For real?"

She reaches down and plucks the ring from my hand. "I'm not letting you out of the contract," she says. "I have a feeling that being *really* married to you, I'm going to earn every penny and then some."

"Is that a yes?" I ask hopefully.

She nods. "Get up, Prince Charming. If anyone sees you like that, they'll start asking questions, and you'll have to contrive some new line of subterfuge to throw them off the scent."

I stand up. "Are we friends again?"

"We're *fake* friends," she says. "I'll act like your friend as long as you act like a decent human being."

Fair enough. It's a starting point. I reach forward, taking her hand in mine, pulling her close. "Fake kiss me so I know we're alright."

"Don't press your luck, Prince," she quips, smiling. "I'm still carrying around about six gallons of fake moral outrage. I need to let it soak before I'm up for fake smooching."

"Can I at least fake hold your hand and fake walk you home?"

"I guess that would be alright, since home is just down the hall." She leans down, slipping her heels off, then hands them to me. "Make yourself useful," she says. "Carry those."

We're both dressed in semi-formal wear for the portraits. She's lovely in a sunny yellow skirt that brings out the golden highlights in her hair. She's beautiful no matter what she wears.

"I can't wait to take that dress off you, Duchess," I tease, leading her toward the corridor, away from the cameras and lights. "And after that, let's talk about taking a short holiday somewhere you've never been before. Just the two of us."

"Sounds like fun," Norah says, feigning disinterest. "Just you and me, six guys from the royal guard, plus Duncan, and a thousand paparazzi from all over the world."

She has a point.

Back in our apartments, she goes her way to change clothes, leaving me to go my way. I'm pulling my tie and shedding my shiny shoes when I hear Norah's phone ringing in the library. She must have left it there this morning. I lift it just before it rolls to voicemail, seeing the caller is "Eric." She's even got a photo of him that pops up along with his name and number when he calls.

Why is this guy calling her?

Just then a text notification appears. I click it. It reads:

You really should have taken my calls. Now I'm pissed. And I'm in London. I will see you tomorrow, one way or another. Don't ignore me. We have too much history.

WHAT THE HELL? *He's coming here? Who the hell this guy?*

"Explain it to me like I'm a six-year-old," Owen says. "From the top."

I sigh again, frustrated that Owen is taking this so weirdly. "We've known one another since we were kids. Our parents are dear friends. We went to the same school from kindergarten through graduation," I say. "It's not any more complicated than that. We went to the same summer camp. When he couldn't get a date for the prom, I went with him. We've been friends since forever, and we dated—briefly. He's the ex I told you about the night we met."

"And he loaned you money?" Owen asks. "How much money?"

This is where it gets difficult. I haven't told Owen about Eric cleaning out my account and closing the credit card. It all happened to coincide with us reconnecting. I just sort of let it all go, figuring that Eric would go away.

"He didn't loan me money, exactly," I say. "He arranged for me to get a credit card, issued from his firm, after mine were cancelled when Barney Mackoff swindled my parents. I was stuck in Europe without a card or access to my bank accounts back home. Eric helped me. But when I got to Anglesey and spent money on clothes, he got angry."

"You spent your money," Owen says. "Not his money."

I nod.

"Who was paying the credit card bill?"

"He paid it from my bank account in Charleston," I tell Owen, unsure how any of this detail matters in the grand scheme.

"So, what's his play? Why is he coming here?" Owen asks, pouring himself a generous shot of Anglesey whiskey.

I wish I knew the answer to that question. I'm almost afraid of the answer at this point. "I don't know, Owen," I say. "He's hurt. He's angry at me. He wants to talk. I just don't know."

Owen sits down in a big leather club chair. He's thinking, and that's a little disturbing. "So, you have plenty of options here," he says. "We can deny him access at the border when he tries to cross. Or we can wait until he shows up in Cymrea, have him picked up and deported. Or you can meet him at the palace gate and tell him to fuck off to his face, just before I have him arrested for stalking and threatening the Duchess of Brynterion, fiancée of the acting king, Crown Prince Owen, Vanquisher of Upstart Competitors."

I can't help but laugh, even if Owen isn't laughing with me. All of those ideas are absurd and juvenile. "You're better than that," I remind Owen. "And so am I. If he shows up, I want to talk to him. I want to hear him out and set him straight. That's the right thing to do."

Owen frowns, setting his untouched drink on the table beside him. He's about to burst out in a pout. "If you're seeing him, then I'm meeting him. *Officially*," he says between clenched teeth. "Bring him in. Invite him to tea. I think Conspirator's Hall, in the south wing, is an appropriate place to receive him. Lots of paintings of beheaded traitors and hung upstarts. He should feel right at home."

It's astonishing to me that Owen is being like this; he's not an insecure man. I settle on the arm of his chair, slipping my hand into his. "You can meet him and posture all you like. And then I'll send him on his way," I say. "But honestly, he's an old family friend. He's mostly harmless, and it would make me happy if you'd try to be polite. Please don't threaten him with the guillotine."

Owen squeezes my hand, thumbing the big ring on my finger. "You're my *real* fake fiancée, and I want to keep you that way. I don't like it that another man has ideas about you."

"Ideas are all it is, Prince Panties-in-a-Wad," I assure him. "What's your calendar look like tomorrow? I'll work him in around your other state secrets."

"I'm free after two," Owen pouts. "And as soon as we've disposed of this peasant, you and I are getting on the royal jet and going somewhere I don't have to have to think about kingly things like tax revenue, or nobles and their demands, or old boyfriends coming out of the woodwork to lay prior claim to the only woman in the realm worth having."

"Where are we going?" I ask. "Have you decided?"

He shakes his head, sipping his whiskey. "You decide. Somewhere you've never been. Somewhere exotic."

"Hm," I muse. "I've never been to Greece. I've never seen the Mediterranean."

Owen brightens, sitting up from his pouty slouch. "We've got a villa on a little island near Mykonos. It's beautiful, and if you want to do the touristy things, it's just thirty minutes from Athens by air."

"You own a house at Mykonos?" I ask, finding it hard to believe.

"On a tiny, private island half a mile away. We don't deal with the tourists unless we want to," Owen says. "You'll love it!"

I'm sure I will.

Now that our travel plans are settled, I can deal with Eric Wimple and his out-sized sense of self-importance. I reply to his text.

Missed your calls but got your text. Been busy. We'll receive you tomorrow at 2:30. Go to main palace gate and show ID, they'll escort you from there. Did you happen to pack my missing $25k? You were the last person seen with it. Asking for a friend.

I HAVE no idea when he'll get the text, or where he is. All I know is, it takes a gigantic pair of wrought-iron balls to steal money from a person, strand them in a foreign country, then get indignant when they find their own way through the land mines you've laid for them. Eric was always guilty of theatrics. I wonder what in the hell is motivating this little show. It'll sure be entertaining to find out, assuming Owen doesn't have the royal guard arrest him and throw him in the dungeon.

∼

"YOUR ROYAL HIGHNESS. Miss Ballantyne. Your visitor, Mr. Eric Wembley, has just checked through the main gate and is being parked. Shall I show him into the Conspirator's Hall when he arrives?" asks our head butler Townsend, who is absolute overseer of all things related to the royal household.

"Yes, Towns," Owen replies. "Thank you."

I think it's ridiculous that we're to receive Eric in the one room in this expansive palace dedicated to people executed by the crown. On the other hand, it's also funny, given the state Eric must have worked himself into to come here.

We make our way to the south wing, a place hardly visited anymore except by tourists and morbid historians. Tea is ready and waiting when we arrive.

I gaze up at the walls and am appalled at the number of headless corpses documented in paintings hanging floor to ceiling. "This is a grim room," I observe. "We should have a Halloween party in here. With an authentic replica of a gallows, and maybe a pile of fake heads in the corner."

"You joke," Owen observes. "Rooms like this serve as a reminder to all of us. Life is fragile. Choose your battles wisely."

"Is that what this room is for?" I ask. "I thought it was about intimidating your opponents and reminding them what ruthless, bloodthirsty stock you come from."

"That too," Owen admits. "That's why we've been around for seven hundred years."

"Your Royal Highness and Miss Ballantyne," Townsend announces, stepping into the grand hall with great pomp. "Mr. Eric Wembley of Charleston, South Carolina."

The next thing I see is Eric slouching in, looking around like a lost puppy in a great big, noisy kennel. He's dressed in white slacks and a rumpled Oxford shirt with a seersucker jacket appropriate only in Charleston. He's looking around like a kid who lost his mom in the grocery store.

"Eric!" I say, stepping forward, feeling slightly sorry for him despite all the drama that's passed between us.

He sees me, and in that instant all his questions, doubts, and insecurities melt away. He's once again transformed into the arrogant, preposterous New York banker. "Is this real?" he asks. "You expect me to believe that this is where you live? It looks like one of your photosets. Are you paying by the hour, or a day rate? I think Merchant Ivory or Netflix would love to scout this pile as a location. Maybe my employer could backstop some financing for it?"

I pause ten paces away, contemplating his insult. I consider where it's come from. This palace, with its ancient fortified walls, its mirrored halls, and its acres of history can be intimidating to someone—like Eric—who has no legitimate family history of his own to cling to. His grandparents, like my own, were successful merchants. That's it. Before that, the genealogical record is sketchy at best.

"Or maybe you can tell me what you're doing here?" I ask, matching his preposterous pretense. "For the record, the royal palace of Beaumaris isn't for rent. And yes, I do live here, along with a dozen other members of the royal family."

Eric laughs. "This is rich," he says. "Six weeks ago you couldn't manage a credit card on your own and were couch-hopping across Europe. Your credit rating is shit. You're unemployed and your family is bankrupt. Now you're a tabloid-cover porn star with pretensions of grandeur."

I'd forgotten just how deep Eric's cruel streak runs. I'm just about to say so when I see his focus shift behind me. He hadn't noticed Owen before.

Owen walks forward slowly, taking his place beside me, waiting for a proper introduction.

"Crown Prince Owen, this is my friend Eric Wembley. Eric, this is Crown Prince Owen, acting king of Anglesey."

Owen does not offer his hand. Instead he adds, "Acting king *and* future husband of Norah Ballantyne, the future Duchess of Brynterion, the future Princess of Anglesey, possibly the future Queen of the Realm."

Really? Princess and queen are not in the contract. This is new information.

"Now that we've all reconnected, perhaps we can get to the point of your visit. What do you want?" Owen asks.

Eric grins, sizing up Owen. He's not intimidated in the least—or he's not letting on that he is. "I want to spend a little alone time with my old friend," he says, eyes flashing confidently. "This is quite a fancy place you have here. I noticed a park mentioned in the brochure they gave me at the gate." He returns his attention to me. "Norah, would you like to take a walk? Give me a tour of the park?"

I glance up at Owen, who's not in the least pleased. I slide my hand into his. "We won't be long," I assure him. "I'll see you upstairs shortly."

He nods. "Take Duncan."

It's ridiculous to think I need a bodyguard on palace grounds, but if it makes Owen feel better, I'm willing to concede to his request. It's a small thing.

Duncan follows us discreetly at twenty paces as Eric and I make our way into the courtyard garden and onto the path leading to the park.

"Insecure little prick, your prince," Eric observes. "What does he think, that I'm going to kidnap you? Or ravish you while we stroll through the shrubbery?"

"Eric, really—what do you want? And where is my money?"

"Your money is safe," he says. "What I want is your attention."

"You have my attention," I say. "What do you want with my attention?"

"I want you to explain to me how you live with yourself after leading me on, playing me for years, making me believe you always intended to come back to me. And now this. I have to read about your engagement on Twitter? I get to see pictures of you fucking on Facebook?"

He's unbelievable. "Eric, I never led you on. You let yourself believe something you wanted to believe. I was never coming back to you. That was—and is—all in your head."

"I came to Paris," he says. "I hung out with your weird friends."

"Exactly. I didn't invite you—you just showed up," I remind him. "We're childhood friends. I wasn't going to be rude and tell you to get lost."

"We dated."

"For a month. Please stop this."

"And now you expect me to believe that you're in love with a pompous ass like that buffoon up there. I know you better than that. You used to laugh at people like him."

"I still do laugh," I say. "And I'm laughing at myself. But yeah, Eric, I really do love him." Saying it aloud, even if it's just for the sake of getting Eric to back off, makes this thing Owen and I have that much more real. Saying it sounds right—it feels right. It's the first time I've allowed myself to believe it, but it feels good. "I think I loved him since the first time I saw him," I say. "It just took me a little while to get used to all the trappings..."

"You're such a bitch, Norah," he spits, cutting me off, stopping on the path, his expression tilting to outrage. "You strung me along while always scheming for something better. Just using me as a backstop. Using me whenever it was convenient..."

That's not true, but now that I see the intensity of his anger, any interest I have in convincing him of my sincerity disappears. I don't have to sit still and let an arrogant, puffed up little shit like Eric speak to me like that.

"I think this has gone far enough," I say coolly. "You can keep the money, Eric—I don't need it anymore. Don't contact me again. Our friendship is done."

I turn to walk away, but Eric grabs my arm, roughly pulling me back.

I see Duncan bolt into action just as Eric sneers, "You don't say when we're done. I say..."

Duncan puts himself between Eric and me while pressing a thumb forcibly into Eric's wrist. Eric whines, letting go of me.

"Take a step back," Duncan snorts, shoving Eric backward.

From out of nowhere, four other royal guards appear. Two step up to flank me while two more join Duncan, flanking Eric.

"Escort him off the palace grounds," I cry, tension rise in my throat. "Our conversation is over."

"It's not over," Eric shouts while the guards herd him away. "I say when it's over!"

Duncan returns to my side as soon as Eric is out of sight. "Are you alright, ma'am?" he asks, his expression grave.

"I'm fine," I tell him. "I had no idea he would behave like that. I'm sorry..."

"No, ma'am, I'm sorry he was able to get close enough to get a hold on you. I should have been more vigilant. It'll never happen again, ma'am. I promise."

"It's okay, Duncan, really—I'm fine."

Duncan looks almost as shaken as I feel.

"Let's keep this between us, shall we?" I ask. "I don't think Owen needs to know every detail."

Duncan's brow creases in a neat vertical line just between his dark brows. He hesitates. "Ma'am, I won't volunteer any information. However, if the prince asks I'm obligated to tell him. You can count on the fact that he'll ask."

Well shit. "Fine," I say. "I understand."

The shock of this little altercation has left me shaky and slightly sick to my stomach. I feel vaguely lightheaded. I need a few moments to myself, to calm down and collect myself before facing Owen and the barrage of question that I know are coming.

I make my way back to my apartment and to my bedroom. I kick off my shoes and climb into the big, canopied bed, flopping down right on top of the expensive, hand-embroidered spread. My stomach is a knot, crampy. My head aches from the anxiety of dealing with Eric and his hurled accusations. I've heard Eric say hurtful things about other people, but I've never been the object of his jibes. That reaction was over-the-top, not at all like him. Unless, of course, I never really knew him at all. I've had other people —people we both grew up with—tell me he has a ruthless, vindictive side. I never saw it. I didn't really believe it. Now I understand.

My phone buzzes in my hip pocket with a text alert. I lift it and see Eric has sent me a text. Hopefully it's an apology for behaving like a psychopath.

You're going to regret this. I'm going to make you wish you'd never been born.

I ROLL my eyes at the text. He's such a drama queen.

I hadn't planned on a nap, but I'm so tired all of a sudden. I just need a little quiet time. I drift off to sleep, thinking about Eric and his meltdown, wondering what I could have done to earn such a crazy rant and the threatening text that followed.

The maids have all our things packed for the trip. Our bags are stacked in the parlor, just waiting for me to call the valets to take us to the airport.

I haven't seen Norah since her friend Eric was here. Townsend informed me he left the palace and that Norah had gone upstairs for a nap. That's out of character for her, but she's been moody for the last several days. I want to get her away from this place, if only for a little while, so we can spend some time just getting to know one another better.

I spent all morning in a meeting with the Minister of Finance, going over next year's budget. We have a trade deficit that's starting to become concerning, which means I'm going to have to spend the next several months working with economists and business leaders from all over the world to try to develop a plan to address our revenue challenges.

Unlike my royal peers in the rest of the world, I actually have to lead my country, participating in every decision impacting our people. I wish all I had to do was show up for ribbon-cuttings and charity balls. That would be so much easier.

"I see you're almost ready to go," I hear my mother say from behind me.

I put down the report I'm reading and turn toward her. "I'm going to go fetch Norah shortly," I say. "Then we'll head out to the airport."

Mother nods. "Who was your visitor earlier?"

Nothing gets past her. "Eric Wembley," I say, retuning to my report. "Friend of Norah's. Upstart. Peasant. Thorn in my side."

Mother laughs, walking around my desk, facing me. She's wearing a Cheshire Cat smile. "Ex-boyfriend?"

I shrug, not looking up. "Norah says no, but I can tell he's interested in her. And she won't let me put him in the dungeon. She's insisting I be polite. I did my best."

"As much as this annoys you, Owen, keep in mind it's very difficult for an average bloke to compete with you. I doubt this young man poses much of a threat."

I look up from my report. "Mother, I think I'm in deep trouble."

She crosses her arms over her chest, regarding me with caution. "Why is that?"

"I'm really in love with her."

My mother smiles reservedly. "I can see that. I've been able to see that for some time. Don't be afraid of love, darling. And don't be afraid of losing it. Just cherish every moment you have it near. You'll be fine."

Sitting back in my chair, I lay the report down on my desk. "She runs hot and cold. She's angry with me right now."

Mother nods. "I'd be angry, too," she says. "That stunt you pulled with the paparazzi was juvenile and disrespectful. You can't treat your wife-to-be like a pawn in a game, or like an employee."

"It's complicated, Mother."

"I know it's complicated. Don't make it more complicated by creating drama. If you love her, always look out for her best interests even when they conflict with your own, and just be there for her. Tell her, without equivocation, how you feel about her."

It sounds so simple. It's never that simple.

"Don't over-think things, Owen," Mother says. "And don't underestimate yourself. Your greatest strength isn't that you're going to be king—it's that you have the heart of a lion. Show her that heart and the strength behind it, and she'll treasure you more than you ever imagined possible."

WANDERING upstairs to look for Norah, I run into Duncan coming down with his travel bag. "How did things go with that Wembley character?" I ask, pausing him on the stairs.

His face, usually impassive, belies some hesitation on the subject. "It might be best to discuss it with Miss Ballantyne first, sir," he says. "Rest assured, he won't be returning to the palace."

That's a relief. "I'll talk to her," I say. "But I'd like a full, written report from you on everything you observed or that he did during his visit. You can work on it on the plane."

"Yes, sir," Duncan says, nodding.

I find Norah in her bedroom, curled up on top of her bed, fast asleep, purring little snores like a contented kitten. She's so adorable, and I hate to disturb her, but we need to get going if we're going to make Mykonos before midnight.

"Wake up, sleepyhead," I croon, stroking her hair. "Time

to wake up so I can whisk you off to a fairytale island adventure."

Norah blinks and then rolls, facing me. She meets my eyes with a lazy, blank expression. She really was dead to the world. "Hey," she whispers, stretching like a cat. "Hmm. What time is it?"

"Almost six," I say, brushing back an errant curl from her cheek. "You've slept the afternoon away. You okay?"

She sits up, shaking off sleep. "Yeah, I'm fine. Just tired. We've had an awful lot going on these last few weeks. Must be catching up with me."

"Everything's packed and ready," I tell her. "Whenever you're ready, we can go."

"Okay," Norah says, yawning. "Sally packed my things. I just need to grab my camera bag and laptop."

It occurs to me as I'm admiring Norah, and amused with her lazy afternoon, that she seems pale. She's got small, dark circles under her eyes, and her lips are pale as well. "Are you sure you feel okay?" I ask again. "You're usually bounding with energy."

She smiles at me, patting my hand. "I'm fine. Just a little worn out."

I'm not so certain. Something seems *off* with her.

~

"THIS IS AMAZING," Norah purrs, running her fingers along the gleaming teak paneling lining the interior walls of the jet.

"Is it?" I ask, laughing at her wonder. "It's just a jet."

I settle down in a big leather chair in the main cabin, waiting for the glass of whiskey I know is being poured by a member of the cabin crew at this precise moment.

"It's not 'just a jet,'" Norah corrects me, gazing around at her surroundings. "This is beautiful, and lush. It's like something out of a movie."

A pretty blond wearing a cobalt blue royal air polo and short black skirt hands me my whiskey, then turns to Norah. "Ma'am, may I get you something to drink?"

Norah nods to my drink. "Whatever he's having," she says, smiling broadly.

When the girl is gone, she leans forward to me. "You've never flown coach in your life," she says, eyes wide and bright with glee. "This is nuts. You have no idea how lucky you are."

I reach forward, taking her hand in mine. I lift it, pressing her fingers to my lips. "I'm starting to understand how lucky I am," I say, holding her gaze. "You're starting to make me understand."

"What's gotten into you?" she asks, sitting back, strapping herself in. "You're awfully sweet this evening."

"Nothing's gotten into me," I say. "I'm just realizing some things. Like how much I enjoy having you around. How much I like making you smile instead of you calling me names."

"Prince no longer has his panties in a wad?" she quips, grinning slyly. "Good."

"What happened with Wembley?" I ask, sipping my whiskey.

The jet begins slowly rolling toward the runway, engines winding up, causing the plane to vibrate.

Norah shakes her head. "Nothing good," she sighs. "He was an ass. Duncan intervened. And I'll be thrilled if I never hear his name mentioned again."

"Duncan intervened?" I ask, surprised. "What did the guy do?"

Norah squeezes my hand, shaking off my question. "Don't worry about it, Prince Overprotective. He's gone. He's not coming back. And I'm over it."

I can't wait to read Duncan's report.

A few minutes later we're in the air, circling high above Anglesey. It's my favorite view. The island is beautiful from the above, dotted with castles and estates, modest houses and farms, all surrounded by sandy, windswept beaches and sheer, stone cliff walls on the coast. A more picturesque place never existed.

Mykonos is a little less than six hours flying time from Anglesey. We'll land in the dark, but we'll wake up to the bright, warm rays of the Aegean sun. With any luck, we'll get to watch the sunrise while eating breakfast in bed on the yacht.

Twenty minutes into the flight, Norah is nodding on my shoulder, sleeping. She hasn't touched her drink, so I help myself. She still looks pale and she's obviously exhausted. We could both do with a break from the palace intrigue and scheduled demands we've been running through for the last several weeks.

By the time we land in Mykonos, it's almost midnight and the airport is desolate. We're met by household personnel, who drive us straight to the port at Chora. Norah is dead on her feet as we board the yacht that will take us to the tiny island where our villa stands high on a rocky cliff, a hundred feet above the water. We'll sleep on board the ship tonight. Tomorrow, we'll move to the villa and spend some serious time doing absolutely nothing at all.

Norah is almost as taken with the yacht as she was with the jet, but not quite as animated in her expressions of glee. She marvels at the luxury and size of the thing, but before she's completely prone on top of the bed in our spacious, well-appointed berth, her eyes close and she snoozes in perfect time with the rhythm of the vessel's rocking on the sea. I pull her shoes from her feet and find a blanket to cover her with, then head back above deck to have a look around.

I find Duncan and three other of our security detail in the galley, having a snack. When I come in, they all stiffen up like the pope has just joined them.

"Relax guys," I say. "Eat."

I help myself to the hummus, flatbread, feta, and green olives arranged in a platter at the center of the table. It's almost impossible to find decent Greek food in Anglesey, and I'm looking forward to eating well while we're here.

"Tell me about Wembley," I ask Duncan. "I asked Norah. She told me you had to intervene?"

Duncan nods. "I wrote up a report," he says. "It's in your email. The short story is the guy is a loose cannon. He said some terrible things, and when Norah turned to leave he grabbed her and yanked her back."

I stop chewing, putting down my flatbread. "He put his hands on her?" I ask in disbelief. "Where the hell were you?"

"Too far away to prevent it, sir. Flat-footed. I underestimated the threat, sir."

Well, at least he admits it. "Shit," I say. "What did you do with him?"

"Per Miss Ballantyne's instructions, I had him escorted off the palace grounds. Then I took it upon myself to keep surveillance on him while he remains in Anglesey."

"And?" I ask.

"And he's still in the country. He's staying at a hotel on the north end of Cymrea."

I nod, returning to my meal. "Keep me posted on his whereabouts," I say. "Put surveillance on his phone and computer. If he sends so much as a postcard, I want to know what it says. Understood?"

Duncan nods. "I'll issue the command to the secret service tonight."

When I return to our berth, I find that Norah has awoken at some point in my absence and gotten herself undressed and under the covers. I peel off my clothes, letting them fall to the floor, and climb in bed beside her, pulling her soundly sleeping form against mine into a tight spooning position.

The idea that Wembley laid hands on her—that he violently handled her—sits deep in my gut, growing hard like an angry boil. It frightens me to confront the idea that danger came so close. It angers me that he would dare hurt Norah. I've lived twenty-eight years on this Earth without a best friend, a lover, or a companion. I never thought I needed any of those things. I lived like an island, the world swirling around me but not really touching me.

Then I met Norah. The idea of losing her is too hard to bear. My mother's words ring in my ear: *"...cherish every moment you have it near... tell her how you feel..."*

I press my lips against the back of Norah's neck, pulling her close against me. "I love you, Duchess. I love you more than anything in the world."

Norah sleeps on, not stirring, just breathing sweetly in my arms.

14

I wake in an unfamiliar place, hearing the gentle slap of water against a hard surface, feeling the rise and fall of the rolling tide supporting this vessel. I barely remember getting here. Opening my eyes, I try to get my bearings. Early dawn light rises over the flat line of the ocean just beyond my open balcony door. A warm Aegean breeze flutters the curtains, filling our cabin with salty, ocean scents.

Owen stirs beside me, his hand lifting, pulling back my hair. "Good morning," he whispers in my ear.

I roll over to face him, coming eye-to-eye with him in the pale morning light. He's sleepy still, smiling dreamily. My hand settles on his chest, fingers threading through thin curls of hair at his breastbone. I blink his beauty into my slowly-waking brain, studying his cheeks, the turn of his jawline at his throat, the way his eyebrows don't quite match. The dimple on his right cheek that only appears when he smiles.

His skin is hot to my touch. The feel of it, and the scent

of him next to me, make that place low in my belly and between my legs ache.

"I want to kiss you, Norah," Owen says, his voice husky with sleep. "But only if you want me to."

I lick my dry lips, then bite the lower one. "I think I'd like that," I say.

He rises up on an elbow, coming over me. "I'm not going to be able to stop with just one kiss," he says softly, his voice lower than the wind coming in over the sea. "I'll never be able to stop with just one."

Owen's lips and mouth open me like an unread volume, drawing out wordless images and scenes from a dream half-remembered. I melt against his weight, merging into him. We make easy love, our bodies rocking in rhythm with the rolling tide beneath us.

I fell in love with his beauty the first time I saw him. I surrendered myself to that beauty so I could taste it and feel it, possessing it as my own. Now I'm falling in love with the man, surrendering myself—my whole soul—to his gentle, decent nature. I'm letting him possess me in a way I never thought I'd want or enjoy. When we're like this, with our bodies and minds in unison, breathing, heaving, grasping at intimacy, unafraid of the vulnerability we both feel so keenly, we're perfect.

My body responds to his like no one else's I've ever known. I receive him into me, not ever wanting to let go, as if he completes me. With tears in my eyes, I hang onto him tightly, crying out against him as waves of his perfect pleasure fill me, wash over me, possess me completely, drown me in warmth and safety—fundamentally altering who I am when he's inside me like this.

When our bodies finally still and untangle, no words are necessary. We lie together in the quiet dawn, drifting on the tide, fingers touching skin. I close my eyes with Owen's arm wrapped around my shoulder, my cheek pressed against his chest. His breathing lulls me into the most contented sleep I've known since childhood.

When I open my eyes next, Owen sleeps soundly beside me, but the sun is rising high in the sky, and I've slept too long. I hear voices outside our open balcony: strange voices, alien accents carrying across the open water, lifting in the wind. I rise, pulling on a thin robe, and go to the balcony overlooking the island ahead of us. Small, brightly painted boats motor across open water from Mykonos—the big island, gleaming, stark in the sun—headed toward our small island with just one bleached building crowning its black, volcanic cliffs. The boats carry men wrapped in colorful shawls, wearing working clothes. Once landed on the beach, the boats are dragged above the tide line and abandoned by their pilots and passengers, who walk in a marching pace up into the hills behind the white villa, disappearing from view.

It occurs to me to get my camera and capture a few fleeting shots of this mini-invasion. I frame photographs, using the zoom lens to narrow my focus on the weather-worn faces of men tanned dark, wrapped in faded cotton to shield them from the relentless sun. Their eyes are blue, green, and brown. Their long, unruly hair curls in the wind with the kiss of sun, bleached golden.

I snap photo after photo of the men, capturing their bold colors and plowed faces as they cross the impossibly blue water to reach the beach.

"What are you doing?"

I turn. Owen stands behind me—tall, naked, gorgeous, sleepy.

"Taking photos," I say. "Where are these guys going?"

Unafraid of appearing nude for everyone to see, Owen steps up to my side at the balcony railing. "They work in the olive grove," he says impassively. "There's a huge grove on the island. It provides a small income supporting the villa."

"All these people work for you?"

Owen nods. "If you ask them, they'd say they work for the olives. The estate has been in existence since the 14th century, when some ancestor of mine shipwrecked on the island on the way to a crusade and discovered an olive grove in need of a master. He skipped the crusade, built a villa, and claimed the island for the Anglesey crown. The Greeks have never disputed our title to the island because we've never gotten involved in their complicated politics, and we pay excellent wages."

"We should go see the olive grove," I say, turning my gaze up to the hills above the villa on the cliff. "I'd love to hike up there."

"Maybe tomorrow morning," Owen says. "By the time we get situated in the villa, it'll be mid-day, and it gets ridiculously hot up there. It's a better early morning walk."

"Okay," I agree. I'm anxious to get off this boat and get to the villa. I want *terra firma* beneath my feet. I've never been prone to seasickness, but the gentle rising and falling of the deck—even in this calm blue water—has me feeling slightly queasy.

OWEN WASN'T EXAGGERATING about the heat. It's barely eleven in the morning, but the temperature feels like July in Texas, complete with a salty, dry wind sucking every ounce of moisture from my skin, leaving me feeling crusty. Climbing the steep, stone-cut stairs from the beach to the villa starts off as a fine walk, but halfway up I'm breathless, thirsty, my thighs screaming from the exertion.

"We're almost there," Owen encourages me, seeing me struggle to lift my feet to take each step. "Let's rest a few minutes here."

There's a turn in the stairs with a little landing overlooking the beach below, and the wide open Aegean Sea beyond. The water is a color of blue I've never seen, defying adequate description. It's one of those rare shades that's impossible to capture on film or reproduce in a painting. You have to see it to experience it. It can't be conveyed in words or pictures.

"You're dehydrated," Owen says. "You're not drinking enough water." He hands me his water bottle. I take it and guzzle greedily, then feel my belly turn again with that queasiness I experienced earlier this morning.

The change of geography has my body discombobulated. I'm hungry, but sick to my stomach. Thirsty, but drinking just makes it worse. Everything has a slightly *off*, metallic after-taste. And I'm inexplicably exhausted, bloated, and tender. I feel almost as if I'm going to start my period, but that's not possible as I'm on the pill, in the middle of a pack—not at the end.

Then again, I didn't get a period between the end of the last cycle of pills and the beginning of this one. It didn't strike me as odd then, as I had too much going on to think about it. In hindsight, maybe...

No. I can't be. That's ridiculous.

Owen slips his hand into mine. "Just a little further," he says patiently. "Then you can chill by the pool with a glass of wine and a fantastic Greek spread for lunch."

I might have to skip the wine.

OWEN and I spend the better part of the afternoon nibbling fresh tomatoes and salty olives, sumptuous mozzarella cheese, and cucumbers served with a smattering of dips and salads I can't put a name to, all of them delicious. While we eat, lounging by the canopy-shaded pool, we talk about nothing and everything.

Owen asks me about growing up in Charleston, and what made me want to become a photographer. I tell him about the photography exhibit I saw when I was a child, images captured in Charleston in the 19th century. I was captivated by how much had changed, and yet how so many of the city scenes were familiar to me, one hundred and fifty years later. I fell in love with moments in history and felt the need to freeze them forever.

He tells me about growing up in the shadows of his father and older brother, always feeling like the extra on a surreal movie set. He was sent to boarding school in Scotland at seven years old and was expected to fend for himself without parents or the nannies who cared for him in the palace. At the school he was "just another little kid among three hundred." He was anonymous. The school, at first bracing and strange, became a refuge. He flourished.

After graduation he went into the Navy for two years of required national service. After that it was college, then back to the palace, which he found alien and confining.

"I genuinely hate all the tradition and pomp of the place," Owen admits. "All the butlers and valets with their powdered wigs. People scurrying around with odd functions that have no purpose in the twenty-first century." Owen looks over his sunglasses at me, laughing. "Did you know there's actually a person at the palace whose title is 'Gentleman of the King's Stool?' His job two hundred years ago was to collect and clean chamber pots, and wipe the king's ass, powder it, and then bury the king's poop in a special pit reserved just for him."

I laugh with him. "And what's his job now?" I ask, curiously interested.

"He stocks the toilet paper and keeps the bowl sparkling," Owen replies, shaking his head. "I wonder what the reaction was when the palace got indoor plumbing? The guy who had that job must have thought his life was over."

"That's pretty funny," I say. "So why is there still a 'Gentleman of the King's Stool?' I would think the maids could handle restocking and scrubbing."

"Hereditary position," Owen says. "His father had it before him, going back hundreds of years. We can't get rid of most of these positions until someone dies without heirs or moves out of the country."

"That's ridiculous," I say. "That must cost a fortune!"

He nods. "A fortune," he repeats. "But I guess there's nothing to be done about it."

"You're king," I remind him. "You can do anything you like."

Owen rolls his eyes. "Oh, if that was really true. Every time I've broached making some small change to improve the household or the national economy, I'm met with the same answer: 'it's tradition.'"

"You can make new traditions," I say. "The monarchy and the country have to adapt. You don't have to look far to see what happens to those who don't adapt to changing times."

Owen nods, biting his lip. "You're right," he says. He reaches forward, squeezing my hand in his. "One thing I'd like to change right away is the tradition that says the monarch has to be engaged or married. It's a ridiculous tradition."

I chuckle. "Thanks," I respond, my tone dry with sarcasm.

Owen shakes his head. "That's not a comment on you, or the institution in general. It's just that not everyone is suited to it. It's discriminatory at its foundations. What if I was gay? Or what if we don't have any sons? There's never been a female hereditary monarch. Anyone of these things could create a national crisis."

I realize all these questions of national importance weigh on him more than he lets on. Owen wants everyone to believe he's a carefree royal brat, but it's not the case. He brought a stack of documents to read on our holiday. He works more than most people do. In fact, if you count as work all the times he has to dress up and make an appearance somewhere he'd really rather skip, he's working nearly all the time.

That's why this small holiday was so important to him.

"You don't have to solve all these issues at once," I say. "We can take them one at a time." I smile at him. "One royal edict a month should clear your conscience before the first year of your reign has passed."

Owen grins sheepishly. "I think I should probably wait until the coronation before I start issuing edicts."

A few hours later, when Owen has briefly left me to check his email, I go in search of Duncan, and a favor. I find him hanging out with several other of the security detail in the kitchen. They're all dressed in shorts, t-shirts, and hiking boots, sweaty and sunned, obviously having just returned from an exploration of the island.

I get him alone in a side room, away from the cook or

anyone who could overhear. "Are you going to Mykonos anytime while we're here?"

He nods. "A few of us are going to head over there in an hour or so to have dinner and drinks. Why?"

"I need something, and I wouldn't ask if it wasn't an emergency."

"Okay," he responds cautiously.

"Does Mykonos have a drugstore or something like it?"

He nods.

"I need a pregnancy test."

Duncan's eyebrows raise. His jaw drops. "Oh," he says, suppressing an awkward smile.

"Yeah," I respond. "More like '*oh shit.*'"

DUNCAN DOESN'T RETURN from the main island until well past midnight, but he doesn't come back empty-handed. He sneaks the little package into my purse when Owen isn't looking. Twenty minutes later I'm in the bathroom, staring at a little pink plus sign, wondering what in the hell Anglesey's policy is on unexpected, early royal deliveries.

Oh shit. Oh shit. Oh shit.

15

OWEN

Duncan's report on Eric Wembley was comprehensive and disturbing. I read the whole thing with bile churning in my gut and my fists clenched. He updated it to include the secret service findings: Wembley has sent Nora six text messages and two emails since he was removed from the palace. The first one was sent within an hour of the incident. I'm certain she saw it, but she didn't mention it to me. She hasn't looked at her phone or opened her computer since we've been here, so it's unlikely she's seen the rest. I hope I can keep her from seeing them; they're vile and threatening.

Norah is napping now. We took a walk up through the olive groves this morning just as sunrise broke. It was an easy hike, and well worth it for the scenery. The groves themselves, which cover several hundred acres, are majestic and ancient, but we also paused to enjoy a smattering of Greek ruins at the top of the tallest hill. Two thousand years ago there was a temple on this island. Judging by the quality of the stone columns, flagstone floors, and still-beautiful sculptures, the temple was an important one.

Norah was beside herself with enthusiasm, drinking up the scenery and history, taking hundreds of photos of the landscape, the ruins, and me. But as soon as the sun started to heat up in earnest, she withered completely. I had to set her down in the shade while she fought off a bout of nausea. As soon as we returned to the villa, she went to bed.

I'm worried about her. She's not well, and I think it might have to do with Eric Wembley and his threats. If that's the case, I'm not sure what I can do about it except keep him away from her. The secret service is deporting him this evening. Hopefully he'll go away and leave us alone.

Norah opens her eyes, waking suddenly, catching me staring at her. She smiles, stretching. "I see you, Prince Peeping Tom. What are you looking at?"

I rise from my seat, then join her on the bed, stretching out, pulling her close to me. "You, Duchess," I say. "You and your beautiful mane of wild-spun gold hair, and your long, strong legs, and your perfectly round, firm tits that make my head spin when I think about them."

She laughs inside my arms, leaning into me.

"I'm glad we've gotten away from everything," I say. "I'm glad I have you all to myself, without palace spies lurking, or my mother's knowing glances, or my brother's drama, or crazy old boyfriends stalking you."

Norah breathes deeply, then pulls away, sitting up. "He's not my old boyfriend," she says flatly, glaring down at me. "He's just a very old friend who got his feelings hurt. He's harmless. You need to let it go."

I sit up with her. "Maybe he's not an old boyfriend," I concede, "but he *is* stalking you. Before you log onto your computer or check your texts, I hope you'll let me clear out some things he's sent you while you've been napping and playing in the sunshine with me."

She frowns. "What are you talking about?"

"I've had him under surveillance since he assaulted you in the garden. He's sent you a bunch of nasty texts and emails. Threatening messages. Terrible, foul things. I'd prefer you didn't read them."

Norah looks down at her hands, then back at me. Her expression masks a myriad of emotions—none of them altogether good. "You had his phone bugged?"

"Phone and computer," I reply. "He's been followed and observed since he left the palace grounds. Tonight he's being deported from Anglesey."

Norah takes another deep breath. "Should I assume you're also having my phone and computer bugged?"

"No," I say. "Norah, I have no reason to do that. I wouldn't. I did this because he threatened you. He physically accosted you. Putting aside the fact that you're one step away from becoming royalty yourself, I care about you, and I'd move heaven and Earth to protect you."

She blinks, struggling to process this information against what she thought she knew about her friend. "My computer and phone are in my bag," she says. "Have at it. If they're as bad as you say, I don't want to see them."

"Thank you," I say. "Is it okay if I block him from your accounts, so you won't receive anything else he tries to send?"

She nods. "Please."

I go to work on her computer while she watches me, regarding me with a stoic, serious expression. It only takes a few moments. Her cell phone reveals a brand new one from Wembley, sent in the last hour. It reads:

You're a gold-digging whore who's going to get what's

coming to you. A bullet in the head is too good for you. I'm going to make the pain linger like you've made mine linger all these years. Cunt.

IF IT'S the last thing I do, I'm going to see this guy shackled in a dungeon.

When I'm done, I stand and offer Norah my hand. "Let's go up to the roof and watch the sun set over the sea while eating grapes and drinking local Greek wine, shall we?"

The sky overhead has darkened to royal blue, already twinkling with stars. But the western horizon writhes with intense color. A line of crimson sits atop a steel gray ocean. Above, layers of orange bleed to yellows, then fade to a thousand varieties of pink before blending into periwinkle and lavender blues. In the middle of all of it sits the sun's disk, sinking slowly beneath the watery line at the planet's edge.

It's quiet up here above everything. We have an unobstructed view in every direction, from the olive groves behind us to the island of Mykonos ahead, the town coming to life with tourists just arriving from a gigantic cruise ship that dropped anchor offshore. The wind has died down, allowing the sounds of seabirds nesting on the cliffs beneath the villa to rise up to our ears. They're coming in to roost, calling out, squawking a last "good night" before succumbing to darkness and sleep.

Norah and I sit together, hand in hand in silence, just taking in the beauty of this place. It occurs to me that she's the first person who I can comfortably sit in silence with, not needing to fill the air. It also occurs to me that this is the first time since we've been together that we haven't had some spectacle of drama or wrenching anxiety over our heads. For the first time in a long time, I feel like we have a smooth path ahead of us. The coronation is happening in just a few weeks. Norah and I will select a wedding date, probably for some time before Christmas. And after that, we should be able to settle into a reasonable routine.

Once the sun finally sinks into the sea, plunging us in shadows, lit only from a million twinkling stars overhead, I share my musings with Norah.

She listens, still holding my hand. When I'm done, she turns to me in the darkness. "I'm really glad you've had a few minutes of peace to enjoy, aside from all the crazy. And I'm just sorry that I have to be the one to bring it all crashing down on your pretty, princely head."

She's going to say something smart, making fun of me and my meandering philosophizing.

"I'm pregnant."

The words hang in the darkness a moment before they register. She must be joking. It's dark, and I can't see her expression clearly enough to tell if she's joking. Hell, I can't tell when she's joking when I can see her clearly.

"Did you hear me?" Norah asks. "Or have you had a stroke? You stopped breathing."

She's not joking.

"How do you know?" I ask, which seems a reasonable question.

"I suspected, based on how odd I'm feeling. I asked Duncan to bring a pregnancy test back from his trip to Chora last night. It turned up positive."

Oh shit.

It occurs to me that this is a royal mess. We just announced our engagement a few days ago. There's a tradition—a royal protocol—that requires us to wait several months before the wedding. We can't get married too soon after the coronation, for practicality's sake. It takes months of planning to prepare for a royal ceremony like a wedding or coronation.

The scandal around this would be huge. I can see the headlines now, with "Royally Knocked-Up" being at the top of the list of tacky puns the tabloids will trot out to make the most of our situation.

And then there will be the more malicious types who will speculate that the kid isn't mine.

Oh shit.

"Say something," Norah says, her tone impassive.

I have no idea what to say. I have no idea what to do. "Any clue how far along you are?"

"No," she replies. "Not long, though. Maybe a few weeks."

If we get married next week, we might be able to convincingly pull off the story that the baby arrived early. "Shotgun Royal Wedding!" That's what *Today's Mail* will lead with. That or, "An Unexpected Bundle has the Randy Royals Rushing Down the Aisle."

Oh shit. Norah said it earlier: it's time for some new traditions. Screw protocol and practicality—we're getting married *before* the coronation. "How do you feel about a royal shotgun wedding?" I ask Norah. "We'll have to skip some of the carriage rides and beefeaters on parade, but we'll still have a royal throw down—just a slightly smaller one than originally anticipated."

Norah chuckles into the cooling night air. "That's fine with me," she says. "A relief, actually. I was afraid I was going to have to compete with your mother for who could deliver the largest worldwide television viewing audience in history. I just don't think a billion people care much about seeing me get married. Her wedding was the event of the decade."

My mother is going to go into apoplexy when she hears this news. I'm going to need to tell her as soon as possible so she can get started on the necessary plans, but not before we have all the information. "Tomorrow we're flying to Athens to go see a doctor," I say. "No arguments. We need to know what's what before we tell another soul."

She sighs again. "I'm in perfect agreement with both those ideas."

My stomach queasiness is back with a vengeance, exacerbated by an early morning speedboat trip to Mykonos and a quick, up-and-down flight to Athens. The city is hot, crowded, stinking of people, food, and diesel fumes as we motor in a hired limo from the airport across town to the suburbs, headed to an OBGYN's office selected by Owen on the recommendation of his cousin, who lives here and knows everyone.

"His patients are aristocracy and shipping tycoons," Owen says, trying to reassure me as Duncan navigates us into a valet parking area. "He's supposed to be very good, and very discreet."

The waiting room décor has an air of exclusivity, rather than the cold, clinical feel of physicians' offices at home in America. Lovely paintings hang on the walls, and a couple of Greek amphorae that have the appearance of authenticity rather than reproductions sit atop pedestals.

"Symbolic," Owen observes, passing one of those on his way to check me in.

When he returns to my side it's with a clipboard and

pencil, to complete a short questionnaire regarding my medical history.

Before I can complete the questionnaire, I'm called by a uniformed nurse who smiles at me. "The first thing we'll do is get a blood sample," the nurse says, showing me to a padded chair equipped with all the tools of the phlebotomist's trade. She does the work herself, finding a vein effortlessly, filling two vials.

I expect to be handed a cup to pee in before being examined by the nurse, but am astonished when the doctor himself appears straight away. He introduces himself as Dr. Octavio Papadopoulos, which has such a nice ring to it, it makes me laugh. He sits, facing me in his rolling doctor's chair. "You came to me today to see if you're pregnant. Yes?" he asks in a heavy Greek accent.

He's got a big smile, and a big personality to go along with it.

I nod.

He reaches forward, taking my hands in his. His hands are huge, soft, and warm. There's something comforting in his touch. He examines my nails and the skin on the back of my hands, pressing his thumb into the pad of my hand, then pinching the skin between my knuckles. "You're dehydrated," he pronounces. "You must drink three times as much water as you drink now."

With this pronouncement, he looks into my eyes, pulling my lower eyelid down to examine the color below. "And you're anemic. You must eat three servings of leafy green vegetables every day. Broccoli and spinach are ideal, along with at least one serving of lean, red meat. You're American?" he asks.

Again, I nod.

"You people eat like shit. Only fresh fruits and vegetables from now on. Only good-quality meats. No more McDonald's or Kentucky Fried Chicken."

"I don't eat that stuff anyway. I eat pretty well," I say defensively.

"Eat better," he pronounces. He hands me a plastic cup, pointing toward a toilet across the hall. "Put the sample in the window when you're done."

Once I've produced the sample and returned to the office, I find him setting up an ultrasound machine. "My nurse has gone to fetch your partner," he says. "Hop up on the table and show me your belly."

A moment later, Owen appears in the doorway. The doctor repeats his introductions, then adds, "I know who you are. We'll act as if you're both strangers for the sake of professionalism."

Owen smiles, amused with the man, slipping his hand into mine as he moves in close beside me.

The gel is cold on my belly, but otherwise the examination is painless. The doctor smiles, finding what he's looking for. "Marvelous," he says. "Yes, you're exceedingly pregnant."

"How far along?" Owen asks, his eyes glued to the monitor, looking for something recognizable in the puzzle of digital fuzz.

Dr. Papadopoulos cocks his head to the side, slowing, then stopping with the wand in place. I hear a loud *who-whosh-who-whosh-who-whosh* come from the monitor. "Hear that?" the doctor asks.

We both nod.

"I'd say nine or ten weeks along," he says, answering Owen's question.

Oh shit!

Owen looks down at me with question in his eyes. He's doing the math in his head.

"Paris," I say, as stunned as he is. We did sort of go out of our way to be reckless.

"Look closely," the doctor says, pointing to a tiny image on the screen.

Owen leans in, squinting.

"See here," he says, his fingers moving across the screen as he speaks. "This is a head. And this is also a head. And here is a pair of legs. And here is another pair of legs. Tiny hands here."

"Oh shit," Owen croons.

Twins?

He looks down at me, disbelief coloring his face. "Twins," he says. "Oh good Lord."

He returns his attention to the doctor and the image on the small screen. "You can't tell what sex they are, can you?"

Dr. Papadopoulos shakes his head. "Maybe by next week. Certainly in two weeks, if everything goes normally."

He holds the wand steady and hits a button on the machine. An instant later, a digital printout appears with the ultrasound images fixed on it.

"Oh, please print another," I beg. "We need two!"

He prints another, handing both to me, smiling. "I hope this is good news?" he says, wiping the gel from my abdomen with a clean towel.

"It's unexpected," Owen says, squeezing my hand. "But good news. They're healthy?"

The doctor nods. "Appears so. The young mother-to-be needs to eat healthy food and drink much more water. We talked about it earlier before you came in, but I'm making it your responsibility to see to it, too. No alcohol. No raw seafood."

He offers his hand, helping me to sit up. "As soon as you're home, make an appointment with a trusted OBGYN and follow his or her instructions to the letter. If you have any problems or concerns while you're on holiday, call me day or night."

He hands both me and Owen a card with his numbers and email address, along with a bottle of prenatal vitamins. "You're all done," he says.

The doctor shows us out to the waiting room where Owen pays the bill and I stand waiting, stunned, trying to think what it means to be carrying twins under normal circumstances, much less this weird arrangement Owen and I have contrived.

Twins complicate things. Being pregnant at all right now complicates things. Being ten weeks pregnant makes everything incredibly awkward.

Oh. Shit.

The drive back to the airport is quiet. Owen holds my hand but has almost nothing to say. He looks as if he's carrying the weight of the world on his shoulders. He's grim, lost in thought.

The flight home is the same. Initially, I chalk it up to the presence of Duncan and the other members of our security detail, but it gradually dawns on me that he could have closed the limo window to speak privately with me on the way to the airport. Once on the jet, the detail is in the rear cabin while we sit alone up front.

This pregnancy presents Owen with too many complex problems to handle at once. To begin with, moving the wedding up will cause a scandal even before the pregnancy is announced. Then there's the fact that the babies will come far too early to be able to pass off as incidental early delivery. Then there's the issue of twins: two children cannot inherit a single crown. There can be only one crowned prince, which would pit our children against one another from the first day they're born.

I've heard Owen describe how he felt as the "spare," always in the shadow of his brother. At least his brother was older—imagine if they'd been identical in every regard except for the luck of which one was delivered a moment or two before the other.

Owen's already been made acting king. His succession to the throne is a closed matter, and he doesn't need a fiancée any longer. He doesn't need me or the royal mess I've just brought into his already demanding, complicated world.

His silence speaks volumes. He's thinking of ways to send me back where I came from.

Before the jet lands in Mykonos, my heart is slowly breaking. It's breaking for myself and the feelings I've developed for Owen, for the dreams I was finally allowing myself to entertain about a life we might have together. And it's breaking for these two fragile beings inside me, babies whose father sees them as complications, as scandal, as threats to his long-fought-for position. If these babies never know a father who loves them, that's the most heartbreaking thing of all.

All that said, if I really do love Owen—and now I know I do—I must do what's best for him. If these two inconvenient little lives threaten him, then I must give *him* up, because I'll never give *them* up.

17

OWEN

The tabloids will savage Norah. They'll cast her as careless—or worse: a conniving upstart with pretensions to the throne. The scandal will be massive. Unmarried, pregnant, carrying the king's twins. *Twins!* Two children, identical in every way, but only one "crowned." The other a matching spare.

The situation is awful. It's enough to threaten the whole monarchy and tear our nascent family apart. There's an element in Anglesey society now who think we're an expensive anachronism. They've been rattling the sabers of constitutional democracy for decades, and this will give them just enough fuel to fire a revolution.

I can't let it happen. My cousin David wanted the job. He can have it. Mother will be crushed, but so be it. I love Norah, and I wouldn't do anything to make our children grow up to hate one another.

Abdication is the only rational solution.

We'd have to leave the country and resign our citizenship. There's no way David would permit me—and especially my children—to stay. I can move some money around so that financing our lives afterward won't be an issue. The problem is where to go. Norah's family in Charleston would welcome us. I can't imagine living in the United States, but I may not have a lot of options. It's difficult to emigrate anywhere these days without years of petitions and paperwork filings. We're going to need to move fast. At least if we're married, the United States will take me provisionally and I can begin the process of obtaining permanent resident status.

"I know you have a lot on your mind, but I've come to talk."

I turn. Norah's standing in the doorway. I've been sitting under the canopy by the pool with a glass of whiskey in my hand, just watching the blue Aegean Sea, lost in thought.

I hold out my free hand. "Yeah, we should probably talk about what to do," I say, urging her toward me.

She takes a step toward me, but doesn't take my hand. She's wearing an odd expression, with her arms crossed over her chest defensively. "I know what you're thinking," she says. "And I understand."

Really? Good. I was afraid she'd be upset.

"I'll forget about the contract. I don't need any money. I don't even care about the money. I thank you for taking care of my mom and dad. I wish I could repay that, but..."

"Norah, what in God's name are you talking about?" I interrupt her sharply. This has the sound of a *leaving* conversation. She's wearing the look of a woman about to *leave*.

"It's too much scandal. It's too many things at once," she says. "I know how hard you fought to get the crown, and how fragile your hold on it is. I... we... we won't be the cause of more scandal. Just help me get back to Charleston. Back to my family."

"You're out of your mind," I pronounce, then take a long shot of the brown liquor in my glass. "Maybe it's the hormones surging through your system. I've heard that women get weirdly irrational when they're pregnant."

Norah just stares at me, fighting what look like tears trying to pool in her beautiful eyes.

I stand and go to her, encircling her in my arms, holding her tight. "You're not going anywhere without me," I say, speaking into her hair. "Our kids are going to know their father loves them."

In a moment, Norah is hugging me back as tight as she can and bawling like a baby into my chest. Her sobs heave against me. Her tears soak through my shirt, dampening my chest.

"Oh, baby. Please don't cry," I urge her. "There's nothing to cry about. No matter what happens, we're in this together."

This only brings on another round of fathomless sobs.

"*Shhhh*," I soothe, stroking her hair, holding her, rocking her in my arms. I've never had a woman cry in my arms. I've never made a woman cry at all, though I've made plenty of them angry as hell. This is different. It's terrible. "*Shhhh*, please baby. I love you so much. Please don't cry."

More sobs follow, but in a few moments she settles down, just heaving hot breaths into me.

I pull her back to my lounge chair, hauling her onto my lap, still in my arms, still stroking her hair and her hand. "It's going to be okay," I tell her. "I have a plan that'll make it all work out and avoid unnecessary scandal."

Norah looks up at me, her eyes bloodshot, lids swollen and red. Her nose is snotty and swollen, too. I mop it with my sleeve, then tuck a wild lock of straying hair behind her ear.

"I was never meant to be king," I remind Norah. "I'm not really cut out for it. And clearly, I'm probably not going to be the traditionalists' choice if they get wind of this."

Norah's eyes grow wide. A furrow digs deep between her brows. "No, Owen," she says.

"My cousin David would..."

"Your cousin David is a creep and would become a tyrant. You can't quit!"

"Norah, the papers will have a field day with this. They'll blame you. They'll say awful things. They'll call our children bastards. They'll..."

"Screw the papers," Norah spits, scrambling out of my lap. The sobs are gone, and the fight has returned to her. All the fire is coming back into those icy blue eyes. "The papers can say whatever they want. It doesn't change the fact that you're the king and these babies are your children. If anyone needs proof, I'll happily submit to a paternity test."

She scowls at the notion of me quitting. "People get pregnant by accident every day. It's only a crushing scandal to people who don't live in the real world. If we don't treat the babies like a scandal, and don't allow anyone else to, then the only ones scandalized are the uptight toadies of an anachronistic enterprise that's needed an overhaul for the better part of a century."

She almost stamps her feet. "I say we proudly announce the happy news the very first chance we get, tradition be damned. If anyone fails to congratulate us, you can exile them to Paraguay, too."

I shouldn't laugh, but I can't help it: Norah makes me laugh. She's found a way to turn this catastrophe into an opportunity for long-needed modernization of how the monarchy behaves and what the people should expect of it.

She doesn't care for rules and traditions that make no sense, whereas I've been raised to accept them *just because.*

"I'll tell you one more thing, too," Norah says. "There's no reason in the world that a pair of twins can't share the title of crown *princes,* and no reason they can't be co-regents. Two heads are always better than one. This way they can be partners, supporting one another, instead of lifelong competitors."

She's astonishingly creative in her solutions. I need to give her a cabinet position; I bet she could manage to get some stuff done while knocking a few old crony heads into the current century.

"That will be my first royal edict," I say. "That solves the biggest problem I've been pondering all day."

"Maybe we should hold back news of the fact that we've got twins until after the edict? Just so no one gets ahead of us."

I laugh. "We'll see," I say, then urge her back to my lap. Once she's settled, I kiss her cheek. "The first person we tell anything to is my mother. She's going to have a meltdown. But she's a strategic genius who personally invented the idea of turning a scandal into an opportunity for gaining the public's sympathy and using the political capital to effect change on an unchanging system. Once she gets over the initial shock, she's our best ally."

I'm counting on it. My mother is a royal pain and a diva, but she's also the People's Princess, and my biggest cheerleader.

~

NORAH and I head up to the roof at sunset, watching the magic like we did before. I take her hand in mine as the glowing orange disk takes its plunge below the waterline, sad that the light show is over.

"Think of all the billions of people who've watched the sun set just like that, since the first of us stood upright," Norah muses, peering into the violet twilight. She turns to me, smiling slyly. "Stone-aged men and women, watching the sun slip beneath the waves, then taking each other's hands and wandering off into the darkness to make babies together. We're all the same."

She's right, of course. The only thing that's changed about humanity is we've managed to complicate life so profoundly with nonsense that matters a lot less than a stunning sunset.

"Come here," I urge Norah, begging her onto my lap. "I need to see what you're prattling on about. I think it might involve something more than just holding hands."

When I've got her on my lap, her legs spread around my hips, I let my hands admire her contours, tracing her curves, feeling her soft places under curious fingertips. Her eyes, shadowed in the darkness, reveal nothing to me. Her silhouette against the Milky Way sky reveals the most beautiful women I've ever beheld.

Sometimes I want to hold her like a baby, and sometimes I want to rock her easily beneath me. Tonight, knowing she's carrying my children, knowing I put them inside her and she's determined to protect them and bear them, I'm so inexplicably compelled with pride and possessive lust, I have no words for what I feel.

Men are fragile creatures. We walk the Earth trying to convince ourselves and others that we're alpha beasts, but we're just frightened creatures beating our chests, howling at the moon. When a woman like Norah comes into our world, we're humbled, and heated, and determined to somehow catch her attention long enough to make an impression.

And sometimes we do.

I want to mark her, to claim her like she claimed me that night in Paris. I press my lips against hers, sucking hungrily, feeling her heartbeat lift and skip under my fingertips at her throat. My tongue presses in, exploring while my hand binds her hair in a knot between her shoulder blades, tilting her head back just so, so I can invade her more completely.

Breathless, overheated, I pull her closer against me, feeling her heat, bringing a sweat to my skin that begs for relief from clothing.

"We need to take this to the bedroom," Norah whispers, heaving hot breaths against my neck. "No more public displays. No more exhibitions for prying cameras."

She's right. There's no telling who's floating around out on the sea, with a long lens and nighttime optics.

Owen backs me onto the bed, peeling my clothes off, casting them aside as we go. He tugs his shirt off before pushing me down onto soft, downy sheets, then stalks in over me like a hungry lion. "You're so fucking beautiful," he breathes, lips and teeth grazing my breasts. "And more perfect than I deserve."

This is like Paris with the tables turned. He's taking the lead and ramping it up to a level of intoxicating heat that's unexpected and ridiculously sexy.

"I want you to come for me," Owen says, his voice graveled with lust as he slips inside me, shoving in deep, filling me with instant, shuddering pleasure. "I want you to come crying my name while we do this."

His palms circle my ass, fingers digging in hard as he pulls me tight against him. I'm on top, but he's in total control. He sets the pace, his hands commanding my movements. I'm on his lap, straddling him, face-to-face as his eyes bore into mine.

"God, you feel so fucking good," he heaves, his mouth slacking open. "You own me."

He says that, but in this moment of pure, animal heat, I'm pretty sure it's Owen who owns me.

Without warning he flips me onto my back, roughly kicking my knees apart. A second later he's inside me again, hauling in with long, precision-timed strokes, his cock teasing parts of my sensitive anatomy that I wasn't previously aware of.

My orgasms come in breaking waves, a tsunami of flooding pleasure as I cry against his neck, my gripping fingers bruising the backs of his arms. "Oh God, Owen, *oh...*" I whimper, tears forming in the corners of my eyes, dripping down.

"That's it, Duchess," Owen heaves breathlessly, driving himself into me without mercy. "Call my name."

An hour later, I'm still calling his name again and again, crying in time with his cries.

"*Agh... ah... Norah... oh fuck... baby...fucking hell.*" He slumps deflated against me, melting into the sheets, completely spent, lungs heaving for air.

A few minutes later, just as I'm about to drift into an exhausted sleep, Owen's hand falls to my belly, enclosing it in his protective shield. He snuggles against me, pulling me close. "Take care, babies," he mumbles against my neck, smiling sleepily. "That was your mum and da making love —*fucking*. That's how you came to be, you little princes."

A few moments later Owen sleeps, snoring sweetly. I follow not long after, threading my fingers into his.

Owen's taken to heart the doctor's instructions concerning my diet. Hummus and flatbread have been replaced by sizzling lamb kebabs cooked outside over open flames, quinoa tabbouleh, and tomato-rich ratatouille. Olives are still permitted because they're loaded with iron, but garbanzos have taken a back seat to lentils and black beans, which the cook says are high in iron and other nutrients. I'm inundated with a tsunami of spinach and a variety of cheeses high in calcium to ensure my bones remain strong. My only permitted beverage is artesian well water, which I'm allowed to sweeten with local honey and flavor with lime or lemon.

While I would generally revolt against anyone regimenting any of my choices, it's hard to complain when the regimen is so delicious.

Owen pops an olive in his mouth, chews the succulent, salty fruit, then spits the seed into a bowl by his plate. "I'm going to bring the cook home with us," he says. "I think Med cuisine is the answer to your nutritional deficits, and I love it. The royal menu could do with a makeover. Sausages, boiled beef, and haggis have seen their heyday. If we're changing things up, let's start with the basics. We should put avocado trees in the royal greenhouses."

"That's revolutionary talk," I tease. "You'll have the peasants rising up with pitchforks."

Owen grins at me.

A second later my phone, sitting on the table beside us, vibrates. I've been sending family and friends photos from our holiday. I posted an entire album of pics from the olive grove excursion, including the Greek ruins. Chantal in Paris has been conversing back and forth with me all day. My mother has *hearted* everything I've posted. My father likes them, too.

I lift the phone to have a look. The message isn't from Chantal, or Sinead, or even my mother. It's from Eric.

Happy holiday. And fuck you, cunt. Pretty pictures. Pretty vapid. Your pretty prince's henchmen are pretty clueless. I'm back in Anglesey after only 72 hours away. Border security here is worse than west Texas. Amazing how easy it is to smuggle contraband in. Sleep tight, Duchess. See you soon.

I SHIVER IN MY SEAT. This isn't the Eric I knew. This is some twisted, disturbed version of my childhood friend.

"What is it?" Owen asks.

I lay the phone down on the table, pushing it across toward him.

Owen lifts the phone, reading the message. His face draws tight, angry. A moment later he summons Duncan, showing him the text. "Get the SS on this. I want him found and arrested."

When Duncan is gone, Owen returns to me. "He can't get at you," he says. "I promise you. You're safe."

I hope he's right. If Eric was able to get back in so quickly, with so little effort, I wonder. And I wonder how, after Owen blocked him from my phone, he was able to get through again.

"He got a new phone," Owen says. "New phone, new profile. He can get new devices and create new profiles, starting over fresh as many times as he pleases." Owen sighs with resignation. "I hoped he'd give up and go away. That was wishful thinking."

The next morning, the messages keep coming without abatement. Eric teases—threateningly—with photographs taken just outside the palace gates, showing him engaged in easy, lighthearted conversation with palace guards.

Another series of texts come through in the late afternoon, featuring a video of Eric on tour with a group, being shown around the interior of the palace. At one point in the video, Owen's mother, Her Royal Highness Princess Dalia, makes a brief appearance to welcome the crowd of tourists.

Eric shakes her hand, bowing, then turns to his camera, grinning coldly. "See how close I can get? I could have slit her throat or blown her brains out." He winks at the camera. "Saving my energy for the ones I love most."

Owen is livid—rightfully so. He and Duncan get on the line with the palace's head of security, along with the chief of the SS, the chief of police for Cymrea, and the chief of border security. They all point the finger at one another, no one taking responsibility—save Duncan, who admits he should have circulated a photo of Eric to every agency in the country.

"I need each of you to work cooperatively," Owen states calmly. "Share information. I don't care what agency picks him up. Every agency will get credit. Get him. I want him off the streets. Am I understood?"

A half-dozen "yes, sirs" rattle over the long-distance line.

Owen has also seen to increased security at the palace and a cessation of public tours until this issue is resolved.

"We need to go home," Owen says to me, putting his phone down. "There's so much going on that needs my attention."

I need his attention, too. I need the quiet of our rooftop sunsets, and the lack of court protocol hanging like a sword over my head. When we go back it's going to be nothing but outraged courtiers and spin doctors. I'm going to be thrown into the fire. I just want a few more days of fantastic escapism offered by these islands and their exquisite seaside views.

"I've got a country to run," Owen says, pleading. "Right

now, that country has been invaded by a man who wants to hurt my wife and unborn children. I need to do something about that. I've also got meetings piling up, a trade deal to negotiate with the Brits, and I really want to sit down with my mother and figure out what our first steps are with moving the wedding up and announcing the pregnancy."

"Just a few more days," I beg. "Just a few more days of *just us* without the world crowding in."

Owen heaves a frustrated sigh. "Duchess, we have to go home. This issue with Wembley is serious. All these issues are serious. I'm king. It's my duty to deal with it all."

I could pout. I want to. I could fume, and that might be fun. But at the end of the day I know Owen is right: we can't hide ourselves away on a tiny island in the Aegean, ignoring the world or the messes swirling around us like hungry sharks.

I'm dreading what Owen's mother will say. She's held this monarchy together through infidelity, untimely deaths, insanity, and a deposed king. She's done it on the sheer force of her will and her incandescently bright personality alone. One more self-inflicted crisis may be enough to cause her to throw up her hands and run screaming. She has the right to do that now that she's resigned as co-regent and Owen is acting king, and I won't blame her a bit if that's exactly what she does.

OWEN IS unsuccessful in convincing the villa's cook to abandon her family and move to Cymrea to work at the palace. She sends us on our way with bags of avocados and almonds, cases of jarred olives, gallons of olive oil, and an address for a Mediterranean food importer in London who can work with the palace chef to keep Owen happily supplied with all the tabbouleh and hummus his heart desires.

The return trip to Anglesey is mercifully brief, as I sleep through most of the flight. As we circle Cymrea on our landing approach, I peer out the window, looking down on the fairytale landscape of my adopted home. Gray slate rooftops shine in the sun. The spires of countless churches and the cathedral reach into the sky with grandeur. The narrow, cobbled lanes meandering through the oldest part of the city harken back to a much simpler era, when people walked everywhere and when they all knew their neighbors. It's still like that in much of Anglesey. Cymrea is a safe city, peopled by generally contented residents who value their traditions.

I wonder what in the world they're going to make of me and the scandal I'm about to dump on the head of their much-loved, new king-to-be?

I hope they don't hang me in effigy in Cathedral Square.

When the plane lands, we're met on the tarmac by a fleet of royal limos bearing heavy security. An imposing man in a crisp, three-piece suit steps forward in front of the rest of the royal guard. Owen greets him with a brief hand-shake, then demands "an update."

The man is never introduced to me, but he rides with us to the palace in our limo, giving Owen a full report on everything that has not been accomplished in the days since Eric slipped back into Anglesey and began thumbing his nose at every attempt to find and detain him.

The man reveals that so far, they have no idea where he is. Geo-tracking is of no use because he's using disposable phones he purchased abroad (they're illegal in Anglesey). As soon as he drops a text or video, he also drops the phone in the trash.

"He's obviously using false identification and cash," the man says. "This makes him nearly impossible to find."

"We've got his image," Owen says. "We know what he looks like. Have we broadcast an alert on television and on the Anglesey emergency network?"

The man blinks, swallowing hard. "No, sir," he replies. "That felt... excessive."

Owen's jaw flexes tight. "Excessive?" he asks, repeating the word through clenched teeth. "This man has issued death threats against my fiancée. He discussed slashing my mother's throat and putting a bullet in her head. He's guilty of high crimes against the Crown. Do whatever it takes to find him."

The man clears his throat nervously. "Sir, perhaps its best to proceed cautiously. While the man may be guilty of high crimes, he has not been *found* guilty. Further, he's a U.S citizen, and as such he poses an awkward diplomatic problem. The embassy is..."

"*I said find him!*" Owen snaps. "I don't give a shit about courts or lawyers, and I don't give a shit about the Americans. *Do you understand me?*"

"Yes, Your Royal Highness. Perfectly."

I've never seen Owen angry before. It's frightening. Based on the shocked expression stretching the face of the man sitting across from us, he's never seen Owen angry, either. He looks like he just got punched in the gut.

After a few moments of awkward, very tense silence, Owen turns to me. "Until this is sorted out, I want you to stay in the royal residence. No exploring other parts of the palace or taking walks in the gardens. Stay inside and keep security near you always."

"But I have to…"

"You *have* to do this," Owen interrupts. "We don't even know that he hasn't hidden himself somewhere on the grounds or even inside the palace itself. He could be anywhere. It's not safe."

He returns his address to the man facing him. "Call in however many men you need from the Army. No one sleeps until every single room, corridor, cabinet, and sock drawer in the palace has been searched and secured. Then move to the outbuildings and the grounds. I want this organized immediately."

"Yes, sir."

19

OWEN

Mother stands at the front steps alongside Townsend, my valet, and half a dozen other staff ready to welcome us home. She's wearing a grave expression as well as her favorite power suit. She calls that look (a feminized version of a man's double-breasted business suit), her "roll with the big boys' body armor." It's appropriate. I know she's up to speed on the situation with Wembley, as she gets the same security updates and briefings I receive.

"What a clusterfuck," she says, hugging me as soon as I step out of the car. "I'm glad you're home, as Neville there doesn't take instructions from me anymore."

She glares past me at Neville Chambers, the head of secret service.

"He updated me in the car," I say. "What did you ask him to do?"

"I told him to put that deplorable creature's face on a wanted poster and broadcast it from here to the North Sea. He said he couldn't do it."

I huff in frustration. "Well, he's doing it now," I say. "I just chewed his ear off for not doing it sooner."

Mother smiles. "Well done."

"Hold onto that happy thought," I say. "As soon as Norah and I get settled in, we all need to talk. We have another situation brewing."

Mother's smile instantly vanishes. Her shoulders slump. "Oh good Lord. What now?"

"Upstairs," I say. "In the residence. Behind closed doors."

Norah slips up beside me, shrinking under my arm as if she wants to disappear.

"Darling, you look pale," Mother observes, then her face freezes. She blinks. She looks at me, then back to Norah, then back to me. "Oh, for heaven's sake," she exclaims. "Could this week get any worse?"

"Be careful what you ask for," I warn her. "There's more to tell."

We meet in my library, as it's swept daily for listening devices. Mother won't sit down, so neither do I. Norah, on the other hand, is happy to sit as far away on the other side of the room as she can.

"I know *how* this happened," Mother says. "What I want to know is *how in the hell did this happen?*"

It's time to come clean about everything.

"We met in Paris in April," I say. "We met. I spent the night. I left. I really didn't expect we'd ever see one another again."

Mother rolls her eyes, shaking her head in disbelief. "One of your anonymous little excursions to the other side of the wall. Son, if I told you once, I told you a thousand times: *wear a condom!*"

"Yeah, thank you," I say. "Not helpful."

Mother turns to Norah, walking right up to her, looming

over her. "So, what's your story in all of this? How did you find out who he was? How did you track him down?"

"I didn't track him down. He tracked me down," Norah replies. "*Persistently.*"

"It's true," I say. "It was all just dumb luck. She was in the country staying with a friend of hers from college at about the same time you organized that ridiculous yacht party. Her friends had an invitation to the party at Brynterion that weekend. Duncan saw Norah there, recognized her from Paris, and arranged for her and her friend to come on the cruise. That's when we reconnected."

"That was less than a month ago," Mother says. "You two decided to get engaged the second you reconnected?"

"Not exactly," I say, hedging. "We came to an arrangement at first." I look to Norah, who's staring back at me like a deer in the headlights. "It was nothing but a business arrangement designed to last only until we got Lloyd to come to his senses."

Mother finally sits down. She's absolutely overwhelmed.

"Things kept spiraling with him, and at the same time, I realized I was developing genuine feelings for Norah. I told you that much."

She nods. "Yes, I recall that," she says. "You managed to avoid the news that she's pregnant, however."

"We just found out," I say. "Just a few days ago."

Mother turns to Norah again. "You're at least nine weeks pregnant and you only figured it out a few days ago? How can that be?"

Norah shrugs. "I was on the pill," she says. "Sometimes I don't get periods. I didn't think anything of it, especially with everything else going on."

"Ten weeks," I tell my mother. "The doctor said nine or ten weeks."

"You're going to be a plump bride," Mother observes wryly. "I think it's time to bring back the Empire waist."

"And we're having twins," I say, finally spilling the news.

Mother turns slowly toward me, her jaw slack and her eyes wide. "Twins?" she repeats.

I nod, waiting.

Mother laughs. She laughs right out loud. She laughs, giggling, until she's breathless, tears forming at the corners of her eyes. When she finally regains her composure, she sighs heavily, throwing up her hands. "Well," she says, "this is going to be fun to sort out."

The three of us sit quietly together, letting Mother process the news. In a few moments she asks, "Have you told anyone else?"

Norah and I both shake our heads, then I add, "Duncan probably knows, and the doctor who did the ultrasound knows."

"I'm assuming you paid him handsomely for his silence on the matter?"

"He gave me his assurances," I reply. "He didn't charge extra for them. I trust him."

"You're a fool," Mother says flippantly. "How did you find him?"

"Philip in Athens referred him."

"So, your cousin Philip probably knows also, or at least suspects. Plus all the housekeepers and staff at the villa. Secrets get out, Son. There's no way to keep them when we live in a goldfish bowl."

She's right, of course. She's always right. "What do we do?"

Mother stands up, shoving her hands in her jacket pockets. "We get you two quietly, legally married as soon as possible. We announce the fast-tracked, official wedding, which probably can't be held in the cathedral because the archbishop won't allow it, then we announce the babies. And then we hold the coronation as scheduled."

"That gives us a month," I say. "Can we do it all that fast?"

Mother cocks her head at me, smiling dryly. "Is that a challenge?"

"Yes," I quip. "I challenge you to handle the press and make them spin all this as good news."

"Count on it," Mother promises, smirking smartly. "I'm going to go make some phone calls now. You two try not to cook up any more outrages in my absence. I'll be back with a justice of the peace before dark."

Once Mother is gone, I go to Norah, who's still cowering in the corner. "That went remarkably well," I tell her, slipping my hands around hers, crouching in front of her. "Don't you think?"

She nods anxiously. "Was she serious about the justice of the peace?"

"My mother doesn't joke about anything," I say. "Are you ready to get married?"

"Are you?" she asks.

"Been ready," I say, smiling up into her big blue eyes. "Can't wait. And then we'll do it all over again with the guests, the dress, the cake, and the cameras. Alright?"

"I hope your mother doesn't hate me for ruining the big church wedding she was planning."

"I'm going to tell you a secret: my mother hates the archbishop. She abhors the idea of giving him the satisfaction of lording over another royal wedding like he lorded over hers. I think she may be happy about that detail. We'll still do the carriage ride around town, playing to the crowds, but we can skip the bowing and scraping and sermons. That works better for me."

"Me too," Norah agrees, allowing herself a small smile. "I never wanted a church wedding, or a big wedding. Just something nice for family and friends."

I laugh. "Right," I say. "We're still royals. It's a long list, even pared down to a fraction."

NORAH and I are in my library, going over drawings and reports left for us by the architect and renovation group hired to oversee the reworking of our apartments, when my mother, as good as her word, turns up with an odd little man in a black barrister's smock, wearing a white powdered wig and an expression of abject terror. He's clutching a black leather folio between his hands, his eyes downcast.

"Justice of the Peace Jones, this is His Royal Highness Crowned Prince Owen, Duke of Brynterion and Cymrea, Acting King of Anglesey," Mother announces, listing a fraction of my formal titles, but more than she ought to.

The little man bows, taking a knee.

"Rise and put yourself at ease," I say, offering my hand.

He's trembling. His handshake is as weak as a fish. "Your Royal Highness, I am so honored..."

"Yes, yes. You're so honored," my mother interrupts. "Justice, this is Miss Norah Ballantyne, the Prince's fiancée."

He gives Norah a small bow, saving his knees for higher dignitaries at a later date, no doubt.

"Let's get to it," Mother says, "You two come stand over here."

Mother arranges us all exactly where she wants us.

When I look up, I see Duncan in the library doorway, holding up his phone, recording us.

Mother is covering her bases from every angle. She's clever, and suspicious, and I'd hate to be her adversary.

The legal marriage ceremony takes less than five minutes. The justice of the peace signs the paperwork, which is witnessed by Mother and Duncan. He hands me a copy, then folds the second copy, sliding it into his folio. "I will file this with the registrar after 2:00 PM tomorrow, as you have instructed," he says. "And I do hope if I can be of further service, ma'am, you won't hesitate to call."

"Thank you," Mother says, nodding dismissively.

The man lingers, looking at Mother with deep inquiry darkening his eyes. She lowers a brow. "Our business is concluded, Mr. Jones. Walk away."

And just like that, it's done: Norah and I are legally married.

"Tomorrow morning at eleven sharp we're sitting down with the *Telegraph*," Mother says. "They're coming here for an exclusive interview with the two of you. You'll announce your engagement and you'll both be casual, engaging, down-to-earth. I'll have the interview questions by breakfast time. We'll practice until it's time to do the taping. You'll both stick to the talking points. No surprises. Understood?"

We nod. *She works fast.*

"What's all this?" Mother asks, looking down at the piles of architectural drawings and renderings of room designs and décor produced for our renovation project.

"We're going to redo the apartments," I say. "Add a kitchen, modernize Norah's end. Open things up so we're not so separated."

Mother rolls her eyes, shifting on her spiky heels, hip pointed out. "Owen, you should have brought this up with me. These people have done a great deal of work for nothing."

I don't understand. Norah slumps, disappointment deflating her posture.

"You two will be moving upstairs into the king's chambers. You're not staying here. This is the *spare's* quarters. It's almost the worst apartment in the residence."

"But..." I hesitate, "if we move up there, where will you go?"

Mother smiles. "Darling, I'm very much looking forward to your coronation so I can move on with my life. I'm moving out. It's your turn now—yours and Norah's, and your children's. You don't need me lurking the halls, casting shadows. I'll always be available for advice, but I won't be the hovering dowager that my mother-in-law was. Plus, I'm still relatively young, still considered a beautiful woman. I've got time to sow a few wild oats yet."

What?! "You're leaving Beaumaris?" I ask, astonished. "Where are you going?"

Mother shrugs. "Probably to the west country," she says. "There's a certain duke I've known since I was sixteen years old who always captivated me. His wife recently left him for a twenty-three-year-old rugby player. He friended me on Facebook, and we've been chatting. He breeds horses. We have a few things in common like that. It's a start."

I'm astonished, but happy for her if that's what she wants. My mother was miserable while married to my father; her children were her only refuge, and she dedicated herself to us. She's long overdue for taking some time for herself.

"Have you seen this duke?" I ask. "Recently, I mean."

Mother nods. "We've met several times over the last few months. Discreetly."

I smile. "I'd like to invite him to our wedding as my *particular* guest," I say. "And I'd like to shake his hand."

Mother smiles at me. It's a genuine smile, not one of her Cheshire Cat, knowing grins. "Are you sure?" she asks. "It could cause another scandal. The Queen Mother in company with a divorced man."

"Mother," I say, "we're re-writing all the rules with this generation. Tell your duke to break out his best suit. I'm looking forward to meeting him."

~

"THAT WAS A REALLY sweet thing you did with your mother," Norah says as we're snuggling down to go to bed. "Not many sons would be so magnanimous about welcoming their mother's boyfriend into the family fold. Especially *this* family."

I nuzzle her fragrant hair, enjoying her warmth against me. Her skin is as soft as a whisper. "My mother deserves any happiness she can carve out for herself. My father treated her horribly. He only saw her as a producer of heirs. He never saw her intelligence or her savvy. I hope this man sees it all. If he does, he's got all my support."

"You're a good son."

There's a hasty rap on the bedroom door, causing Norah and me both to jump. I pull up the sheets to cover her, then pull on my pajama bottoms to answer the door.

It's Duncan, dressed in sweatpants and a t-shirt, in bare feet, looking frazzled. "They picked him up, sir. We've got him."

"Where?" I ask.

"At police station number three, about four blocks from the main gate of the palace. He was observed reconnoitering the palace boundaries, presumably looking for a weak spot to gain entrance. He was picked up by the city police."

"I'm getting dressed," I say. "I want to see him. And have my secretary call the American ambassador—I want him there, too. Get dressed. We're going to the police station."

I close the door and go to Norah. "Get some rest. I won't be long. I promise."

"Don't go," she asks. "Come back to bed. I can't sleep without you."

"I have to," I say. "I need to deal with this personally. I won't be long."

Police station three is a typical 19th-century edifice updated to reflect the standards of mid-20th century modernity. In short, it's a cracking crumble of stone overlaid with drywall and more layers of blistered paint than is altogether acceptable. I need to increase the city police's budget.

Eric Wembley is being held in a cell reserved for "special cases:" foreigners, tourists, the insane, and royals or nobles gone astray. I don't do jail cells, so I ask that he's brought to an interview room for our tête-à-tête. A police captain delivers him to me still handcuffed, wearing a jailhouse-issued lime green jumpsuit and a smirk on his face that makes me want to punch him.

"I must really be somebody to get your royal ass out of bed at this hour," he boasts. "How's your not-quite-so-royal piece of ass doing? She putting out proper?"

He's shorter than I recall. He seemed taller before, or maybe that's just my mind playing tricks on me.

"Are there cameras in this room?" I ask the captain.

He nods. "Yes, Your Highness," he says. "Afraid so."

"Lucky for you," I say to Wembley. "You know what I did for fun in the Navy? I beat the shit out of guys who wanted to intimidate the royal brat. I was taught to fight by an IRA soldier-turned-Catholic priest who lost his faith. Do you have any idea how much anger that man held? He taught me to punch until bones broke and teeth fell out. I had to fight every day like that."

As Wembley blanches, I turn back to the captain. "Can you find us a room?"

"Sir, that would not be a good idea. The American ambassador is on his way."

I offer Wembley a cruel smile. "I called him," I say. "I summoned him here. I didn't trust myself. I could have kept you awhile on my own terms, put you in the dungeon at Beaumaris. But I knew your ambassador would be displeased if I returned his subject to him in less than working order."

"You're a posturing prick," Wembley spits.

Am I?

A stunning, unexpected right hook to his jaw drops him in a heap on the floor. "You forget where you are, sir. This is Anglesey. I do what I please *and that is the law.*"

The captain, standing beside me, does nothing to impede me.

"Get him up," I instruct.

The captain goes to the floor, lifting Wembley to his feet with great exertion. Wembley doesn't look any worse for wear except for the bleary expression on his face.

"What was that?" I ask. "You were saying something about my wife?"

Wembley spits a wad of fresh, crimson blood on the floor. "Your whore," he says.

I deliver another right, this one a powerful, straight-on punch to his face. I feel the bones of his nose crunch, collapsing on impact. He reels backward, once again falling to his knees in a heap.

"Get him up," I say.

"Sir, the ambassador has arrived," the captain says. "He'll be here in three minutes."

"Get him up," I repeat.

Once more the captain lifts Wembley on unsteady legs.

My hand stings from the blows I've landed on the flesh of this piece of trash. "You were saying?" I ask.

"Don't," Wembley begs, his nose spewing blood, his eyes unfocused. "Please don't."

That's what I thought: a garden-variety bully with the pain tolerance of a newly-minted nun. I launch without drawing, landing a powerful upper-cut against his jaw, sending his cranium rocking backward at velocity. Wembley drops like a sack of potatoes onto the floor, out cold.

"Tell the American ambassador I said to get this bag of garbage out of my country and never let it near my borders again. If I see him here after this, I reserve the right to wind his bowels around the street signs at the head of Old Town and mount his severed head on a pole in Cathedral Square."

"Yes, Your Royal Highness," the captain responds, his voice quavering.

I pass the American ambassador coming in as I'm leaving. He pauses for salutations, but I offer him none. All I offer is, "Get that trash out of my country before I declare war on his home state." I say this as I breeze by, only pausing for Duncan to open the door of my limo.

I have no idea what the fallout will be from my premeditated violent actions, nor do I care. That creature stalked my home, threatened my family, and disturbed my peace. In my own country—a country I rule—I'm well within my rights to dispense justice as I see fit.

On the way back to the palace, I call my newly-hired personal secretary to deliver an unvarnished account of my meeting with Eric Wembley, with instructions to release it, along with all the texts and videos he sent, should the press get wind of my visit to the police station.

"If the Americans lodge any sort of protest or objection, tell them to respectfully piss off," I instruct. "Anglesey existed six hundred years without an American embassy on our soil. We've got the EU, the UK, and the East Asian Alliance. Tell the Americans I don't appreciate their criminals coming into my country under false papers, threatening my family."

I lay my phone down on the seat, lifting my bruised hand to my lips, sucking fresh blood from open cuts on my knuckles.

"The American ambassador has taken custody of Wembley," Duncan informs me from the front seat of the limo. "They're taking him directly to the airport and putting him on a diplomatic charter flight to New York."

"Thank you," I say. Finally I'm rid of him. Finally we can return to things as they were. *He's gone.*

Norah is sound asleep when I slip naked into bed beside her. She doesn't need to know what Eric Wembley said about her, or what I did in response. All she needs, right now, is the security of a safe roof over her head, good food for our babies, and the knowledge that I will break international treaties of centuries-long standing to protect her.

I slip my arms around her, pulling her small body to my embrace. I nuzzle her hair, breathing in her scent. I fall into sleep knowing I've done my duty to defend my family against all enemies, foreign and domestic.

20

NORAH

I open my eyes to an early sunrise beautifying my window view. Traces of pink light wash the sky, and misty fog clings low to the treetops in the park in front of the palace. Blinking away sleep, I feel Owen's breath against my neck. He's wrapped himself up in me, in a tangle of arms, legs, and sheets. He's warm.

I unwind myself from his embrace and turn to face him. He usually rises before I do, so I rarely have an opportunity to study him like this. Sleeping, his face is relaxed, unmarred with the concerns that often plough his brow and narrow his eyes. Right now, he looks ten years younger: full lips, smooth, boyish skin, and impossibly long, thick eyelashes. I hope our children look like him. If they do, they'll be beautiful.

Owen adjusts his position, raising his hand up to his chest. It's then I see the bruises and cuts, the smears of dried blood across his torn knuckles. It looks like he put his fist through a concrete wall—twice. The cuts are ragged and pink, slightly swollen.

I rise and pull on a robe, then ring the bell for Sally. She appears, surprised I'm awake this early. She's more surprised when I ask for a first aid kit to accompany our morning coffee. "Is everything alright, ma'am?"

"Yes, I think so. Owen has just hurt his hand somehow. I need to tend to it."

Ten minutes later, while Owen sips his coffee, reading the morning papers, I clean his wounded knuckles with peroxide and cotton balls. "How did you do this?" I ask for the third time.

He sighs again, leveling me with his Prince Pompous gaze, then turns *Today's Mail* around so I can see the front-page. "King of Pain? HRH Crowned Prince Owen Goes Gloveless Against Handcuffed Stalker in Police Custody."

Below the headline there's a photograph of a bruised and bloodied Eric being hauled out of a police station by two tall men in business attire.

"The man on the right is the American ambassador," Owen says. "The one on the left is my Secretary of State. It seems I've created a bit of an international incident."

Something tells me Eric had it coming. I only wish Owen had seen fit to rise above it.

"Did it make you feel better?" I ask him while dabbing antibiotic ointment on his cuts.

"Immensely," he replies, setting the paper down. "Are you angry with me?"

"No. I'm not angry. Disappointed maybe."

"That's worse," he sighs. "That'll take a while to recover from. Longer than the skinned knuckles."

I bandage Owen's hand with cotton pads, then wrap it with a self-adhering medical tape. When I'm done, it occurs to me that we're going to be taped for an interview in just a few hours, the bandage is impossible to miss, and the headlines can't be avoided.

As if he's reading my mind, Owen says, "I've already issued a formal apology with a detailed accounting of what happened, and why. My press secretary and security director have sent the ambassador and the press the complete log of messages, videos, and emails Wembley sent to you. The security footage from the police station is being released to the press. I'm not proud of any of it, but I'm not running away from it either. That asshole got a fraction of what he deserved. Every man and half the women in this country will support me once they've seen the full story."

"You had time to do all that, but not wash the blood off your hand?" I ask, repressing a smile.

"Priorities," Owen quips. "I wanted to get back to you in bed."

We spend breakfast and two hours afterward rehearsing the Q&A Princess Dalia prepared for our interview. She's put together an excellent spin on our situation, painting us as too hopelessly in love to spend another second alive in this world without being bound together in matrimonial bliss.

We're to reveal that we've already been legally married, which was Owen's decision; he was concerned if something happened to him before we were married I would lose my royal status, leaving me vulnerable to stalkers like Eric without the financial resources to protect myself. We're then to announce the date for a formal wedding ceremony, which will be a small affair of close family and friends, rather than the anticipated state wedding everyone was expecting. The date is set just a week before Owen's coronation.

If the reporter goes off-script and asks if there are any other reasons for moving the marriage up, Owen and I are instructed to both remain silently smiling, creating an awkward silence the reporter will want to fill by moving along to something else. Princess Dalia admits the silence may be interpreted as an admission, but she's confident that when the announcement about the pregnancy comes, most people will be happy rather than scandalized.

"Half the couples in Anglesey with small children are unmarried. Regular people don't care about the paperwork or the church blessings. This will make you two appear much more like regular people."

To put a fine point on that distinction, Owen's wearing jeans and an open-collared shirt, and I'm dressed in a sleeveless, cotton sundress for the taping. We're instructed to behave as easy-going and down-to-earth as possible, and to hold hands.

Princess Dalia stands behind the cameras during the whole thing, arms crossed, silently watching her production take shape. Everything goes just as choreographed, none of us deviating from the scripted questions or answers until the very end, when the interviewer takes a chance at raising the ire of the Princess.

"It would be remiss of me not to bring up this morning's headlines," she says, sitting forward to address Owen. "And I can't help but notice your bandaged right hand. Can you explain why you repeatedly struck a man in handcuffs? A man who was helpless to defend himself? Who was in police custody and being dealt with?"

Owen lifts his hand, opening his fingers, flexing, then turning it to show the bruising. He lowers his hand, placing it on his other one, over mine. He leans a little forward, speaking calmly but deliberately in response to her question. "I lost my cool with a man who assaulted my wife. Who repeatedly threatened to harm her. Who, after being deported from the country, managed to sneak back in using false papers and carrying burner phones to elude our police. He managed to slip through our security and get inside the palace, and he got close enough to my mother, Her Royal Highness Princess Dalia, to—in his own words —'slit her throat or blow her brains out,' and then he followed up by threatening to do precisely that to Norah."

"I understand all that," the interviewer replies. "But Your Majesty, he was in handcuffs. He hardly posed a threat to you or anyone else at the time."

Owen nods. "Agreed," he says. "It was the wrong thing to do in the moment. But even in handcuffs he persisted, hurling threats and insults at my wife. I'd challenge any man in this country who comes face to face with someone who so violently threatens their family not to react in the same way. It would be the rarest of men who could rise above it. I'm Crown Prince and soon I'll be the king, but I'm still human, and like any man I'll defend my family and my country to my dying breath."

A few moments later it's all over. The bright lights are turned off and the cameras powered down.

The interviewer from the *Telegraph* sits back in her chair, regarding us with satisfaction. "Thank you," she says. "We'll edit today and broadcast at eight tonight."

Princess Dalia steps forward, offering her hand. She appears slightly miffed with the last question, but I can tell by the way she circles her arm through Owen's she's swelling with pride at how well he handled his response.

"One off-the-record question, if you'll allow me?" the interviewer asks.

We all stop, holding our breath.

"We don't do off-the-record," Princess Dalia responds, her tone chilled, a tight smile pressing her lips.

"Everyone is going to speculate," the lady from the *Telegraph* says. "That speculation is going to wind up in print within hours of this broadcast. Wouldn't it be better to spin the speculation your way?"

"Go on," Princess Dalia says cautiously.

"If you'll give me an exclusive first look at the new prince or princess, I'll spin the speculation as a giant leap forward in the monarchy's progress into the 21st century, leaving behind all those stodgy old social mores that are no longer relevant in normal people's lives."

Princess Dalia nods, smiling awkwardly. "While the palace has no official comment on that matter and doesn't even know what speculation you may be referring to, we'd be happy to offer you an exclusive first look at any offspring the happy couple may have in the future. Your paper and news channel have always been among our favorites to work with."

"Perfect," she responds. "I'll be in touch."

An hour later, when I'm alone in the library sending my mother an email with the wedding date and travel details, Princess Dalia has herself seen in. She strolls into the parlor with a train of people following, all of them carrying armloads of gowns and boxes of *stuff*. She begins arranging the people into stations around the room.

"Ah, there you are, dear. Come here!"

I walk forward with trepidation. My one refuge has just been invaded by a hive of activity bearing all manner of silk, lace, and satin finery, and oversized catalogs of every description.

"We have a shotgun wedding to plan, dear. Many decisions to make, very little time. Step into the whirlwind."

Before we get to the dresses, we select the invitations, the flowers, the food, table dressings for the rehearsal dinner, the pre-wedding brunch, the reception, and the formal dinner afterwards. For some reason I'm required to select a china, silver, and crystal pattern, and even a linen design.

The Princess advises me without pressuring me, while her secretary follows, taking notes. "You don't have wretched taste," she says, meaning it as a compliment. "I've seen girls with ten times your pedigree who couldn't match a dinner plate with an appropriate piece of silverware to save their blue-blooded lives."

"Art and design school," I say. "Bachelor's degree in making sure things match and balance."

"Impressive," she quips. "On to the dresses."

We spend the balance of the day trying on gowns designed for a fairytale wedding. Acres of silk, lace, and miles of ribbon fill the parlor, with piles of delicate slippers spilling into the library.

We make an elaborate mess of the place, and have fun doing it. The Princess is all business, but I find myself enjoying the business of becoming a bride, even if it is a shotgun wedding.

"I'm still searching for a venue," the Princess says, examining me in my favorite dress from among the dozens I've tried. "It's got to be somewhere with enough space to accommodate the reception, but not so large that we're forced to invite the whole country. The palace is too large and *too royal*. I'm drawing a blank."

"How about a private house?" I ask. "That's common where I come from."

The Princess considers the idea. "The problem is we'll have nobles sparring with one another, creating jealousies between them. Someone will feel slighted by whatever choice we make."

"What if I choose?" I ask. "I don't know any of them, so I can't slight any of them."

She regards the idea with interest. "What are you thinking?"

"My friend Sinead's house near Brynterion," I propose. "If it wasn't for her and her husband, Earl Hereford, Owen and I would never have reconnected, and I'd be a girl out in the world in a great deal of trouble."

She smiles. "What type of house does this Earl Hereford have?"

"Huge," I say. "And ancient, and beautiful. It's hundreds of years old. I don't know what style it is. It's a mix. I do know that its main hall was originally an abbey. I think Sinead said it had twenty bedrooms in just one wing."

"What's this house called?"

"It's Hereford Abbey," I say, "not far from Brynterion Castle."

"I think I know that place," the Princess says. "Let me look it up before we make the inquiry. If it's the place I remember, it would be perfect. And you're correct, no one could take issue with you choosing the home of your friend."

It would make Earl Whatsit's life to host a royal wedding at his ancestral home. Sinead would love it, too. They're already at the very top of my guest list. This way, they won't have travel expenses.

"I like this dress the best too," the Princess says, admiring me. "We'll hold off on fittings until we're closer to the date."

She unzips me, helping me out of the gown, handing the dress off to the young woman in charge of them all.

"I'm sneaking out of the palace for dinner tonight," the Princess says. "But tomorrow morning, the three of us need to go over the guest lists, so don't go to bed until you and Owen have made yours. Each of you need to select an equal number of bridesmaids and groomsmen. Understood?"

I nod.

"Don't let Owen blow it off. He'll try to. We need to get the invitations out *last week*. There's no time to lose."

"Understood," I say. "Can I ask a favor before you go?"

"Of course."

"I really want to make an OBGYN appointment. Do you have anyone you'd recommend?"

The Princess nods. "Of course, darling. I'll make an appointment for you this week. We'll catch up on it in the morning. You'll love her. She's my doctor. She delivered both Lloyd and Owen."

That's such a relief.

~

IT'S ALMOST seven in the evening before Owen returns from work, looking haggard. Being king isn't all it's cracked up to be, and this, our first full day back since our blissful Aegean holiday, has been non-stop for both of us.

He leans down, kissing me sweetly on the cheek before wandering to the bar to pour himself a drink. "Mother has you doing something," he says. "What is it?"

"Guest list," I say. "You have to do one, too. We're meeting about it in the morning. All three of us."

"Can't make it. I'm having a showdown with the Minister of Finance tomorrow morning over police department budgets. I did a tour of Cymrea's police stations today, and it was appalling. The buildings and jails look like something out of a Dickens novel. They're archaic, and filthy, and crumbling. Next week I'm touring the city's schools. Would you like to come with me? I'd like your opinion. I went to a very unconventional private school in Scotland. I have no clue what a normal elementary or high school should look like."

Really? "Yes!" I exclaim. "I'd jump at the chance to make myself useful."

"Monday and Tuesday," he says. "Put it on your calendar."

I laugh at the notion. "I don't have a calendar," I say. "I don't have anything except several boxes of books."

Owen strolls over. "That's right, I was going to have your things brought from Paris. I completely forgot. I'll take care of that tomorrow."

"It's okay. I really don't need anything. The palace is fully functional, non-stop entertainment. At least, it has been so far."

"What did you do today?"

I tell Owen about my day filled with crystal patterns and china, flowers and tablecloths and bed linens, dresses and shoes and bouquets.

"You did all that in one day?" he asks, settling down beside me at the table, looking over my guest list.

"That and more," I say. "Your mother is a force of nature."

"That she is."

We order dinner served in the apartment so we can tune in and watch ourselves on the television, delivering our happy news to the world. Owen cringes at his televised self, but he looks dashing and at ease on the screen, answering question with his fingers threaded in mine throughout the whole thing.

I'm less impressed with my own performance, but Owen assures me I'm far too self-critical. "You're going to break a million hearts," he says. "Now that they've gotten a good look at you and heard you speak, they're all going to see how brilliant you are, along with being the most beautiful women in the realm."

When the interview gets to the very end, Owen watches himself deliver his speech about defending home and family. He nods his head, agreeing with himself, then adds at the end, "Can't wait to see tomorrow's headlines." He turns back to me. "I'm surprised Mother wasn't here for this. Where is she?"

I grin. "I think she's gone out with her duke," I say. "She said she was sneaking out for dinner."

Owen smiles, shaking his head. "Amazing." He looks up, eyes bright. "How do you feel about moving upstairs? The king's suites are... *expansive*. We'll have to do some remodeling and redecorating. It would be more convenient, as the office is up there, with all the people I work with every day. And there's a nursery."

"I'm fine with wherever we live," I tell Owen. "I never expected to live in a palace. I'm not complaining about this place, but if we're supposed to move, I'm fine with that, too."

Owen looks around at his minimal space with all its glass, chrome, and black leather. This apartment, just like the one at Brynterion, is stripped down to the essentials: a physical protest against the notion of decoration.

"It's probably time to put away my chrome and steel 'spare' resentment and soften the edges a bit. Babies need soft surfaces and warm places. I doubt a toddler would like this any more than I liked the Louis XIV gilt or baroque furnishings I was always being told to keep my hands off of. I want our children to *feel* at home when they're at home. I don't want them raised like relics in a museum."

"Let's make them a home, then," I say. "Let's clear the

slate, saving what works, tossing the rest. We'll build something comfortable for the four of us inside the king's suites."

Owen's expression warms. "You know, for a gold-digger who only agreed to marry me for my money, you're turning out to be a pretty good pick."

21

The invitations are sent and RSVPs received. The cake is made, sitting in a walk-in freezer in the kitchen at Hereford Abbey. The flowers are on their way. Some of the guests coming in from outside the country have already begun arriving in town, including my future in-laws, who flew in from South Carolina two days ago. They're *interesting.* So far, they've spent almost all their time in Anglesey sightseeing. There's plenty here to see, though they haven't spent a lot of time with Norah, which I find curious.

The wedding is in two days, and the coronation is just one week away. I've never been a man who developed anxieties around events, but the last few weeks have been so tense in their build-up to what's about to happen—first with the wedding, then the coronation—I seem to have perpetual butterflies in my gut. The only thing that eases it is a shot of my favorite whiskey at the end of every day, combined with spending a few hours just talking about things with Norah. She makes things feel *okay.*

The day after our big television debut announcing the

fast-tracked wedding, the papers and the internet exploded with speculation about Norah's *condition*. The kind people at the *Telegraph* were as good as their word, leading the frenzy with a lengthy editorial speculating on "this thoroughly modern young couple" forging a new path for the monarchy, shedding all the nonsense and hypocrisy that made our grandparents miserable. The rest of the press fell in line, and public opinion is solidly leaning in support of us. More than 80% of the people polled said they hope we *are* pregnant.

Speaking of public opinion polling, 95% of those polled said they would have punched Wembley, too, if given the opportunity. That story dropped from the headlines faster than a certain American president's popularity rating.

Today's big anxiety-inducer promises to be a challenge —and controversial: my brother's psychological evaluation in the Swiss hospital has concluded, and he's returning home. The doctors, while agreeing completely with all of us that he's incompetent, delusional, and generally unglued, have also concluded that he poses no risk to himself or to others. He's annoying and impossible to have a rational conversation with, but he's not going to hurt anyone.

Mother is determined to return him to the breast of his family. I'm worried he's going to turn the family into a group home for the unhinged. Time will tell.

He's arriving here at Brynterion by three o'clock. We're all supposed to greet him out front. I hope he's not still wearing those ridiculous saffron robes. He used to have such great fashion sense. Before he turned to The Exalted Order of the One True Toth, he was a bit of a clothes horse and a fixture on the international club scene from Milan to London.

I don't understand what happened to him. Sometimes I

wonder if the stress of becoming king just became too much, sending him straight over sanity's edge. Lately, I wonder if I'll manage to hold it together well enough to get through next week.

It's not enough that I'm getting married. It's not enough that I'm about to be officially coronated king of Anglesey in an insanely choreographed ceremony whose rites and rituals go back to the Dark Ages. It's not enough that the ceremony takes place at the cathedral in front of thousands of guests, as well as a live television and internet audience that will number in the billions.

On top of all this, we're in the final phase of negotiating a new trade deal with the United Kingdom following their exit from the European Union. The Brits have had a hell of a time since leaving the EU. The French in particular have been punitive regarding food imports. This has opened an opportunity for our farmers to export more products at higher prices into the UK. Meanwhile, the French, who having been punitive with the Brits *on principle*, are now left with unsold farm commodities that we're more than happy to take off their hands at fire sale discounts.

While we're working on that deal, we're also looking at a massive internal infrastructure initiative that will upgrade everything from our schools and municipal buildings to bridges, roads, power generation, and waterworks. I'm still trying to figure out how to pay for it, and that's proving a challenge. The nobles, who control 90% of the nation's wealth, don't want to put in their share for the improvements, claiming their children don't go to public schools, and they can do very well without the national electric power grid; their homes—stately mansions on thousands of acres—either are or can be powered with solar and wind, installed at their own expense.

Meanwhile, the 90% of the population of Anglesey who don't live on estates or out in the countryside are struggling to make ends meet on flattened wages, in a country with a rapidly aging infrastructure, and their taxes keep going up.

We've got to do something different, but I'm struggling with just what to do.

"Penny for your thoughts?"

I look up from my paperwork, which I've been gazing at for twenty minutes without comprehending a single line I've read.

Norah leans on the doorframe of my library, arms crossed, gazing at me like she knows what I'm thinking. She's a figure of beauty. The best thing in my world.

"I'm thinking everything about being king sucks, except having had the good sense to offer you the job of my wife. I think you're the best decision I've made so far."

She huffs a small chuckle, strolling toward me. She's wearing faded Levi's and a t-shirt, looking like a college girl headed into her weekend. She's adorable. "It's almost three," she says. "We need to go down and meet your brother."

I look at my watch. It's twenty 'til. "Come here," I say, begging her to me with an outstretched hand.

She comes, taking my hand in hers, and I pull her rather roughly into my lap, making her laugh.

I place my palm flat on her warm belly, under her shirt. "How are our princes?" I ask, leaning over her belly to address them directly. "Cozy in there? Good. This is your da saying hello. Grow strong, little princes."

"They may be princesses," Norah reminds me. We've decided to remain in the dark on that detail, instructing her doctor and nurses not to tell us. We want a surprise when they're born.

"They're first born, heirs to the throne. Regardless of sex, *they will be princes*, even if they're also princesses. Before Elizabeth I was a queen, she called herself a prince."

"They'll be royal brats if you have anything to do with it," Norah laughs. "I'm thinking of sending them home with my mother for the first ten years, just so they grow up knowing the world doesn't revolve around them."

"Not likely," I reply, feeling the underlying truth in her joke. She did grow up knowing that, which I guess is what's made her so adaptable, and so strong. I still think it's sad her mother and father would rather spend their time before her wedding being gawking tourists rather than being with her.

Norah's belly is growing; she's starting to show. She's also glowing. Her complexion, which was always peaches and cream perfect, is now radiant. A month ago, I was smitten with her beauty and her character. Now I'm just stunned, stupefied by my good fortune in finding her.

Norah slips her hand over mine. "We really should go."

"Alright," I concede, "let's go see what the circus brings in."

Downstairs in the main lobby, all the essential characters assemble, waiting for the arrival of Lloyd the Deposed. (That's what the press calls him. I have a few more colorful titles of my own.) Mother is anxious, wringing her hands in anticipation of his arrival while checking her watch every half-minute. The valets and butlers wait patiently, expecting the worst and grimly prepared for it. Earl Hereford and his lovely, rather vivacious wife Sinead, are hanging by a thread. He looks like he just swallowed a pineapple whole, and she's bouncing on her toes like a schoolyard rope skipper.

The only one here who isn't a tense ball of nerves is Norah. She's cool as a cucumber. I'm guessing that's because she hasn't met Prince Preposterous. She has no idea what we're all up against.

At two minutes 'til three, the call we've been waiting for comes, announcing that the motorcade delivering my brother to Brynterion is three minutes out. We head outside, taking our places in line according to station. We wait for the convoy of three black Range Rovers to make its way here, delivering my older brother back into the fold of his family.

Right on time, the vehicles appear on the long drive, then circle in close, stopping yards away from our assembly gathered at the front door. The first one out of the cars is Lloyd's head of security, his equivalent to Duncan. The man has been with Lloyd since he was fourteen years old.

He opens the rear passenger door of the middle vehicle and out pops Lloyd, spinning like a happy dog, looking all around. "Mummy—Mummy—Mummy!" Lloyd cries, seeing our mother. He crashes into her headlong, nearly knocking her down.

"Oh, my sweet darling," she croons, hugging him, trying to catch her balance—*and his.* "Be gentle with your mum, honey. I'm so glad you're back home."

He's like a giant toddler, ripped on cocaine. "Owen!" he shouts. "Baby Owen! Baby Owen. *King! King! King!* Bru-ha! Ha!" He's giggling like a lunatic as he wraps me in a bear hug, spinning me around in circles.

He's got two inches and twenty pounds on me. If he tries to take me to the ground, I'm done. We were both taught to fight by the same ex-IRA soldier. Lloyd knows every move I know, and probably more I don't.

"Pretty. Pretty. Pretty," Lloyd whispers, spying Norah beside me. "Pretty *new* princess. Smart. Smart. Smart!" He stops short of throwing himself at her, and instead stuns me by bowing, then offering his hand, smiling gently at her. He approaches like a charmed child fascinated by a newborn kitten.

Norah shakes Lloyd's hand. "Thank you, Prince Lloyd," she says, a beaming smile stretched from one lovely ear to the next. "It's a pleasure to meet you. I'm glad you're here."

At least someone is.

Mother takes charge, hustling Lloyd to her apartment in the north wing, far away from mine in the front of the house. She promised to keep him contained and out of trouble. By the looks of him, that's going to be a tall order.

"I thought you said he had a tattoo on his forehead," Norah asks as we make our way back to sanity and our rooms upstairs.

"He did," I say. "It was removed at the hospital. It required a specialist with lasers to take it off, and a plastic surgeon to deal with the latent scar."

I saw a remnant of the thing in a few small freckles on his skin which could easily pass for mild blemishes from a sunburn. Well worth the money spent.

"I have a crazy uncle back home in Charleston," Norah observes, giggling. "He graduated sixth grade before the school had enough of him. He's way worse than Lloyd, and we managed to live with him."

What hasn't this girl dealt with? Maybe we can send Lloyd back to Charleston with her parents when they return.

ONE DAY before the wedding and things are tense. Norah's gained five more pounds and the dress doesn't fit. She's with the seamstress now, having the waistline let out. My mother is driving the florists insane with her last-minute changes.

The caterers have lost the coolers containing the oyster stew. Wedding guests keep showing up at the castle unannounced, hoping to pay their respects in advance. And my brother is bouncing off the 15th-century stone walls of this place like a rocket-propelled ping-pong ball on acid.

The rehearsal dinner is tonight, and so far, Norah's parents haven't returned from their tour of the north country. I'm sure they've been enthralled by stone circles and Neolithic mounds, but the clock is ticking, and Norah is starting to worry if they're going to show at all.

"It's okay," Norah says, trying to make light of their absence, "if they don't show, Duncan can give me away."

"Conflict of interest," I say, straightening my tie in the mirror. "Duncan's my best man. He can't pull double-duty. I'm not paying double-time."

"Tightwad," she grumbles, slipping into her satin heels for the dinner. "I guess the honor falls to Earl Whatchamajigger. Sinead will be happy with that."

"*Duke* Whatchamajigger after Friday," I remind her. "I'm elevating him after the coronation. Pretty good turn for a guy who just happened to have the decency to bring you along to a party on a whim."

"His whim, not mine," Norah states. "I didn't even want to go." She stands back, inspecting herself in the mirror. "I look so fat. I'm going to be the fattest bride in history."

She gorgeous. She's barely showing, and only if you're looking for it. She's radiant.

I come up behind her, slipping my arms around, dropping my hands to her belly, sinking my face into her golden tresses. "You're going to be the most beautiful bride in history. And you're my bride. I love you, Duchess. I don't know how I managed to snag you. I don't know how I managed to entice you to be mine, but I'm so glad I did."

Norah leans back into me, heaving a heavy sigh. "You do this Prince Charming thing amazingly well, Owen. You're hard to dislike, as much as I try sometimes. The truth is, there's not another prince in all the world I'd rather go through this nonsense with than you."

If that's as close as I ever get to an "I love you," I'll be satisfied.

By the time the guests begin arriving for the dinner, I've managed to down four glasses of whiskey and am feeling very little anxiety. Dinner is just about to be served when the last two arrive: Norah's parents. The look like they dressed in the car on the way here, but at least they made it.

Mother and Lloyd occupy their seats at the head table, and I'm astonished that Lloyd behaves himself throughout the whole evening.

When it comes time for toasts, Lloyd stands and raises his glass. I anticipate an incoherent ramble, but he shocks me. "To my little brother, who was always a little saner, and to his shockingly beautiful, shockingly intelligent bride, Norah."

I don't know what to make of this brief intermission of sanity. Before I can process it, I find him babbling to some duke he's got cornered about the sacred scrolls of Toth and how baboons will soon rule the world again.

Norah and I are put through our paces after the meal is cleared, with everyone in the wedding party practicing their parts along with us. I catch Duncan making eyes at Chantal, one of Norah's bridesmaids. Chantal, a thin French model, makes eyes right back at him. After the practice, when the band strikes up and the dance floor opens, those two are inseparable the rest of the evening. Meanwhile, Sinead and her Earl rip up the place. Those two have taken ballroom dancing lessons—or have a secret tango fetish. They're the stars of the evening.

By two in the morning, I'm done. I slip my hand around Norah's expanding waistline and beg her to take me to bed.

We slip under the covers, both of us knowing that tomorrow is the day the next phase of our strange life together starts in earnest.

"Go to sleep, baby," Norah whispers, smoothing the sheets over my semi-conscious, badly inebriated body. "I love you. *We* love you. We've all got a big day tomorrow, Prince Perfect. Get some sleep."

22

I tried to eat breakfast but couldn't keep it down. Until this morning, I've done a good job of rolling with the punches, taking things as they come. But this morning it hit me: I'm marrying a man I've only known a few months, who is going to be king of this whole country. I'm leaving behind anything resembling a normal life, my career, my family, and friends. I'm entering a strange new world that puts my life under intense public scrutiny, and I'm bringing two innocent children into that world. They'll be raised in a fishbowl under the glare of spotlights. Nothing about their lives will ever be remotely "normal."

These are the choices I've made. My parents are thrilled. My friends are beside themselves (except Eric, though I no longer count him as a friend). I know in time I'll make new friends. My future mother-in-law is an incredible role model for how to behave in this life, and how to raise a family in it. All that, and I really have come to love and admire Owen. I think he's being honest with how he feels toward me.

Despite it all, the prospects of this new life are intimidating and scary. Right now, this instant, I'm a little sick to my stomach and shaking like a leaf.

Chantal fluffs my skirts, making the folds and pleats fall just right. Sinead is in charge of the train, which is fifteen feet long when fully extended behind me. Looking into the mirror, at my hair all done up in an intricate braid with lace, tiny pearls, and fragrant flowers, I hardly look like myself—I look like the princess in a Cinderella storybook.

"Beautiful," Chantal observes, smiling proudly. She did my hair and my make-up herself. She's also helping Stephen Aubauchan, my old boss from Paris, with the wedding photographs before and after the ceremony. She's my maid of honor and, along with Sinead, one of the very few close friends I have.

"You really are breathtaking," Sinead says, stepping up behind me. "Now if you'll only quit trembling, you'll be perfect.

I can't quit shaking. I've been shivering like a Chihuahua all morning, and not from the cold. I've got ringing in my ears that won't quit, and cotton mouth. It's all the anxiety that's built up to this day.

My mother and father appear, and Mother starts crying. My father looks proud and buoyant, like he just won the lottery.

"It's time," my father says. He's dapper in a gray-tailed tux jacket and white tie. I've seen him in a tux, but not one this fancy or perfectly cut. All the men in the wedding party will be decked out like this. All except Owen; he's wearing his Navy Dress Blues. I can't wait to see him all done up like a real king with a sword on his hip and a golden sash.

Chantal hands me my bouquet with a sweet smile. "Break a leg," she says, eyes flashing with humor.

I wish I could laugh. I'm so spun up with nerves I can hardly think straight.

It's a long walk from my dressing rooms to the main hall where the wedding is taking place, and every step finds my knees weak and my pulse pounding in my ears.

"You look beautiful," my father whispers as we approach the giant hall, filled with a "small" crowd of guests, numbering "only" five hundred or so. Only a few of them are from my guest list.

I hear the strains of music begin, cellos and violins playing the opening bars of "The Wedding March."

"Take a deep breath," Daddy says. "You'll do fine."

It's all such a blur. Owen standing tall and proud in his uniform, with gold piping and medals pinned to his chest, wearing a heartened smile when he sees me, holding out a hand to take mine as I step up beside him. Duncan stands by him, towering and almost as handsome, dressed in his tux and tails, with the rings in his coat pocket at the ready when they're needed.

Owen and I chose not to get creative with the vows. We repeat them as given, and after a mercifully short speech on the power of marriage and family to build great nations, we exchange rings, and are pronounced husband and wife. Owen lifts my veil, locks eyes with me, then tilts in and kisses me with genuine depth and affection. His kisses always melt me; this one is no different. I fall into his embrace, forgetting the crowd or the priest or even my family. I just melt into him for a moment, before feeling slightly light-headed from holding my breath throughout the whole service.

∾

IT's the first week in August in Anglesey, so it's warm as we pose outside in the flowering gardens for photographs. Stephen is a great photographer and I know I'm going to appreciate his work, but he's tedious and a perfectionist and I'm tired by the time we finally call it a wrap.

Owen takes my hand in his, smiling down on me. "You look like you could use a cold drink and a large piece of wedding cake."

I nod enthusiastically. "And a few gallons of water," I add.

We move on to join the reception in the banquet hall, already well underway with plenty of food, music, and dancing.

Duncan peels off instantly, dutifully retrieving a glass of scotch for Owen (as well as himself). Princess Dalia intercepts us before we can make it all the way inside. She's wearing an odd expression, approaching apprehensively. "Owen, Norah, I have someone I'd like you to meet."

Her duke. He's tall and dashing in a black tux and tails, a genuine gray fox with piercing green eyes and an air of confidence in his posture.

The man bows before us as Princess Dalia says, "This is His Grace, Arthur Campbell, Duke of Cambria. Your Grace, may I present my son, Crowned Prince Owen of Cymrea, and acting king of Anglesey."

Owen shakes the man's hand, then introduces me.

"It was a lovely wedding," the duke says, smiling shyly. "And there was never a lovelier bride."

I'm inclined to like him, and I believe Owen is, too. He's generally not forward with new people, but he takes the Duke of Cambria by the elbow, disappearing with him into the crowd, leaving me with his smiling mother.

"Excellent," she says. "Now that that's out of the way, we have work to do."

We do?

Princess Dalia apprehends me, pulling me into a long line of nobles and other important members of Anglesey society who are queued up to meet me, congratulate me, and—oddly, I think—spend a few minutes telling me what gift they've brought for our wedding.

The long line of people waiting for a handshake and introduction goes on for what seems like hours. I can't leave until everyone is greeted. Meanwhile my belly growls, my feet hurt, my head aches, and I'm thirsty. I catch an occasional glimpse of Owen laughing with people he obviously knows well, drinking, snacking on plate after plate of hors d'oeuvres. How I envy him.

Before I'm done smiling and shaking hands with the last of the island's nobility, my wrist is cramped and I'm wobbly from hunger rather than nerves.

Finally getting away, I move toward the buffet table, but am thwarted by a disturbance in the middle of my path. It's Lloyd. He's taken to a tabletop, a glass of champagne in hand, chanting at the top of his lungs the myriad glories of "Exalted Toth." The crowd around him packs in tight, gawking up at him, taking photographs, laughing, egging him on. I'm caught up in the chaos, pressed tight, unable to move through the crowd or escape the way I came.

I'm ensnared in a finely-attired mosh pit. The crowd carries me where they want me to go, and I have no choice but to flow with the tide. I'm shoved closer and closer to the center, into an ever-tighter press of drunken, exuberant admirers of Lloyd the Deposed's performance.

"Norah!" I hear Owen's voice behind me, but I can't turn to see him.

"Help!" I cry out. "Owen!"

A moment later the seas part behind me and I'm dropped backwards into Owen's steady arms.

"Good Lord," he exclaims. "I thought they were going to crush you." He carries me safely away, setting me on my feet far from the melee. "Are you okay?" he asks. "You're pale."

"I'm fine," I reply. "A little flattened, but fine."

"Good. Okay. I'm going to go shut down the entertainment."

A second later he's gone, hurtling himself into the mosh pit, shoving people aside with ease, making his way toward his spectacle of a brother. Another moment later, he drags Lloyd by his lapels off the table, disperses the crowd, and hands Lloyd off to his security detail with harshly worded instructions to "keep him under control or lock him in his quarters."

When Owen comes back to me, he's exasperated and clearly over the evening's festivities. He takes my hand in his. "Let's do the obligatory last dance and get the hell out of here," he says, pulling me toward the raised dance floor at the head of the hall, not waiting for my answer.

I'm so exhausted I'm running on adrenaline and muscle memory, and nothing else. I follow Owen's steps, grateful he's a good dancer and has very strong arms and hands. He's the only thing holding me upright.

"I know this has been an exhausting, insane few months," Owen whispers in my ear as we dance. "And I know it's not perfect. But I do love you. I'm going to do my best to take care of you and our family. Great partnerships have started with arrangements like ours. Maybe someday you'll come to love me, too, in your own way."

I look up at him, heartened by his speech, wishing I had to energy to meet it. "Owen I... I... I don't even know what to say. I'm an exhausted mess. I can't find the right words."

He pulls me close. "It's okay, Duchess. We've got plenty of time."

When the dance is done, we waste no time making lengthy goodbyes. The crowd assembles to see us out to the waiting car, which will take us to the port at Barmouth and a couple nights spent on the royal yacht, sailing back to Cymrea.

I guess I'll get something to eat or drink when we get to the yacht.

The press is assembled in an organized line just outside the front door of Hereford Abbey, positioned to photograph us as we leave the private reception. These are the only press images of the wedding, so we're obligated to stand a moment, posing for the cameras, smiling politely as the rowdy group shouts questions at us.

I'm blinded by the relentless strobe of flashes exploding in my eyes, and feeling dizzy, when out of the corner of my peripheral vision a familiar image catches my attention. I turn to look just in time to see Eric rush headlong at me like a football linebacker ready to tackle.

It happens so fast, no one has time to react. He hits me with a force so intense it knocks the wind out of my lungs. I don't have breath enough to scream. I fall backward with all his speed and weight propelling me down.

I should have told Owen just how much I love him. I wish...

23

I'm looking to my right, smiling for the cameras, blinking in time with the flashbulbs, blinded in the glare, when I feel a hard shove from the left and I stumble. Norah's hand is torn from mine before I know what's hit us. I swing around, recovering my balance, and see a man tackling Norah. She's flat on her back on the flagstones with the man on top of her, his fist drawing back, ready to strike.

Duncan's on him first, grabbing his raised arm, twisting it back, hauling the guy backward. *Eric Wembley!* Rage explodes inside me.

I'm on him next, pounding with stony fists against flesh, feeling bones crunch with each connection made. A second later security surrounds me, dragging me backward on my heels. *That's when I see...*

She's motionless. Eyes open, but nothing in them. He knocked her out of her shoes. They lay on the stones a yard away from her limp body.

I fall to my knees at her side as a crowd encloses us.

"Call emergency services," I hear someone say.

A hand falls to my shoulder. "Sir, we need to get you back inside."

I shrug it off, leaning down, taking her hands in mine. They're lifeless. I reach down to lift her up and feel warm liquid spill over my hand. A pool of blood spreads on the stones beneath her head.

"Oh my God, my dear duchess," I hear a familiar voice cry from what seems a long way away. "Oh God, please. Don't do this. Please don't take her away from me. Not like this."

Somewhere, a thousand miles off, I hear shutters clicking while the strobe of flashbulbs illuminate the horror in front of me in vivid technicolor. I lift Norah into my arms, cradling her against my chest.

Duncan appears at my side. He presses two fingers to her throat.

"She's alive," he says. "Let me have her. I know what to do."

Duncan takes her from me, moving fast back into the abbey. We bypass confused, shocked guests, heading—I realize quickly—toward the kitchens. He clears the main island in the center of the kitchen, laying Norah out. Then he finds the ice-maker. Gathering up towels, he packs them with frozen cubes, then packs the towels around Norah's head. He elevates her upper body, dropping her legs off the edge of the table top.

Before he's done her entire head is swaddled in bulky, ice-packed towels.

"If her skull's cracked, this will slow down the swelling that could cause a stroke or worse," Duncan says, feeling again for a pulse, pressing his head to her breast, listening to her heart.

I look down on her. She's as pale as death. I take her hand in mine and find it cold and moist.

"She's going into shock," Duncan says calmly. "Body temp is dropping. It's normal. It's not a bad thing. Once the ES is here, they'll stabilize her."

I look around. This kitchen is ancient and cavernous. The only people in it are royal guard, all standing at ready posture on high alert, all of them prepared to do whatever is required to defend this room. They're stationed on point at doorways and windows. All looking outward, anticipating assault.

The towels around Norah's head slowly go crimson with her blood. Somewhere off in the far distance, the waling sound of sirens pierce the evening air.

I approach the table bearing Norah's lifeless body with grief and trepidation. I lift her hand to my chest, placing my other hand on her belly. "I'm here, Duchess. I'm here. I love you more than you'll ever know. Please baby, hang on."

A HOSPITAL EMERGENCY room knows no distinctions between class, color, creed, or credit rating. This place is like Purgatory. Everything is leveled. All distinctions evaporate to the barest priorities.

A small woman dressed in sky blue nurses' garb puts her hand firmly to my chest, shoving me backward with remarkable power. "You need to wait outside," she barks, and couldn't care less that I'm her *king*. "The doctor will come to you as soon as he can."

Duncan presses his hand to my shoulder. "Come on, Owen. We'll be in their way. We can't help now."

The waiting room is dingy, lit by dull fluorescent lights.

The floor is dirty. The walls in this place are grimy. The seats are soiled so thoroughly that the pattern of fabric covering them is completely obscured by the left-behind stains of suffering and human exposure.

Twenty minutes pass before Norah's parents and my mother join me here. Mother hugs me, slipping her arms around me in a way that she hasn't done in years. "She'll be okay," she whispers.

I'm not so sure.

An hour passes while we wait in silence, Duncan to my left, Mother to my right, Norah's parents directly facing me, both of them wearing grave expressions.

In that hour, my mind goes places I didn't know existed. I've lived my life mostly alone until these last few months with Norah. In that time, she's become my everything. She laughs at me, and with me. She listens. She shares herself. She never lets me take myself too seriously. She makes waking up in the morning something I finally look forward to. She makes crawling into bed at night the thing I love most, because that's when we talk together, solving the world's problems on pillow-tops. I sleep with her against me. I can't imagine sleeping alone anymore.

And the babies. *Our babies.* We made them together.

I can't do this alone. I can't lose her.

"Sir?"

I look up. A young man in rumpled, stained scrubs regards me with caution.

"How is she? Is she okay? Tell me."

The doctor, a young man not much older than me, sits down across from us. "She's stable," he says. "She's suffered a blunt force trauma to the back of her head, resulting in a hairline crack to the base of her skull. So far, swelling is minimal thanks to the quick thinking of your security people, but that's a temporary measure. She's bleeding internally, which is putting pressure on her brain. She needs surgery to relieve the pressure."

So she can be helped?

"She has other complications," the doctor continues. "She's anemic, which means her blood isn't carrying the full complement of oxygen required for optimal organ function. With a head trauma, the body automatically starts shutting down unnecessary functions to preserve oxygen for brain tissue. I'm concerned because I'm seeing a restriction in blood flow through the umbilicus. Her body is starving the babies, trying to save her brain function."

Oh God... No.

"She needs emergency surgery to fix this. London has an excellent neurological surgical unit at the City Medical Center. We've already called for medevac transport; they should be here within half an hour."

"London!" Mother gasps. "Why can't you do it here?"

The doctor shakes his head. "We don't have the facilities or surgeons trained on procedures like this. Most critical injuries or traumatic brain injuries get sent abroad. Anglesey doesn't have the infrastructure or talent to deal with those sorts of things."

How can that be?

"Can I fly with her?" I ask.

The doctor shakes his head. "I'm sorry, no. Only the patient."

I look over to Duncan. "Call for the jet. Have someone from the household meet us there with some fresh clothes for me—a week's worth."

He nods, leaving the room to make the arrangements.

∽

THE WAITING ROOMS at City Medical Center in London are not dimly lit, with dirty floors, grime on the walls, or stained furnishings. The hospital gleams. The staff are numerous, immaculate, and unwaveringly competent. We're greeted by a family services liaison who explains to me everything that's happened so far, and everything that is going to happen.

"Once she's out of surgery, she'll be sedated heavily to place her in a medically-induced coma. This will give her brain time to heal. It may be for only a few hours' duration based upon her progress, or it may take longer if the injury is more severe."

"What about the babies?" I ask.

"She's being transfused with an oxygen-packed mixture that should protect the babies. The doctors are doing everything they can."

Mother squeezes my hand. "The doctors will do everything possible, Owen. We just have to be patient."

I don't want to be patient. I want the love of my life back in my arms, calling me ludicrous names, and I want our unborn babies to thrive.

While we wait, I observe the comings and goings in this state-of-the-art medical facility. Companies of young doctors-in-training trail seasoned physicians, taking notes, observing. Platoons of nurses and other staff attend to patients. Legions of service staff clean, transcribe records, deliver meals, and some just sit with patients and their families, providing support and counseling.

It's so different than at home. Here, nothing is overlooked. Here, every need is addressed. A volunteer brings refreshments, reminding us there's a restaurant on the ground floor with a full breakfast. Outside the big windows, the sun rises. I can't imagine eating. I'm sick to my stomach. But the idea that this hospital has a capable neurological unit taking care of Norah, along with a fully functional restaurant for staff and patient families, makes me question what in the hell Anglesey has been doing with its money.

"Sir. Ma'am. You have a visitor," a volunteer says, holding the door open on our small waiting room.

I'm astonished to see Mother's cousin Charles come in, flanked by his own security detail.

"Charles," Mother says, stepping forward, offering her hand and her cheek.

Norah's parents stand up stiffly, their eyes wide with instant recognition.

Charles is this country's Crown Prince, and a distant cousin on his mother's side.

"I heard what happened," he says, his tone grave, his cut-glass Windsor accent pinched and nasal. "Awful business. How is Norah?"

"We don't know."

I've met Charles two dozen times in my life. I always liked him. He seems solidly steady, if slightly out of touch. His mother is the Queen of England and a legend. She's the longest reigning monarch in history, making Charles the longest reigning frustrated prince in waiting.

Charles is at least thirty years older than mother. I always fancied him as a dodgy, ancient great uncle.

"We've closed the hospital to the press," he says.

Maybe he's not so dodgy.

He turns to me. "Owen, my security people will work with yours to make this as seamless as possible. After she's out of recovery, we have a fully staffed, pristine rehab facility at Buckingham Palace. We'll take her there to recover if you're amenable. The Queen has extended her invitation."

"We'll see what her doctors say," I offer. "I just don't know yet what care is going to be needed."

"Understood," Charles says. "May I stay with you until she's out of surgery? Until you know more?"

While we wait, Charles and my mother chat about his work with The Prince's Trust, a charity he established decades ago to bring opportunity and social justice to marginalized people throughout the UK.

It occurs to me, listening to him talk about marginalized people in former colonies, that I live in and rule a nation that barely avoided becoming a British colony. The English set their sights on Ireland first, postponing invading and subduing Anglesey for another day. The English Civil War got in the way, and they never got around to conquering us. Just my luck. Now we're trading partners and allies. It wasn't always the case. Something in my DNA bristles at his offer for help.

"I hear you're working on a trade deal," Charles says. "Since all the Brexit nonsense, we're a hungry nation."

I really, really don't want to talk about work right now.

"I envy you," Charles says. "You get to lead on policy and national decisions. All British royals do is cut ribbons and smile approvingly, no matter what the Parliament and Prime Minister do to bugger things up."

He envies me? That's ludicrous.

"By the looks of things, your parliament and prime minister are doing a fair job," I reply. "London is the gleaming capital of the world and still growing. I'm here because Anglesey doesn't even have a hospital capable of taking care of its own people. Don't envy me—I rule a feudal backwater run by a kindergarten of over-indulged nobles."

"Owen!" my mother admonishes me.

"It's true," I say. "Look around. The best thing that ever happened to England was Oliver Cromwell and the guillotine. If I thought offering my head would improve things at home, I'd step right up."

Charles laughs at me. "Well Owen, the thing is, you're the one man in the country who *can* change things. The nobles may be brats, but they're *your* brats—they exist at your pleasure. If you're willing to risk your head, you could take it slowly and simply risk their outrage. Confiscate some lands. Redistribute some wealth. Seize their offshore bank accounts and reinvest the assets into your country."

It would take a very brave man to do that.

The waiting room door opens. An authoritative-looking man in green surgical scrubs appears. He blinks when he sees Charles, nodding to him as if they're old friends. He's got intelligent, stony gray eyes, and short, salt and pepper-shaded hair. He's wearing pristine Adidas track shoes with his scrubs, making him slightly comical—if his face wasn't so grave.

"I'm Dr. Turner," he says, stepping forward, shaking my hand.

"Owen," I say. It's always strange meeting people who are not my subjects. I'm just *Owen*. No title. No last name.

"Miss Ballantyne is in serious but stable condition," he says. "The pre-surgery CT scan showed extensive swelling and bleeding in the occipital lobe of her brain, with a three-inch fracture of the cranium at the same location externally. In surgery, we were able to release the pressure caused by the bleeding and stop further hemorrhaging by surgically repairing the torn vessel."

"When will she wake up?" I ask.

"We're going to do another CT scan in six hours to make sure there's no addition bleeding or persistent swelling," he says. "We're keeping her sedated until we make the determination that the swelling is completely gone. That may take several days. Maybe longer."

"Is she going to be okay?" I ask, hearing the desperation in my voice. "Are the babies okay?"

"She'll recover," the doctor says cautiously. "Brain injuries are tricky. She went a long time between the injury and receiving proper care. It's impossible to say what the short- or long-term damage might be until she wakes up. It's likely she may have some vision issues, at least initially, as the injured lobe controls vision and the processing of visual information.

"She's pregnant, and there's an ongoing risk to the fetuses," he goes on. "Some of the medicines we've administered are contraindicated with pregnancy. The fetuses' heart rates are elevated, and there's indication they are in distress. All we can do is wait and watch closely."

Mother slips up beside me, circling her hand around my upper arm. "Doctor, my son and Norah were just married this morning. Please take very good care of her. She's wife of the acting king of Anglesey, and mother to the next monarch. She's..."

The doctor nods, smiling awkwardly. "Yes ma'am," he interrupts. "Believe me, ma'am, all my patients are important. I do my very best for each of them."

"Can I see her?" I ask. "Can I be with her?"

Dr. Turner nods. "She'll be placed in a room as soon as she's out of surgical recovery. Someone will come get you. It won't be much more than an hour."

Many hours later, long after my mother and Norah's parents have retired to Buckingham Palace as guests of the Queen and Prince of Wales, I remain with Norah, determined to stay with her.

They had to shave her head for the surgery. Her long, sun-kissed tresses, wild with curls, are no more. She's gaunt, gray under florescent lights above her bed. She's connected to machines measuring her heart rate and blood pressure, machines monitoring brain activity, and other machines dripping medication into her veins. She breathes slow and shallow, her chest hardly rising and falling. Her fingers, wrapped in my own, are soft and slack, without muscle tone. She's as still as a stone.

I lay my hand over her belly, on the small rise that's just starting to show.

"Be strong," I urge them. "I'm here. I'll always be here for you and your mum. I love you all so much. Please, all of you, be strong and come back to me."

24

NORAH

The midday sun warms my face while a salty breeze coming off the blue North Atlantic keeps the heat from being too oppressive here on my spot at the beach. I shade my eyes against the brightness, peering through amber lenses at the twins rough-housing in the surf with their "da." Owen's having a high time of it, picking up one, lifting him high overhead, then tossing him into the deep with a magnificent splash. He picks up the other one, repeating the game. Both boys squeal, pealing with laughter, then come up for more of their father's manhandling.

I watch them play a long time, soaking up the view of my beautiful husband—the king—hip-deep in the ocean in his swim trunks, his toned torso flexing with the weight of a ten-year-old boy in his grip. He's easy to look at. I'm lucky to have him. I'm lucky to have all of them. Three beautiful men who dote on me as thoroughly as I dote on them.

Owen tosses Henry into the low waves, then throws up his hands. "I'm done!" he calls. "You two monkeys try not to drown yourselves."

Ellis dives under the surface, coming up alongside his brother.

They swim against the incoming surf, bobbing in the waves, playing together like they've done since they were babies. Ellis and Henry are physically identical, but two very different children in almost every other respect. They're our "matched set," as Owen likes to say. Henry is contemplative and steady. He likes puzzles and complex games. Ellis is bold and a bit of a risk-taker. There's no challenge he won't attempt. Together, they complement one another perfectly. Ellis runs faster, but Henry can run longer, and he never quits. Henry writes wonderful little stories to entertain his brother, and Ellis illustrates them beautifully. Both boys are learning to play the piano. Henry prefers Chopin. Ellis revels in banging out Mozart.

Owen comes up the beach toward me, dripping wet. He drops on the blanket beside me, then leans in and steals a kiss.

"You're beautiful, my queen, laying there half naked with your long legs begging me to rub sunscreen on them."

"Do," I encourage him, grinning. "Get me warmed up for later, after we put the boys to bed."

"I love you so much, baby. Please come back to me. Please wake up. Norah..."

"I LOVE YOU SO MUCH, baby. Please come back to me. Please wake up. Norah, I'm right here. Wake up, baby."

Owen's voice jars me from a dream. A happy, warm vision of him and our boys, all of us together.

"Norah, wake up, baby..."

I blink, trying to focus my brain. The sound of forced air from a ventilation system *whooshes* overhead and a steady *blip, blip, blip* from some electronic machine keeps rhythm nearby. The air in my nostrils is infused with the scent of cleaning products and plastic. *Where am I?*

I force my eyes open, feeling the painful glare of greenish fluorescent lights in my face. I grimace.

"There you are," Owen says. His hand holds mine firmly. "God, I've missed you so much."

The room is a fog. I can make out large shapes and colors, but few details. The world comes to me through a veil. I recognize Owen's face only because his voice is attached to it. I can tell he's smiling by his tone, but I can't see the crinkles that always form at the corners of his eyes when he's happy.

"Hi, Duchess," he says, squeezing my hand tighter. "How do you feel?"

"Hi," I say, hearing my voice crack, feeling dry in my windpipes. "Thirsty."

Where am I? How did I get here? What day is it? We got married. I remember that—but not what came next.

Someone puts a plastic cup in my hand. I reach forward with my other, feeling for a lid and straw. I find the straw, and navigating it to my lips, suck hard, swallowing cool water until the cup is drained.

I feel groggy, disoriented, and curiously lightheaded. Something's not right about my head. I lift a hand, reaching up, but Owen's hand intercepts it.

"Not yet," he says softly, guiding my hand down, laying it on my belly.

The babies. Are they okay?

I press fingertips against my tummy where the babies are, feeling familiar firmness.

"They're okay," Owen reassures me. "You're okay, too."

"Norah?"

An unfamiliar voice calls my name from my right side. A fuzzy figure in white is nearby. I try hard to focus, to make some sense of all this, but none of it makes sense. I can't see anything clearly. I don't know anything.

"Norah, I'm Dr. Turner," the strange voice says. "You're in City Medical Center in London. I'm a neurosurgeon here at the hospital. I know you're probably disoriented and quite sleepy. You've been asleep for some time. I need to ask you some questions. Is that alright?"

He wants to ask me questions? I have no answers.

"Owen, what's happened?" I beg. "How did I get to London?"

"We'll get to all that," Owen says, placing his hand over mine. "Let's humor the doctor for a few minutes, then we can talk."

"How's your vision?" the doctor asks. "Any blurriness or unusual effects, like tracers or shadows?"

I nod. "Everything's blurry, like a fog. I can't see any detail, just shapes and soft colors."

"Okay," he says. "That's normal and probably temporary. It should gradually resolve itself. Do you have any obvious blind spots or dark spots?"

"No," I tell him. "Should I? How would I know?"

"You'd know," he says. "Norah, what year is it?"

What? I answer his question—a silly question—and six others just as silly following it.

"What's the last thing you remember?" he asks.

I remember my feet hurt and I was hungry, and Lloyd dancing on the table, chanting about Toth. I recall floating over the floor in Owen's arms. He told me he loved me and would always take care of me. I remember I didn't tell him I loved him back, and regretting it later. That's the last thing I recall. Standing in front of the cameras, knowing I should have said I loved him, too, regretting not having done it.

"The cameras," I say. "I remember us posing in front of the cameras."

"That's very good," the doctor observes. I believe he addresses Owen with his next statement. "If there's memory loss, it's likely to be mild and temporary."

Twenty minutes later, Owen and I are left alone. He sits on the edge of my bed, grasping my hand snugly in his. He begins filling me in on exactly what happened in front of the cameras, and what's happened since. I've been asleep for six days while the swelling in my brain subsided. The babies have had a rough time of it, but they've held on. They're still in some distress, but the doctors are cautiously optimistic.

"I thought I was going to lose you," Owen whispers, anxiety stretching his voice. He sounds exhausted. "I'm terrified for the twins. I'm so sorry this happened. I never imagined bringing you into my world would put your life at risk. That it would put so many precious lives at risk. I'm so sorry."

"You've got nothing to be sorry for," I tell Owen. "Knowing everything I know now, I'd do it all again. I'm exactly where I'm supposed to be, *with you*. Our babies are going to be fine. They're going to be strong and healthy little men who are the pride and joy of both of their parents. Owen, I love you. I've whispered it in your ear while you slept and said it silently to myself a hundred times. *I love you*. It's been difficult to say because it's all happened fast, and it scares me because I've never been in love before. I love you *so much*, and I'm so lucky to be with you."

He lifts my hand to his lips, kissing my fingers. A hot tear drops to my knuckle, then another and another. "God, I missed you so," he says, sniffling, wiping tears away with the back of his hand. "I'm so glad you're back."

I smile, extending my fingers to touch his face, feeling

those earnestly shed tears. "Prince Poignant, are you crying for me?"

He nods, not letting go of my hand. "Yes, Duchess. I'm crying for you. I haven't told you the worst thing yet." I hear a smile in his tone.

"What's that?" I ask, doubting there's anything much worse than what I've already heard.

Owen takes my hand and moves it toward me, then places it directly on top of my head.

I feel stubble—razor-sharp stubble like Owen's chin. *Holy shit, they shaved my head! Where is my hair?!*

25

OWEN

"They're smaller than they should be at this stage," the OBGYN says, studying the sonogram images of our twins. "But twins *are* often smaller, and developmentally, they're exactly where they should be. We've got ten fingers and ten toes on each baby. They're sucking their thumbs. One of them looks like a swimmer; he's doing the breast stroke."

Norah smiles. "Sometimes I think I feel that."

"Usually at this stage you can't feel the flutters yet, but it's tight in there with twins," her doctor responds. "They'll be boxing each other in a few more weeks. You'll feel it."

She wipes the gel from Norah's belly, then packs up her gear. "It's been great consulting with you, ma'am," she says. "I'll send this to your regular OBGYN in Cymrea as soon as I get back to my office, along with all my other notes and images. I've kept her abreast of things while you've been recuperating in London. Don't hesitate to call me if you have any questions."

"Thank you for everything," Norah says, squeezing her hand before she departs. "I'll miss you."

Being guests of the Queen of England, living in Buckingham Palace, has had its advantages. Norah was released from the hospital two days after she was brought out of the medically-induced coma. Since then, for the last ten days we've been in residence at the royal palace in London. We've had the benefit of a team of physicians and healthcare support personnel who are on call to every member of the royal household. Norah's surgeon from City Medical Center, Dr. Turner, has made house calls to the palace to check on her, ensuring she's progressing as she should.

I postponed the coronation to stay with Norah while she recovered. A lot of people back home in Anglesey are upset with me about that, as the country has never been without a coronated monarch longer than six months. Sometime back in the 17th century, some judge made a pronouncement in the legal statutes claiming that the coronation must take place within six months of the prior monarch's death. That tiny footnote has come down to this century as law. I sent a note to the Privy Council and the Barristers Court, telling them that as Crowned Prince, acting king, and the next monarch, *I alone* get to decide what the law is in my own realm, and they could bloody well wait for my wife to recover before I return home for the ceremony.

These last ten days at Buckingham Palace, spending time with the English royal family— particularly my cousin Charles—have been enlightening. Charles is no stodgy old toad, sipping brandy with his sycophants— he's a radical force of nature who's had almost 60 years to contemplate what it means to reign as king. He's as opinionated as any dock worker or bricklayer, and just as hardworking. Last year he attended 600 official engagements on behalf of the crown. He's traveled the whole world, from the rural reaches of Zimbabwe to the peaks above Tibet, and sat on the dirt floors of carpet weavers in Iran, sipping tea. He has a few ideas about how the world *ought to be* organized versus how it *is* organized, and he's been more than generous in sharing his philosophy while I've been a guest under his roof.

Listening to him talk of all he's seen and the people he's met has given me a few ideas of my own. The one thing he's made me realize is that I, as sitting monarch of Anglesey, really do have the power to effect change in my country. It's my job to create a better place, and to upend old traditions that don't work, while creating new ones that do.

He put it to me succinctly last night: "Do you want to pass on all the problems and inequities for your children to deal with, or would you prefer they come up in a country they're proud of, a place they can continue to refine? You can keep to tradition and let things decline further, leaving it for them to clean up or lose their heads over, or you can start the work for them. Which kind of man do you want to be?"

I know which kind of man I want to be. I know what I want for my children, and their children, and all the children in Anglesey.

Once I'm officially crowned king, I'm going to make sweeping changes to how things are done, starting with the healthcare infrastructure of the country, and going on from there.

"I'm ready," Norah says, seizing my hand.

Norah's parents left, returning to Charleston a week ago. My mother returned to Anglesey a day later. Now it's time for me and Norah to give Buckingham Palace back to its owners and return home to Beaumaris Castle, the palace, and re-start preparations for the coronation.

∽

'THE BEST LAID *plans of mice and men go often askew.'*

I think it was Robert Burns who wrote that line. It's so true, and true for kings as well as men and mice. In my absence from Anglesey, and in response to postponing the coronation, some of the more radical elements of the peasantry have gotten busy agitating. I've come home to talk of a general strike to protest lack of employment, low wages, and high taxes—the economic trifecta that has brought down every European monarchy before ours.

The nobles are in an uproar; they want the ringleaders rounded up, arrested, and the movement crushed before it can get started.

In an emergency convening of the House of Lords, I sit patiently for hours listening to a roomful of pompous old blowhards—men who have never worked until their backs ached or worn blisters on their hands—deride the workers, complaining about the tiny sliver of our national budget that goes to things like emergency food assistance for the unemployed, and early childhood healthcare.

I listen until I can't listen anymore. When I've heard enough, I raise my hand for silence. It's my turn to wax authoritative. "I'm going to allow the strike," I tell them, then watch a wave of dissent roll around the room. "I'm going to go a step further and support the strike, because I'm inclined to agree with the workers. More than that, I'm going to call a meeting with the strike organizers, and I'm going to listen to their suggestions on what needs to happen to improve their lives and modernize this country."

I've shocked them all into stunned silence.

"Anglesey is going to join the modern era," I say. "You dukes and baronets can contribute. You can become part of the solution. Or you can oppose the effort, and I—along with the seven million working people in this country—will recognize that you're part of the problem."

The way they're looking at me, I suspect Marie Antoinette saw the same expression in the eyes of her opponents, but for very different reasons.

"If we don't change willingly, embracing it, they *will* change it for us. Suppressing this unrest will only embolden it, throwing fuel on the flames. This way, we manage it. We structure it, and no one loses their head."

I allow my eyes to wander around the room, pausing on each familiar face. "You're intelligent men and women. You're all accustomed to running large households and businesses. I'm asking each one of you to do his or her duty as a leader, and work with me to put together a plan to take this country forward for everyone's long-term benefit, and for the survival of the country. I want your suggestions."

I leave the Lord's Hall with the hive of nobles buzzing behind me. Some of them are agitated, some angered, and a few are inspired and intrigued. This is the first time I've taken my privilege as king to oppose the nobles on any issue, much less one of national importance. It's something my father rarely did. He was a diplomat, a conciliator. I'm sowing my autocratic seeds. It's necessary to do this now, at the very beginning, to demonstrate that I won't let them steamroll me on other—possibly more important—issues down the road.

In truth, this strike is a small nuisance; I could make it go away without many repercussions. Buy endorsing it and engaging with the leaders, I gain an opportunity to demonstrate to the people that I am their king *first*, and not just a blue blood with a crown who disregards them.

It's a tightrope walk between the two pillars of this society. I need them both to support me, or we all fall down.

"Boldly played," Norah says when I tell her about the meeting and what I did. She's still recuperating, spending more time resting than she'd like. She's bored and restless, tired of being waited on and coddled.

"Let's go for a walk in the park," I suggest.

While she's been recovering from her head injury and worried about the babies, I haven't wanted to trouble her with all the issues I'm facing. It occurs to me that she's got an objective perspective, coming as she does from another country, and she might have some insight I haven't discovered on my own.

Late August always brings the first chilly threat of autumn in the evening air. The days are shorter, the sunsets more vivid, the shadows longer. Anglesey's summers are miraculous for their flowers and warmth, but they're all too brief. The fall will come soon, and that season is the briefest of all. By November the skies will hang low and gray, heavy with fog and rain. It will stay that way until April.

I slip my hand around Norah's expanding waistline, pulling her near. I begin telling her about the things I want to accomplish as king, starting with improving our healthcare system. "How do I get a thousand skilled specialists to relocate here? How do we even begin to build the hospitals and clinics we'd need to house them?" I ask. It's a question I've asked myself a thousand times without arriving at a sustainable answer.

Norah shrugs. "You can't," she admits. "There's no short-term way to do it. Rural communities all over the United States struggle with the same question. Lucky for you, you don't have the same limitations they have."

"What do you mean?" I ask her, pausing by an apple tree, plucking a ripe fruit for my wife, then one for myself. They're luscious, sweet and juicy.

"You have money. Lots of money. And you have nobles with even more money."

"They don't want to part with *their* money," I say.

"You have to give them the right incentive," Norah says, a smile turning her lips. "Let me tell you about the introduction of the personal income tax and the 16th amendment to the United States Constitution."

What follows from Norah is a lecture on motivating the wealthy to expend their income for the common good, instead of on yachts, mansions, and gilded swimming pools.

"Vanderbilt University. Duke University. The Kenan-Flagler Business School at the University of North Carolina," Norah says, then rattles off a dozen more names I don't recognize. "Almost every major university, museum, library, hospital, and arts facility in the country came into fruition because of the first real income tax law. The wealthy would rather have their names sprawled across the gates of a university or on the side of a teaching hospital than pay a smaller amount in taxes to the federal government. It's great PR for the rich, and it serves a necessary purpose in society. Building things puts common men to work. Schools and libraries educate the common man's children. Those children grow up to be doctors, teachers, business owners. They spend money, feeding into the economy, raising wages and GDP for the whole nation."

That's brilliant.

"What you need is a think tank to help you come up with ideas like that, and an evil genius marketing and data analysis firm to help you sell the ideas and defeat the people who oppose you."

"A think tank?" I ask. I *sort of* know what that is, but I'm not sure I know how to put one together.

Norah grins at me. "Make me organizing chairman of your think tank, and I'll help you pull it together."

"Hired," I say, not kidding at all. In five minutes she's already conceived one idea that's a thousand times better than anything I managed after weeks of puzzling on it.

"Excellent," she giggles. "I'll start tomorrow."

"You're going to want an office and your own secretary soon, aren't you?" I tease.

She nods. "Yes, but not until after your coronation. We need to get it made official ASAP. If you piss off the nobles before you've got that crown, they may just depose you and pull Lloyd back into the job."

I know she's joking, but there's a ring of cautious truth-telling in her tone.

"Yeah," I say. "The nobles are pushing for me to name the date. I don't know why they're so hell-bent on a cere-mony—it's just crazy tradition. I've already signed all the papers."

She smiles sweetly at me again. "You haven't spoken the vows in front of them, pledging your fealty to Anglesey. They want to see you holding that scepter, wearing that ermine cloak, having that ancient crown placed on your head by the archbishop. That's what a king looks like to them. They need it. I think the people need it, too."

I pause in the lane, taking Norah's other hand in mine. "How did you get to be so wise?" I ask her. "How do you know about things like think tanks, and income tax law?"

She grins. "Since we're married, and you can't easily get rid of me, I'm going to go ahead and tell you: despite my stunning beauty and astute fashion sense, I'm a closet nerd. I spent my childhood in libraries. I love books and newspa-pers, history and facts. I never thought any of that would ever be useful—just entertaining and interesting. But sometimes the trivia packed in my brain comes in handy."

"It does," I agree. *She's going to make an excellent queen.*

"Ooowww!" Norah squeals, jumping, lifting a hand to her belly. "Oh, my word!" she says, big blue eyes going wide with surprise. "They're boxing! I think they're really boxing in there."

26

NORAH

I t's amazing who will return your phone calls when you say you're calling from the royal palace at Cymrea on behalf of the Crowned Prince and acting king of Anglesey. Over the last month I've had tremendous luck putting together a board of directors for The King's Society, the think tank Owen and I talked about that's going to help us remake this country. Melinda Gates was thrilled to put me in touch with some incredibly bright thought leaders who have worked on economic development programs all over the world. She even said that the Gates Foundation may be interested in helping us seed fund the first endowment for the newly-proposed Medical School at Queen's College, here in Cymrea.

Sir Richard Branson has been helpful, as has a brilliant man named Scott Levi at the Research Triangle Institute, an organization that provides research, development, and technical services for projects like ours, all over the world. They have a fantastic track record in the United States, working to transform rural economies into high-tech development centers. We're all going to do great things together.

But first, we have a coronation to get through.

Having interesting work to do has been great for my confidence, which is good because my hair hasn't grown out much, but my belly sure has. I'm just shy of eight months pregnant, and so fat! Tomorrow I'm supposed to kneel before my king, swearing an oath to be his "liege woman of life and limb," and I'm not entirely sure I'm going to be able to get up again.

We've practiced the ceremony half a dozen times with all the central figures who have parts in the production. It's all very choreographed and highly ritualized, and it's rather silly looking with a hockey stick standing in for a scepter, a rugby ball for the globe, and a polo helmet for the crown. Owen's been fitted for his crown, but he won't get to have the real item placed on his head until tomorrow. The palace functionaries are absolute sticklers for tradition.

One person who is breaking with tradition is Owen's mother. She could, by all rights, stand beside him while he takes his place on the throne. She's opting instead to watch the proceedings from the audience. She's officially retiring from public life as soon as Owen is crowned and has already moved out of the king's apartments upstairs. She's living temporarily in an apartment in the west wing. Soon she's moving to a country house in Saxony, very near a certain handsome duke.

Our architects and carpenters are remodeling the king's apartments to make them a proper home for Owen, me, and the twins. The work is coming along nicely and should be done before the babies are born.

Generally, everything is going swimmingly well. The only fly in the ointment is Lloyd, who can't seem to stay out of trouble. Last night he snuck out of the palace by himself and managed to scale the fifteen-foot-high wall enclosing the grounds. He ran around on top of it for hours, chanting, howling at the moon, babbling at the top of his lungs about The All-Exalted Toth. He entertained a lot of regular people on the public side of that divide. Before the royal guard could get him down, every paparazzi in the country had collected hundreds of photos and lots of hilarious video. Lloyd was all over the news this morning, upstaging the plans for the coronation.

Owen was not amused.

"Mother's moving to the west country," Owen said at breakfast this morning, glaring at the newspapers. "We've got a country to run, a palace to manage, and twins on the way. I don't know what to do about Lloyd. We can't possibly keep him here. Maybe we should just send him back to Bora Bora."

I asked Owen to give it a little more time before he made any permanent decisions on that question.

We're all dining together tonight, a formal affair with members of the coronation party, the archbishop, the Minister of State, the Minister of Defense, and the Lord Mayor of Cymrea. Owen is terrified that Lloyd is going to make a scene this evening, and he insisted that he not come to the coronation.

"He usually behaves when I'm around," I observe as Owen and I dress for the evening. "I'll stay near him tonight while you and your mother entertain the guests."

I'm wearing a calf-length, Empire style black gown that hides my growing girth better than anything else I've tried on in a month. Owen slips diamonds and sapphires around my throat and onto my wrist, fixing a new pair of sapphire earrings in my ears.

"You look good in jewels," he says, running his fingers

through my too-short, tight curls. "You look good naked, too. I can't believe how sexy you are pregnant."

"Keep talking," I say. "I need to hear that right now. I feel like the broad side of a barn."

Owen laughs. "Not yet, Duchess. You still have a month to go. You'll get there, but you're not there yet."

My plan to keep Lloyd distracted during this very important dinner starts off a little rocky. Before the soup bowls are cleared he attempts to engage the archbishop—a stern, pious fellow with a single eyebrow and an enormous nose—in a theological discussion about the Dead Sea Scrolls, and how they were *actually* written in the first century by ancient devotees of the cult of Toth who were exiled to the desert by a Roman prefect who ruled Egypt at the time.

The archbishop nearly chokes on his endive as soon as Lloyd starts expounding. Personally, I would love to hear how this tale unfolds, but I have a job to do, and I can't allow the entertainment factor to get in the way of my royal duty.

"Excuse me, Prince Lloyd," I say, interrupting, batting my lengthy eyelashes at him. "I heard a rumor running around that once upon a time, you trained in personal defense with a former IRA soldier. Is that true?"

Lloyd stops talking. He looks at me oddly, blinks, and then he smiles slyly. "Why yes, it is true," he says. "Before I discovered the truth of Toth, I engaged in many useless endeavors like fighting, drinking to excess, and entertaining myself in various ways that would be impolite to discuss in the present company."

"What was it like?" I ask him. "Hanging out with a genuine ex-terrorist?"

His eyes brighten. "Diverting," he says, turning slightly toward me, now ignoring the archbishop. "I was a sheltered child, as you might imagine, and was unprepared for some of the crueler aspects of adolescence. My father thought it would be a good idea to teach me how to defend myself. I believe I took the lessons a little too much to heart. I excelled in the brutal arts."

I manage to keep Lloyd engaged like this through four courses and dessert. Since he doesn't drink, and I can't drink, I ask Lloyd to walk with me in the park while everyone else retires to the parlor for after dinner drinks.

"You're awfully nice to me," Lloyd observes as we amble along, security following closely in case he decides to jump the fence again.

"You're a little odd," I admit, laughing. "But you're easy enough to be nice to. And you're certainly interesting."

I see his eyebrows raise and a smile briefly cross his face. "Norah, my dear, you don't know the half of it," he says, his voice low so our shadows can't hear. "I know what you're doing, and I respect it."

"What am I doing?" I ask, genuinely curious what he thinks.

"You're running interference and doing it well."

I'm shocked by his sudden burst of lucidity. I don't even know how to respond.

"I'd like to come to the coronation tomorrow," Lloyd says. "I swear on the Good Book of Toth I'll behave. I just want to watch Owen get that crown put on his head."

Okay... *Now I'm just confused.* "Why?" I ask.

"Just ask Owen if I can come. Tell him I *swear* I won't embarrass him. Tell him it'll mean more to me than anything in the world. I'll sit with Mother. I'll be a perfect prince. He'll never know I'm there."

Later, after our guests have departed, after Princess Dalia and Lloyd have gone off to their own rooms, I tell

Owen about my strange exchange with Lloyd, and his request.

"He swore?" Owen asks, his expression drawn with concern.

I nod. "He said, and I quote, 'Tell him I swear I won't embarrass him.'"

Owen stands silent a moment, contemplating. "When we were kids, if we swore on something, it was our code that it was a huge deal and we couldn't break one another's confidence," Owen says. "It was our leveler. If you swore you wouldn't tell, no matter how bad the lie was, you couldn't tell, no matter what. Even as crazy as he is, I don't think he'd swear if he didn't mean it."

"He really wants to be there," I say. "It's important to him. I'm not sure I understand why, but he seemed sincere."

Owen shakes his head, shrugging. "As long as he's got six royal guards with him to haul him out of the cathedral if he goes nuts, I guess it'll be okay," he says. "I can't see the harm in it, and in a way, his presence lends some additional credibility to my claim to the crown that's rightfully his."

A few moments later, Owen calls Duncan to convey the news that Lloyd is permitted to attend the ceremony, and to oversee Lloyd's security escort, making absolutely certain he doesn't break his promise.

"I know something you don't know," Owen says smugly as we crawl into bed together.

"What's that?" I ask.

He grins, twirling his fingers in my short curls. "You've been there for all the rehearsals for the coronation. When we get to the end and the Minister of State gets to the very end and says, 'begin the elevation proceedings?' That's when we stop rehearsing."

I nod. "Yeah, I always thought that was odd, that we stop when he says 'begin.'"

"Tomorrow," Owen says, "we'll keep going. There's a short list of people who will be *elevated* to noble rank after I'm coronated. I'm elevating your friend, Earl Whatsit, and Sinead to duke and duchess. I'm elevating a handful of barons and viscounts from the House of Lords who've been supportive of my ideas, up to marques and dukes. Duncan is going to receive an earldom, along with a knighthood. I'm reestablishing the Order of the Garter, which was traditionally a collection of king's advisers composed of commoners. Duncan is going to be in charge of reconstituting that order, creating a think tank of Anglesey's best and brightest commoners to help us connect with the general population."

"And none of them know?" I ask. "Not even Duncan?"

"None of them know," Owen says. "Duncan may have an inkling that something is up, as I asked him to invite anyone he wanted to see him in the procession. He invited his mother and your friend, Chantal. I think they've been seeing one another since the wedding."

I suspected as much. That makes me smile. "Duncan will be so proud," I say. "He's the best."

"He is," Owen agrees. "I owe Duncan everything. He's my guardian angel."

"He's mine, too."

No nation's leader wants a general strike to occur. It's an expensive, inconvenient disruption to business and governance. It's going to cost the country millions. The fact that the strike leaders have scheduled the thing to take place tomorrow—the day following my coronation—is symbolic. The nobles are still outraged: they're asking me to bring out the army if the protesters block the streets or if the thing goes on more than a day or two.

I'm not going to do it. I haven't asked the leaders to call off the strike. Instead I've asked the organizers to sit down with me, my cabinet, and members of the newly formed King's Society to work with us to draw up wage and human rights legislation, self-governance guidelines, a reformed tax code, and about a dozen other high-priority issues.

Initially they didn't believe we were sincere. After seven meetings and agreement on the first draft of what I hope will become Anglesey's fledgling constitution, they now know we're sincere.

I receive stacks of mail every day. Most of it's handled by

my secretary's office. This morning, as Norah and I are having breakfast, the butler delivers a letter. "This was sent down for you, sir. The secretary's office said that you should see it immediately."

Norah looks on curiously as I open the correspondence. It's from the Worker's Organizing Committee.

Your Royal Highness, Crowned Prince Owen, Acting King,

We the undersigned write to you today on behalf of our membership, and as unofficial representatives of the people of Anglesey.

We offer our congratulations on your upcoming coronation and wish you the greatest success as monarch of our nation.

Your willingness to listen to your people, to empathize with their concerns, and your determination to enact genuine reforms has demonstrated to us that you are indeed our king.

We anticipate that you will continue to act as our king, working to balance power, reform the economy, and invest in the country and its people for the benefit of the people, not just the privileged few.

In celebration of your coronation, and in hopeful belief that change is coming, we have called off the general strike previously scheduled to begin at noon tomorrow. There will be no work stoppage, no protests or demonstrations.

We look forward to a long and mutually beneficial relationship working with you and the government.

Our kindest regards...

I'M HUMBLED. I don't even know what to say. I hand the letter to Norah for her reaction.

She reads it silently, with a smile slowly creeping over her lovely face. "Owen, this is wonderful," she says. "Look at what you've done."

"I haven't done anything yet," I reply. "We're just starting."

"You've listened to them. You've engaged. You've heard them and you're putting things together to act in their interests," Norah says. "You're going to be a great king, and they know it."

As it turns out, the Worker's Organizing Committee didn't just send that letter to me—they also took out full page ads in Anglesey's two leading newspapers, posted it online, and put up posters on every street corner all over the country.

It's probably the biggest compliment I could ever be paid. With any luck, it will have the effect of bringing the nobles who oppose the constitution and all the newly proposed legislation to heel. Representative democracy, livable wages, and fair taxation are coming to Anglesey, whether the rich old blowhards in the House of Lords like it or not. We're going to accomplish it without a revolution, or even a single street protest. That may be a first in world history.

THE ROYAL PROCESSION from the palace to the cathedral is an ancient tradition. It's done on foot, with the entire royal family marched down the middle of Cymrea's streets through a huge crowd of Anglesey's citizenry gathered behind police-guarded barricades to see the spectacle. Five hundred years ago, the procession was conducted this way to force the new king to come face to face with his people, and to feel his vulnerability against their numbers. It still has that effect today.

There's a sea of humanity surrounding us as we walk the half-mile in the glum, gray chill of early November to the place where I will finally be crowned king of Anglesey.

Norah holds tightly onto my arm. We're both dressed for the event, me in my Navy Dress Blue uniform, and Norah in a conservative suit and faux fur coat, tailored to make her as comfortable as possible despite being heavily laden with twins.

The people call our names, waving and smiling. They throw flowers and take photos as we pass by. Lloyd and my mother wave back, but I'm required by custom to remain impassive. That's fine, because I'm much more concerned with keeping Norah upright than I am about waving at people.

By the time we reach the cathedral, ascending the steps to go inside, Norah's almost done for. "I have to sit," she says as we pass through the giant, thousand-year-old oak doors.

This procession is choreographed so tightly that if we stop, it throws the whole clockwork out of sync.

"I'll take care of her, sir," Duncan says, stepping up.

"Go," Norah says, taking Duncan's arm. "Go on!"

With my mother and Lloyd behind me, I march slowly forward into the nave of the cathedral, my cadence dictated by the rhythm of a single drummer keeping a slow, steady beat on his instrument ahead of me. He's the only person permitted to march ahead of the king. He represents *the people* marching before their monarch, leading and defending, but always in the lead.

The cathedral is packed. Every titled noble and all their

families are here. Every church official, from bishops to choirboys. Every government minister is present along with all their families, our entire diplomatic corps, foreign dignitaries invited by the palace, celebrities, and other special guests. There are thousands crowded into this giant church, and there are billions more watching live on televisions worldwide as well as streaming on the internet.

It's overwhelming. I've never felt so many eyes on me.

Reaching the raised dais near the chancel, the drummer steps to the right while the archbishop, resplendent in satin and gold threads, his head covered with a fantastically decorated mitre, steps up from the left.

I move forward, arms at my side, until the archbishop and I are face to face.

Everyone in the cathedral falls silent. The only sound to be heard is the flutter of pigeons in the stone eaves, hundreds of feet above our heads. I've never felt so small, or so scrutinized. My hands tremble. My mouth has gone dry.

"Sir," he calls loudly, his voice echoing against the vaulted heights of this space. "Is Your Majesty prepared to take the oath?"

I take a deep breath, hoping my voice projects rather than cracking like a frightened child's. "I am prepared," I declare.

"Will you solemnly promise and swear to govern the peoples of the Kingdom of Anglesey, and of your possessions and the other territories to any of them belonging or pertaining, according to their respective laws and customs?" he asks.

"I solemnly promise to do so," I respond.

"Will you, to your power, cause law and justice, in mercy, to be executed in all your judgements?"

"I will."

The archbishop gazes sternly into my eyes. He knows the next promise I'm bound by law to make is the most difficult one put to me, and the most controversial in the face of the reforms I'm proposing.

He raises his voice, lifting his chin high so all can hear. "And will you, to the utmost of your power, maintain and defend the rights of the aristocracy and their heirs, to their titles and their lands? Will you maintain and preserve inviolably the peaceful settlement of the nobility without challenge, preserving unto them their rightful place as your counsellors and liege lords of this kingdom, protecting all such rights and privileges, as by law do or shall appertain to them or any of them?"

"All this I promise to do," I say, equaling the archbishop's volume.

The crowd releases an audible, collective sigh of relief.

My detractors have said my intent is to overthrow the nobility and confiscate all their property to redistribute it to the poor, Bolshevik style. The truth is, I'm trying to save the nobility from themselves. With reform, we can preserve the titles and protect the lands. If we carry on as we're going, the people will eventually burn every country estate, palace, and castle in this kingdom to the ground. They'll hang us all from the rafters.

The archbishop steps to the side, clearing my way to the dais ahead and the ancient, ironwood throne where I'll sit before being crowned. Another bishop approaches from behind, wrapping my shoulders with a floor-length ermine cloak. Once it's tied securely across my chest by a valet, I walk forward, and with the assistance of two footmen charged with managing the cloak, I climb onto the dais, turn to face my people, and sit.

A bishop approaches from below, kneeling before me

bearing in his hand the Ring of the Realm, a heavy golden band set with eleven emeralds, each of them representing the eleven different counties that make up the Kingdom of Anglesey.

I tell him to rise. He comes forward. I lift my right hand. He slips the ring on my finger, then kisses it as a bishop below us reads out the symbolic meaning of the item, and the blessing it brings.

Another bishop approaches as before, with the scepter representing royal rule carried horizontally in his two hands. I instruct him to rise. He approaches, eyes down, lifting the thing to my right hand. I take hold of it. It's an object of beauty: a golden rod capped with jewels, crowned with a figure of an open hand representing justice. I slowly turn my hand, moving the scepter to a perpendicular position, letting the base of the thing come to rest near my right foot.

A third bishop approaches in the same way, carrying the blue and green glass orb that represents the Earth and my dominion. This he places in the open palm of my left hand.

Finally, the archbishop comes forward, kneeling like the others, waiting for my command to rise. He bears in his hands the crown of Anglesey, an immense and ancient treasure that's been used to crown the monarchs of this island for as long as there have been monarchs. It's been altered over the centuries. What was once a simple band of gold has grown to receive intricate decoration and hundreds of finely set gems. There's a new diamond added with each monarch who receives the crown. My diamond, a four-carat, pear-shaped stone surrounded by a ring of small sapphires, is the thirty-third diamond set on the thing.

When he rises, he lifts the crown high over my head for

all to see, then slowly lowers it, settling it on my head. I was warned it would be heavy. It is *very heavy*.

As soon as the crown is settled, the archbishop calls out, "God save the King!"

His call is followed by a deafening chorus from the crowd. Every person inside the cathedral and outside on the streets, shouts in unison, "God save the King! God save the King! God save the King!"

The bells of the cathedral chime, filling the nave and the whole world beyond with pealing, celebratory rings. The ringing continues for three minutes precisely, when the chimes are silenced. Outside these halls, church bells around the city and the country continue ringing for the rest of the ceremony, which includes the *elevations* portion of the event, where I trade my scepter and globe for a massive, sterling silver sword.

The elevations go off without incident, with grateful nobles bowing and scraping, kissing my ring, some of them more emotional about their rise than others. I've saved the two best elevations for last.

"His Majesty the King calls for his subject, Joseph Prescott Duncan!" a herald cries loudly. "Approach and kneel before your king!"

Duncan looks like a deer in the headlights for a split-second, then he presents himself at my feet, kneeling before me.

I read the words that make him a Knight of the Order of the Garter, and then make him an earl with right to bequeath the title to his heirs into perpetuity. He pledges his lifelong fealty to me as my "liege man of life and limb," which as my bodyguard, he really is.

I touch each of his shoulders with the flat edge of the sword, then present him with the sash and medal of the

Order of the Garter, slipping it over his head with great ceremony. He looks down at the thing curiously.

"I'll explain later," I say in a low voice, unable to
suppress my smile. "It's a substantial promotion from the
royal guard."

Once Duncan returns to his place, the last of my
subjects to be elevated is called.

"His Majesty the King calls for his subject, Norah Elizabeth Ballantyne! Approach and kneel before your king!"

For two hours, Norah has been seated in a box with
Mother, Lloyd, and a dozen other members of the royal
family. She's expecting to be called before me, as I've
promised to elevate her to Duchess of Brynterion, plus a few
more noble titles to dignify her with. When she approaches,
she looks a little unsettled and more uncomfortable than
usual. A valet is required to help her kneel.

I speak the lines that elevate her to Duchess of Brynterion, Duchess of Saxony, Duchess of Carnarvon. I then
further name her Princess of Cymrea. I see Norah take a
breath when I've completed the list. She waits for the
command to rise, but I don't give it. I keep her on her knees
another moment longer.

"And I elevate you, Princess Norah, my wife and consort,
naming you Queen of Anglesey, co-regent and ruler at
my side."

An audible gasp rises from the crowd. A murmur
follows, rolling in the air as Norah recites her promise to be
my "liege lady of life and limb." The valet helps her to her
feet. She looks up at me with the strangest expression, as if it
never occurred to her I might raise her so high. She never
expected it; she's truly astonished. She also looks miserably
uncomfortable standing before me, as big as (in her own
words) the broad side of a barn.

"Go sit down," I say, smiling warmly at her. "Before you fall down."

The next phase of this drama requires me to appear outside for the crowd, in all my state: crowned, carrying my globe and scepter. It's hard enough walking with thirty pounds of gold and gemstones on top of your head. It's an athletic event to do it wearing a forty-pound fur cloak, carrying a ten-pound glass ball in one hand, and a twenty-pound gold rod in the other.

I manage it, appearing on the front steps of the cathedral before a screaming crowd of thousands, all waving Anglesey's flag, smiling happily. With my family surrounding me, the cathedrals bells chime again. I am now, finally, formally: His Royal Majesty, King Owen of Anglesey.

Who needs a last name when you've got all that?

THE CROWN, scepter, globe, and ermine cloak go back in their respective cases, to be returned to the Cymrea History Museum where they will remain on display until needed again, which I hope is a long time from now.

Standing in a curtained-off, private area on the west aisle of the cathedral, I wait with the family while the crowd of visitors make their way out. Norah is walking in circles, her hand on her belly, looking miserable. I'm cornered by cousins and uncles offering their congratulations.

I finally manage to excuse myself to get to Norah, when I'm intercepted by Lloyd. He shoves out his hand. "You did well," he says, seeming perfectly lucid. "Congratulations, Your Majesty."

"Thank you," I say, shaking his hand, expecting the next

thing out of his mouth to be an incoherent rant of insanity. I get something else entirely.

"This has been the longest bloody year of my life. Do you have any idea how tedious and difficult it is to sustain an act for *that* long? I can't believe the lengths I had to go to to avoid wearing that godforsaken crown." He sighs heavily, then smiles. "Thank you for being prepared to take it on. You were always more suited to it. Responsibility looks good carried on those broad shoulders."

He grins, slaps me on the back, turns and walks away. Mother glances in my direction, winks at me, then returns to her conversation with Uncle Rupert.

She was in on it. Maybe the whole time. I've been boondoggled!

Norah comes up beside me, taking my hand. "Owen, we should talk," she says, a worried expression on her face.

I'm afraid she's going to protest her elevation, but I'm not hearing of it. She's in this with me: we're partners. From here on out, we're sharing it all equally.

"I'm think I'm in labor," she says, grimacing uneasily. "The babies are coming—*now*."

"What?!" I exclaim. "Now? As in *now*?"

She nods, breathing. "I need to get to the hospital, or I may have them right here in the church."

I look around. "Duncan!" I call, seeing him nearby, talking with another of the royal guard. "We need a car and a clear path to the hospital," I say, pointing at Norah's belly. "Now!"

THIS ISN'T A DRILL, and it's not Braxton Hicks contractions; Norah's water broke in the car on the way to the emergency room. She's only thirty-one weeks pregnant and the babies are coming.

We were supposed to have a special "royal delivery room" prepared for us, but we're early, and the hospital isn't ready. We get to do this just like every other parent in Anglesey does it.

Duncan takes my coat and a nurse hands me a fresh gown and cap to wear into the delivery room. In just a few moments she's squinting, clenching her teeth, and squeezing my hand so hard I think she might crack knuckles.

"Breathe baby. Breathe. It'll be okay," I say soothingly, stroking her still-short hair.

"It's not freaking okay!" she shouts. "It fucking hurts!"

"She's almost fully dilated," her doctor says. "Norah, this is your last chance. Do you want something for the pain?"

She bites her lip, shaking her head. Then she howls with the worst contraction yet.

"Crowning!" the doctor announces. "Coming along fast." She turns to a nurse beside her. "Tell the NICU team to get their asses down here!"

I'm breathing almost as hard as Norah, and I may be just as freaked out.

"Norah, I need you to open up and give me a really good push."

There's banter between the doctor and two nurses, most of it I don't quite follow. What I do know is that the babies are going to be very small—maybe too small. An incubator is brought into the delivery room, accompanied by a small team who wait for the birth.

"We've got twins coming on," the doctor tells the team. "31 weeks. Good vitals. No prior issues. Not sure why they're coming early, but here we are."

Another contraction grips Norah's body, causing her to push hard.

"And... we've got a boy!" the doctor declares, cleaning him up while leaving the umbilical cord attached. He's tiny, shockingly small. He's pink and wrinkled, and silent, his little arms trembling, tiny fists clenched.

Norah huffs, trying to roll forward to see him.

"Norah, we have to keep him warm and help him breathe," the doctor says. "I'd love to give him to you to hold, but he needs help."

She clamps the cord and cuts it, then passes the baby to the NICU team, who descend on the tiny thing, placing him in a plastic box, attaching all kinds of wires and tubes to his paper-thin skin.

Just a moment later the second baby starts crowning. He comes hard and fast, and unlike the first one, he comes out fighting, then wailing pitifully, his tiny, underdeveloped little voice not more than a thin cry, despite his best attempts at more. He's just as small as the first one, just as shriveled and pink. They look the same, with a downy fuzz of dark hair slicked to their impossibly small heads and dime-sized matching birthmarks on their little baby chests.

"Go with them!" Norah begs me as they start to take our babies away. "Go and be with them and talk to them. Hold them as soon as you can, skin-to-skin!"

I'm loathe to leave her, but I also know she's not in danger. *Our children are.* "I will," I say, squeezing her hand. "I'll be back. I love you so much, Duchess. I'll be back."

"Don't come back," her doctor says. "In a few hours, she'll come to you."

Norah smiles, shoving me off. "Go take care of our boys."

The neonatal infant care unit is small and quiet, with the lights set low to protect prematurely born babies' eyes.

There are six other incubators here with six other fragile babies inside them. Mine get to share their incubator like they shared their mother's womb.

I'm allowed to reach inside the warm box and stroke the babies' heads, hands, and feet as long as I don't touch their ventilators or disturb the cords and wires attached to their little bodies. I talk to them, telling them how loved they are, telling them about today, and the cathedral's bells, and all the people. I tell them how much I love their mother.

After an hour passes and they've settled, demonstrating that they can breathe on their own, a nurse comes to me smiling sweetly. "Would you like to hold them?" she asks. "It's good for them, and they're not nearly so fragile as they look. They're breathing really well."

The next thing I know I've got two tiny babies on my bare chest, all of us covered in a blanket while I rock them, singing a soft lullaby I remember from my own childhood. One of them presses his small palm to my chest while kicking rather firmly with soft feet. The other nuzzles my skin, quietly breathing.

They're the smallest things I've ever seen, and I'm fascinated by them. I breathe in their scent, falling in love with them, rapt by the folds of their ears and the way their small fingers grip mine when I press into their palms.

One of the babies opens his liquid blue eyes, looking up into mine as if with genuine recognition.

"Hi there, little prince," I say softly. "Welcome to the world. You're so beautiful."

He smiles rudely with a gummy baby grin, making a low-volume but high-pitched pinched sound that causes his brother to pay attention. Another set of liquid eyes peer up into my face, and another baby smile melts my heart.

I've never loved anything or anyone so hard; I might sob

just being in their presence. But this is different—this is soulful. I'm holding two brand new creatures. I'm the first person to talk to them and tell them stories, to lay them against my skin—and they're smiling at me. They like me. They know me.

An hour later, Norah joins us. She takes the babies to her breasts, warming them against her skin, talking to them. Feeling her, catching her scent, hearing her voice, the two of them fall fast asleep on her chest, their arms and legs touching, fingers on opposing hands entwined. I snap a picture of that with my phone for the sake of national history.

A few minutes later the NICU nurse comes back. "They need to go back in the incubator," she says. "They've both lost a degree of body temperature. We must keep them warm."

Norah watches closely as our babies are replaced inside their box and reconnected to oxygen. She's as haggard-looking as you might expect, but still beautiful, with glowing soft skin and bright, curious eyes.

A little while later a doctor comes by, introducing herself as the senior resident in charge of the NICU. "The attending will be down for rounds shortly," she says. "But I just wanted to update you. Your sons are strong, and all their bloodwork and vitals look good. They're breathing better than most do at this stage of their development. Their kidney function is good. Liver function is a little low, but we expect it to pick up in a few days. They should be just fine. A year from now, barring something unforeseeable, they'll have no lasting effects from premature delivery."

Norah brightens considerably. I feel a massive weight lift off my chest. I can breathe again.

"You should name them," the doctor says. "Preemies like hearing their names."

Norah smiles. She's known their names for a long time. She swore to me that she knew she was having boys, and that she already knew their names.

"Ellis is the rambunctious one," she says, touching his little hand. "And this is Henry." She strokes his small head while he sleeps.

"*Prince* Henry and *Prince* Ellis," I remind her, slipping my hand over her shoulder, stroking her back. "Crowned princes."

I've never been so damn proud of anything in my whole life, and so proud of their mother, *my queen*.

28

NORAH

I find myself almost hypnotized sometimes with baby eyes and tiny fingers, little baby ears and noses. I'll be doing something useful, like changing a diaper, and the next thing I know an hour has passed and I'm just entranced, staring at my sons, stroking them, talking to them, coaxing smiles and approving coos out of them. People say they love their children, but I'm *in love* with these two. Having them is falling in love all over again, every single day.

"I'll take him, ma'am," Sally says, smiling, holding out her hands.

Sally has been promoted from maid to nanny. She wanted the job, and with nine grown children of her own and none of them in jail, she's certainly qualified for it.

I reluctantly hand Ellis over. She's already got Henry tucked into their stroller.

"Have you seen Owen?" I ask.

She shakes her head. "No ma'am. The last I saw of him, he was headed to his offices. He said he had something important to do before we leave."

"He's always headed to the office, especially when we have to be somewhere," I say, smiling with resignation. "I'll go fetch him."

The twins were only released from the NICU a month ago and we'd rather stay home, but duty calls us to work. The four of us are departing Cymrea this morning for the Royal Tour of Anglesey. Whenever a new monarch is crowned, by tradition he visits all eleven of the nation's counties, staying at the homes of the most prominent nobles in each one. A few hundred years ago, touring was necessary for the nobles to meet their new king. Today, it's more of a PR thing. We're going to take the opportunity to meet with a lot of different people from all walks of life while we're out in the provinces.

Sally takes the boys away while I go in search of my missing husband. I find him just where Sally said I would: in his office, at his desk, silently pondering some official-looking document.

"It's time to go, King Contemplative," I say, leaning in the doorframe, arms crossed.

He looks up. His face is impassive. He sighs.

"What's going on?" I ask. He only gets pensive like this when it's something really serious.

"Do you have any idea how much I love you?" Owen asks.

I raise an eyebrow, trying not to smile. "More than a barrel full of monkeys?"

He puts down the paper and holds out his hand. "Come here, Duchess."

"That's Queen Duchess to you," I remind him, coming forward, laying my hand in his. He pulls me onto his lap, settling a hand on my thigh, circling my hip with his other.

I peer up into his lovely blue eyes, waiting for him to tell me what's on his mind. He stares back, his wheels turning quietly in his head.

Finally, Owen says, "I love you. I love our little family we've made. I love what we're doing. You're my best friend, and a partner to me in every way, and I would be absolutely lost without your steady hand and your resourceful mind."

"Alright," I say. "Thank you. And I feel exactly the same way. And you're not hard to look at either, which is a bonus."

Owen smiles sadly. "I'm struggling with something," he admits.

Now we're getting somewhere.

"What's that?" I ask him, as I fiddle with one of the buttons on his shirt. "Let me help."

Owen leans forward. He retrieves the document he put down a moment ago. "I haven't wanted to bother you with this," he says, worry furrowing his brow. "I wanted to just protect you from it, make it disappear, and maybe you'd just forget about it. But you deserve better than that. And I don't want to make a decision either one of us would regret, so I'm going to let you make this one."

"What is it?" I ask.

He hands me the document. It's an edict rendered by the High Court of Cymrea, a guilty verdict for the crimes of assault and attempted murder. It's from Eric's trial. I never even knew there was a trial. I never asked. He isn't someone I like to think about.

I scan through the document, looking for the sentencing part.

"Page three," Owen says.

"Oh my Lord!" I cry when I find it. "The death penalty?"

I look at Owen, not understanding. "How can that be?" I ask.

He shrugs, shaking his head. "You're the wife of the

king," Owen replies. "A physical assault on any member of the royal family is an automatic death sentence, if convicted. But the jury—all of whom I've spoken to—had several other motivations behind their decision. You were pregnant, and you're very popular with the common people. They're starting to like me a little, but they liked you from the first moment they saw you. Their decision is as much vengeance as it is justice."

"This is awful," I say. "It's terrible."

"Is it?" Owen asks sincerely.

"It is," I reply, confused that he may have another opinion. "Killing him accomplishes nothing except putting blood on everyone's hands. What he did is awful, but doing the same to him is more awful because we don't have the excuse of mental illness or blind rage. This is a cold, cruel thing."

He nods. "Something told me that's what you'd say."

"You don't feel the same?"

Owen bows his head a bit, taking a deep breath. "I feel exactly the same about every other death penalty case I've ever heard of. Except... *him*. I just can't shake the image of you, lying unconscious, with him about to strike you again. My anger toward him for almost taking you away from me... I can't express the rage I still feel when I think about him."

"You can commute the sentence to life, or something less than death, correct?" I ask.

Owen nods.

"Then that's what you should do."

He pauses, thinking. "Life without parole?" he asks.

"Are you asking me what I think is fair?"

Owen nods again.

"Well, King Complicated, if I was dictator—and oddly enough, I might just be—I would sentence him to a term of not less than twenty years in a secure mental health facility where he can get the help he needs. After that, he has to be reevaluated."

"Duchess, you do tend to think things through with precision. This is why I never want to make a decision without you. Invariably I'll do it wrong."

I grin at him, leaning down, kissing him chastely. "Yes, but the beauty of you, among other things, is that you know it. You'll never make a bad decision now that you made me queen."

He smiles. "I liked that kiss. May I have another?"

I cock my head to the side, raising an eyebrow. "We have a motorcade waiting to take us on our grand tour," I remind him. "Can you confine yourself to just one kiss so we're not keeping the whole country waiting?"

"Just one for now," he says. "More later."

I lean in, touching Owen's lips, tasting his morning coffee, the scent of his aftershave teasing my nostrils. I melt against his circling embrace, my senses surging against the warmth of his skin. He breathes me into him, absorbing me, fingers lifting to brush the side of my face, then threading back into the lengthening curls at the nape of my neck. His kisses and caresses clear my head of every other distraction but him. When we come together like this, the whole world slips away in a vapor, leaving just us and the steady cadence of our two hearts beating in sync together, two sets of lungs breathing the same air, two minds joined in one shared occupation.

Our kisses never stop with just one.

29

S EVEN YEARS LATER
"Da, what's that?" Ellis calls from the balcony.
I look up from my work. Ellis is climbing up on
the balcony balustrade like a monkey. He and Henry are not
even supposed to be out there without an adult; it's not safe.

I put down my report and walk out onto the balcony
with them. It's a beautiful, midsummer day. The sun is high
in the sky and warm on my skin. The scent of flowers lingers
sweet in the air. "What's what?" I ask.

Henry and Ellis both point to the west, to the far edge of
town where a giant crane has just this week been brought in
to work on the construction of Cymrea's first skyscraper—
the first of several underway.

"It's a construction crane," I say, explaining to them in
detail what it does and why it's necessary. "When that
building is finished, it's going to be the tallest thing in the
whole country. But it won't be for long, because there are
three more going up near it, and more planned down
the line."

As skyscrapers go, these aren't terribly impressive.

However, fifty floors is something in a city that's only got a few dozen buildings above four stories.

"What are they for?" Henry asks.

"Different things," I say. "Apartments for people to live in. Offices for people to work in. Schools, and a very nice, new hospital. As soon as they're done, you'll both get to tour them, but for now let's come back inside so I can get some work done, and so you two don't fall off the balcony and break your heads. I'm sure I have a sword or something safe like that you can play with."

They laugh, catching my humor. They're like their mother, perpetually amused with me. Instead of swords or throwing knives to play with, I set them up at the chessboard. Ellis is black. Henry is white.

"Think hard on your opening gambit, Henry," I say. "It sets the course of the entire game. Whoever wins gets to choose bedtime reading. Play well."

I'm a lucky man in that I have two smart sons who enjoy the same kinds of things I do. They're both remarkably good chess players for their age, and they keep getting better thanks to their competitiveness. Henry is the sneaky one: he found a book on chess in the library some months ago, and his game rocketed ahead overnight. He beat his brother every time they played. Ellis was feeling rather sorry for himself, and Henry took pity and let him in on his secret. Now they're back to evenly matched, both getting incrementally better at the strategy with every game.

I go back to my work, consisting of our annual economic outlook reports.

It's been a good few years. Wages are up by 25% over the last five years, with unemployment down to just 4% thanks to the building boom going on and new programs we've put in place to bring business and innovation to the country.

The expansion of the three largest colleges in the country to full-fledged universities is having the greatest impact: we're educating the young people of Cymrea, but we've also attracted faculty and students from all over the world thanks to generous employment contracts, assistantships, and scholarships. Those foreign nationals arrive with money in hand, eager to spend it on housing, transportation, dining out, and entertainment. The schools have been a boon to the country's economy all on their own. Everything else we're doing is just diversification.

We've paid for all this by establishing a hefty income tax on anyone earning more than twice the national average income. It worked out just like Norah predicted: the nobles started asking us how they could help with schools, hospitals, libraries, and infrastructure programs, instead of heaving billions into the national coffers.

Remarkably, by making the wealthy pay their fair share, we've jump-started a sustainable, thriving economy without incurring much national debt. We're surging ahead, while other larger, far more developed nations are slipping backwards into a strange, 21st-century brand of neo-feudalism.

"How do you do that?"

I look up. Norah's standing in the doorframe, studying our sons.

"Do what?" I ask.

"Make them sit down so quietly and behave. I sent them in here because they were driving me crazy, tearing through the house like a couple of chimpanzees."

"I threatened to throw them off the balcony," I tease. "Just like my father before me."

She rolls her eyes at me, which is adorable. "I brought this to you," she says, dropping the morning edition of

Today's Mail on my desk. The front page headline reads, "Crazy Prince Lloyd, Now the Toast of Paris Fashion Week."

"He's modeling haute couture for Saint Laurent," she sighs. "Didn't we pay him some obscene amount of money to flitter away and play somewhere below the limelight? Does he actually *need* a job?"

"He's not hurting anybody," I say. "And he's happy. Let him have his fun. People love him for his eccentricities."

Norah sighs again. "You're such a decent human being, I wonder how I deserve you. You have every right in the world to stay furious with him. You can't seem to hold a grudge."

Why should I? I wouldn't have Lloyd as king; I love Anglesey too much. Norah and I have accomplished great things since his abdication, with more great things coming. I wouldn't change anything.

"Let's take the kids for a walk tonight," I say. "Outside the gates, into town. Let's get out of our bubble and go see how the people are."

She smiles. "Excellent idea. I'll let Duncan know. Anywhere in particular you want to go?"

"The new park by the children's museum. The one with all the monkey bars and slides, and that carousel. The kids will like it, and it'll be good for them to hang out with other kids for a bit. Then we'll get some ice cream."

She comes around my desk, plopping herself on my lap. I pull her close.

"Have I told you lately how much I love you?" she whispers in my ear. "Have I demonstrated it properly?"

Her breath tickles my ear. Her implication stirs a tickling somewhat lower.

"Every day, Duchess," I reply, slipping my palm over her belly, feeling the small rise that will be our fifth child.

"Every single day, and it's perfect. I love your demonstrations. I never get enough of them."

"Just checking," she giggles, nipping my earlobe. "I don't want you to ever doubt it."

"Careful, baby," I croon against her neck, pulling back wildly curled locks of spun gold so I can press lips to her flesh. "You're distracting me from the nation's work."

"Owen, I'm the queen—I *am* the nation's work."

That's true. Well then, I can't neglect my duties.

"Boys, your mom and I have work to do," I say, taking Norah's hand, pulling her to her feet as I get to mine. "Stay here until you finish your match, then go to the nursery with Sally and your sisters. Understood?"

They barely acknowledge me, they're so focused on their game.

"C'mon, my queen," I say, pulling Norah along toward our apartments. "Let's go see to the national treasure."

It's good being king. I set my own hours. I work from home. My wife is also my business partner. Sometimes, we even work in bed.

Who needs a last name when I have all this?

DELETED SCENE

OWEN

"Is this where we're going, sir?" Duncan asks, glaring across the narrow, West Bank, Paris street like he's staring down the barrel of a loaded weapon.

Across the way, the art gallery is brightly lit, windows glowing warm against the rain-slicked cobblestones beyond the front door. Giant, monochrome photographs hang on the white walls of the open gallery space. The interior is crowded with nicely dressed people who laugh and talk easily. Strangers shake hands, heads bobbing with smiles and curious, sincere expressions.

"Sir?" Duncan asks again.

I'm thinking. Duncan can wait.

We're parked at the curb, tucked inside the car while I consider the question. I want to go in. I want to stroll up to that big glass and steel door, pull it wide like I own the place, and take on the crowded room without hesitation. I want to melt into the rabble, take all the time I want to study the photographs (if they're any good), or—more likely—roll my eyes at the pretense. I want to rub elbows with strangers and drink cheap champagne served in small plastic glasses. Isn't that what people do at public art gallery openings?

From my concealed position behind dark tinted glass, I see a hundred ordinary faces behind those windows. I also spy a few extraordinary creatures. *This is what I came for, isn't it?*

Several of the women in that room are cock-teasingly hot. Twenty are among the most famous faces—and bodies —in fashion. All of them have gathered in one room, on one night, to celebrate the work of Stephen Aubauchan, the photographer who took them from "pretty girls" into the stratosphere of celebrity fashion.

I collect pretty girls. Tonight, I'd like to up my game. That brightly lit room across the street offers me the best opportunity I'll get to take this little hobby of mine to the next level.

"Yeah," I reply to Duncan, "that's where we're going."

His jaw tightens. He huffs at me. "You realize there's no way I can approve this." But resignation bleeds into his tone, dampening it.

I grin at him. "Whatever. If I get mobbed and torn to pieces, tell Mother it was for a good cause."

Duncan rolls his eyes, shaking his head with disdain. "If that happens, your mother will have my head mounted on a pike at the gates."

He's not even exaggerating.

"Give me the key," I demand.

He places the ignition key into my open palm. He's an old hand at this game.

Duncan goes in ahead of me, casing the place for paparazzi. A few minutes later, he reappears on the side-walk, lighting a cigarette as a signal that the coast is clear. That's my cue to make my way in, join the crowd on my personal quest to identify and seduce the most beautiful woman in the room, get her to take me home with her, and convince her to sleep with me—all without revealing who I am.

Duncan plays along because he knows otherwise: I'll ditch him altogether.

The gallery is crowded, hot, and loud. The high ceilings and stone floors amplify the noise of two hundred voices like the vaults of a cathedral. It's an assault on my ears, which are accustomed to quiet; I don't get to spend much time among the masses.

It's only a matter of time until someone recognizes me. For this game, I've got to work fast: I need to get in, find my next conquest, and get out with her on my arm before someone outs me. If that happens, its game over. And it's what happens more often than not. The odds are always stacked against me, especially in a room filled with people who adore celebrities, buy magazines, and read the gossip rags. They know my face—they just don't expect to see it *here*.

I have a few tricks I use to stay incognito while I stalk the room, searching among the "beautiful people" for the one who's going to take me home. For starters, I peer at the floor —*a lot*. I've been trained since birth to sit up straight, square my shoulders, never slouch, keep my head high, and always maintain eye contact. Doing the opposite of those things dramatically alters my appearance. Also, for this game I always dress down in muddy boots and torn jeans. No one glances twice at a guy wearing worn-out work clothes.

When I identify my object and make contact, that's when I'll turn on my princely charms. My manners shine through the disguise of grubby old clothes. Women are less interested in the outward trappings of beauty than men are.

Us, we like the layers, particularly taking our time *peeling off* the layers. Women are into what's beneath the wrapping. Women are curious creatures.

I'm thinking I may have overdone it a bit with the threadbare Levi's when I hear a voice behind me. "Good God, do they let anyone in off the street? I thought this was a private affair."

I glance back, noting her haughty, solidly upper-class, East Bank accent. A century ago, her ancestors would have disowned her for slumming on this side of the Seine. My critic is an over-made diva beyond her expiration date. Her cheeks glow pink with drink, but the glow doesn't conceal the hard lines etched into her forehead, clawing the corners of her eyes, stamping a cold smile onto thin, pale lips.

I wink at her, smiling boyishly, and move on.

In the corner I spot three towering goddesses, each stunning in her own way. The tallest has long, inky black hair shimmering with rainbow streaks. Her full lips are painted ruby red, her high cheekbones dusted with powder. She's something to look at, and I'd fuck her in a heartbeat, but she's not the most beautiful woman here.

Beside her stands a creature built for the Paris runway. She's a doll, literally: her figure has been starved for the benefit of male designers and photographers who prefer the look of young boys to grown women. She's been enhanced with enough plastic to render her almost alien in appearance. And while she's certainly interesting to stare at, she's not the woman I've come for.

The woman I want isn't a painted fake, posing for the flashbulbs. She's not worried about impressing a soul in this room. I don't know who she is, but I'll know her when I see her, and when I see her, it's *game on*.

I survey every face and figure inside this room, studying

the beautiful ones, finding their better attributes, counting their flaws. I'm just about to move in on a gorgeous specimen of Polynesian glamour when my ear catches a sound that turns my head.

Her laughter rings in the air like the high notes of a harpsichord. Her laugh spreads out above the throng of people, settling like raindrops on a tin roof. Whatever made her laugh still tickles her. She smiles unselfconsciously, laughter pulling a dimple on her right check, creasing the corners of her flashing, sapphire blue eyes.

There's nothing painted or artificial about her—her beauty is genuine. She doesn't need powder, product, or plastic. Her sandy blond locks, wild with curls, are gathered at her back and tied off with a simple blue ribbon between her shoulders. She's dressed in clingy black leggings, a fitted undershirt, and a wispy-thin overshirt concealing just enough curve and silken skin to render her fascinating, and —at least to my mind—the most beautiful woman in this room.

Game on.

She's not alone. One of her companions is a spaced-out looking model in runway chic, her bare feet painted with glitter. The other is a well-dressed guy about my own age with dark eyes, an expensive haircut, salon-polished skin, and a suit custom cut to his tall, skinny frame. He made Beauty laugh, and for that I'm grateful—and also jealous. He holds a glass of brown booze in his right hand, his left making vivid gestures as he speaks. He's got both women hanging on every word.

The clock is ticking. I need to break his spell and cast one of my own. I need her to see me, and then see *into* me.

The threesome has clustered near a wall-sized print of a woman's ample tit rendered in shades of black and gray. It's framed and hung behind glass for the show, a small placard mounted right to indicate the piece's title and the gallery's asking price.

I move behind Mr. Dashing to get a good look at the placard. Mr. Dashing, unaware that I'm only inches away, waves his hand in another wild gesture that ends with him elbowing me in the back.

I fly around. He flies around. Our eyes meet. He's shocked, about to apologize, when his eyes take me in: my untucked shirt, torn jeans, muddy boots, and two-day-old scruff of beard. His jaw sets. His eyes narrow.

"Excuse me," I say, smiling coolly. "Just trying to get a look at the price of this one."

Mr. Dashing smirks, drawing his arms in. "I doubt it's in your price range, friend. Perhaps you're in the wrong place."

"Eric, don't be so rude!" Beauty protests. Her tone, like her laughter, lilts. She's American.

"He bumped into me," Eric snorts.

I do my best to feign hurt feelings. I check out his suit, then glance down at my own grubby attire. I look to the girls. First to the barefoot model, who holds my eyes with an expression of sympathetic curiosity.

I let my gaze fall to Beauty, biting my lip self-consciously. "So... *so sorry*," I mumble, dropping my eyes in mock deference, taking a step back.

He played right into my plan.

Beauty frowns at Eric. "You're an ass sometimes." She steps forward, past him and toward me until I'm standing face-to-face with this stunning creature who regards me with genuine sympathy.

She offers her hand. "I'm Norah," she says, her tone softening on approach.

I take her hand in mine, shaking politely. "Collin," I

reply, using my second name. "I'm sorry—I didn't mean to interrupt you and your friends."

My accent attracts her first. Her eyes brighten, the corners lifting with barely concealed inquiry. "You didn't interrupt anything." She glances back at her companions. "I've already heard all of Eric's stories. I came to Paris for new stories."

She's got an air about her, an easy confidence seeping between layers of closely held secrets. She peers into my eyes as though she's trying to discern mine.

"Have you found any?" I ask her.

Norah smiles—*barely*. "Not really," she admits. "Not yet, anyway."

～

ONE HOUR LATER

Cheap, art gallery champagne leaves a fruity, slightly spicy aftertaste. I discover this on the shadowy landing between the flights of stairs leading up to her flat. Citrus and cherries and a hint of red pepper prick my tongue as I press it past hers, opening her to me, breathing her taste in.

I back her against the wall, lifting her arms above her head. I hold her wrists tight while pressing my weight against her, slanting my mouth over hers, marking her long, pale neck with my teeth and lips. Her breasts, warm and round, flatten against my chest. Her hips rock forward to meet mine.

We don't pause for a tour of her living arrangements. Inside the apartment, she barely manages to turn a lamp on before I shove her onto the bed, rolling those tight leggings over her hips and down her thighs like peeling the skin off a hunted animal. Beneath, I'm thrilled to find milky white thighs willingly spread wide for me. Her heat rises into my nostrils, tweaking my brain, hardening my cock hard behind the zipper of my threadbare jeans.

Her body is perfection, her silky skin pliant and soft, reactive to my attentions. I torture her with my mouth, teasing goosebumps onto her flesh, hardening her nipples with my tongue and teeth. I suckle worshipfully, drawing moans and whimpers from her in even turns, building her up, getting her ready for me.

My fingers descend, slipping between the thin seam of lips protecting her most precious place. She's wet, dripping, her clit hard and ready for attention. That's all well and good, but this game isn't about her—it's about me. I doubt I'll ever get a chance to come back for seconds, so there's not much point in drawing things out. I came here to fuck a beautiful woman, not to rock *her* world.

Norah is as curious and impatient as I am. Her left palm cups the solid bulge between my legs, her right tugging at my button and zipper.

"You want that?" I growl, nuzzling her ear, pressing my cock into her hand. "You want that inside you?"

"I really do." She releases the button, slipping my zipper down to slide her hand beneath my briefs. Her fingers are soft and warm, circling my length with a mixture of gentle and firm strokes.

I shove my jeans and shorts down my legs and kick them off, letting her work her magic on my ready cock.

She's not the least bit timid. She keeps her eyes on mine, pressing her fingers and stroking her thumbs across my length, tracing the ridges and contours with careful attention. "Lay down." She lifts a hand to my chest and presses me backwards.

I'm astonished. She wants to go down on me? *Really?*

That never happens during this game. Blowjobs only happen when they know who I am and they're trying to get into my head. It never works; I know the routine. But this is different—she's not aspiring to anything. *She's just having fun.*

"Lay *down*," she insists, laughing at me. "And don't look so stunned. You can return the favor before we're done."

I do as I'm told, and in a moment, I realize I've completely lost the upper hand in this game. She takes my cock into her mouth, wrapping her lips around me, her tongue finding nerve endings I never knew existed. My mind goes numb, slipping into the bliss of singularly-focused pleasure. My cock becomes the center of the universe for a few brief moments before I lose all control, stifling groans, gripping Norah's soft hair inside closed fists, trying not to choke her while my pumping orgasm explodes down her throat.

Hours later—before we collapse together in exhaustion, before my eyes close on the world—I think to myself: we've done things I've only fantasized about. Norah is ambitious in bed, demanding, fucking incredible in every sense of the word. She's beautiful too, and fearless—a combination I've never come across.

I fall asleep draped in her arms and legs, tangled in her body heat, my skin slick and perfumed with her scent.

I came here to fuck a beautiful woman. Instead, she rocked *my* world.

∾

MY PHONE IS RINGING. I hear it from a long way off, the tones familiar, melodic. "Purple Rain." A song from another time, another prince.

"Jesus, what the hell is that?"

It's Norah's voice that wakes me, not the sound of my phone. I sit up, confused and blinking back sleep. The room is bright with sunshine and barely furnished, scattered with dirty clothes and books.

My phone keeps ringing; it's the ringtone I've set for palace security. It's the only tone I know I can't let go to voicemail. They don't call without a good reason.

I scramble in the back pocket of the jeans I dropped in a rumpled heap last night. I swipe to answer, hoping I've caught the call before it disconnects. If that happens, a whole different set of events get put into motion, none of them good, especially considering I'm naked and in a strange girl's bed. I don't need a mass of armed men bursting in under the assumption I've been kidnapped, ready to shoot first and ask questions later.

"Yes?!" I say, relieved to hear live air on the other end of the connection.

"Your Highness, this is Rowling. I'm sorry to disturb you, sir, but we have a situation developing at the palace. Your mother has requested your immediate return."

"What's wrong?" I ask. "Is she alright? Is she ill?"

"No, sir. Her Royal Majesty is in fine health. I'm sorry sir —I can't discuss this on an insecure line. When you get to the plane, we'll have a secure connection and I'll brief you. The jet is standing by at the airport. Is Duncan with you now?"

I struggle out of bed and to the window, peering down at the street where I parked last night. Duncan leans on the closed driver's side door, looking up at me from behind mirrored aviator sunglasses.

"Yeah, he's here," I say. "Not in the room, but here."

"He has instructions to take you directly to the airport. There's no time to be lost."

"Very well." I end the call, then look at the phone in my hand. The last time I got a call like that was when my father died six months ago. That ringtone makes my guts clench and my heart race. I don't ever want to get a call like that again—it means everything is falling apart.

Something big is going down at home. Something—*I know*—to do with my brother and his bizarre behavior. That's the only reason they'd call me. He's the heir. I'm the spare. They're never supposed to need me, and I'd like to keep it that way.

"Everything okay?"

I turn. Norah is sitting up, her knees pulled to her chest and the sheets drawn tight, covering her from shoulder to toes. Last night she was wide open, shameless. Now, in the mid-morning light, she's the picture of demure—if slightly rumpled—reserve.

She's still the most beautiful creature I've ever laid eyes on.

Game over.

"I've gotta go," I say, reaching for my jeans and pulling them on, then searching for my shirt.

"Why?" she asks, confused. "I thought we'd..."

But I cut her off. "I just do."

What I want is what she wants: I want to stay, let her feed me breakfast, hang out with her, get to know her. That's never going to happen—it can't. It's better to nip any expectations she might have in the bud.

Forty seconds later, I'm on the stairs headed down to the street and back into the over-bearing care of my patient, ever-loyal bodyguard, Duncan.

ABOUT THE AUTHOR

Lexi Whitlow is a small-town girl from Virginia. She spent her early years growing up between Virginia and North Carolina, playing in the dark rich dirt of Eastern North Carolina at her granddaddy's farm. She's a mom of a six-year-old boy and a seven-month-old girl. Life is hectic, but it sure is sweet.

She holds a master's degree in English literature from the University of Virginia, and her mom is so proud she's "using her degree."

Lexi harbors a not-so-secret love for bad boys. She loves fighters, tough-as-nails cowboys, bikers, and criminals. Her husband is a scientist... but he has the heart of a bad boy for sure.

Made in the USA
Columbia, SC
13 May 2018